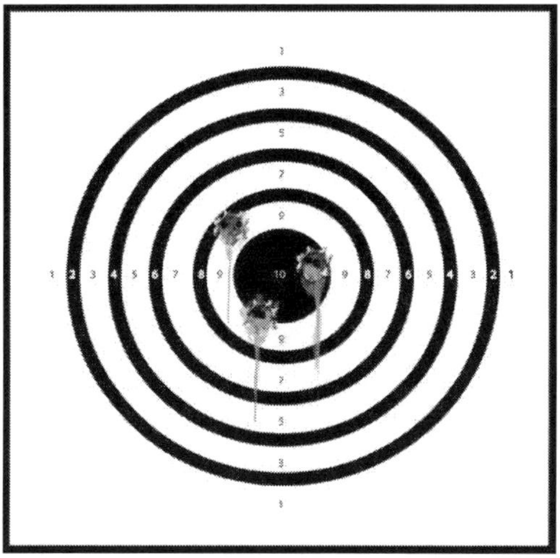

BULLSEYE

A novel of **murder** and suspense

Roger C. Lubeck

BULLSEYE: A novel of murder and suspense

Cover by Roger C. Lubeck

This is a work of fiction. All characters appearing in this work are fictitious. Any resemblance to real persons, living or dead is purely coincidental.

Library of Congress
Cataloging-in-Publication Data Available
LCCN 2011936702

ISBN-13: 978-0983728115
ISBN-10: 0983728119
202 Pages
It Is What It Is Press
686 Carriage Hill Lane
Sugar Grove, Illinois, 60554
www.iwiipress.com

Dedication

To Lynette Chandler,
there is never enough time.

TABLE OF CONTENTS

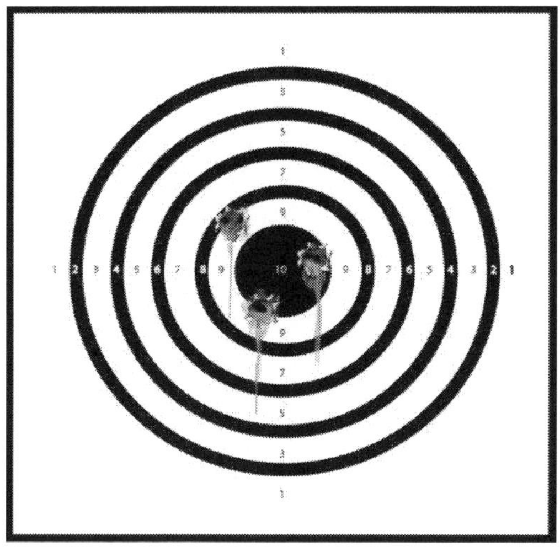

BULLSEYE

A novel of **murder** and suspense

CHAPTER 1

THE TURTLE

Robert "the Turtle" Cederberg was twelve when he spent his summer living with his mother, brothers, and the family's maid in Kingsville Ontario. For the Turtle, that time in Canada was a summer of discovery, a summer of many firsts. On July 24, 1963, the occasion of his thirteenth birthday, he slow danced for the first time with a girl with real breasts. For the Turtle, the experience made his hands sweat and his penis swell.

On August 4, Robert earned his first dollar. Actually, he earned five dollars and thirty-five cents picking wax beans at a local farm, but he missed a significant number of beans in his assigned row and was fired before noon; another first. Later, flush with penny candy, he told his mother that he finished early because they ran out of beans and did not need him anymore; a lie he would use many times in the future, but another first at the time. Robert would not work again for money until he was sixteen, a long time between a first and a second time at anything, but not a record.

Robert used the remaining money from picking beans in the hot Canadian sun, to take Cathy Mathews on a date to a carnival, another first, where for less than three dollars and thirty-five cents he kissed Cathy, for the first time, and then advanced from first base to second base, only to be throw out on a technical error.

On the day before the Cederbergs were to return home to Grosse Pointe, Robert lied to a police officer when the officer questioned him about a dead man, in each case a first time, but not for the last time. Reflecting on those lazy days in Kingsville, eating buttered corn and lemon custard, picking yellow wax beans for pocket change, and swimming out to the sand bar early in the morning, he wondered whether finding the man on the beach that last day of his summer vacation was the event that most shaped his life. In hindsight, it was probably learning to shoot a gun.

Robert Cederberg grew up in Grosse Pointe, a wealthy suburb of Detroit. Robert's parents also grew up in Grosse Pointe, making Robert and his brothers' second-generation Grosse Pointers. Robert's brother Austin was six years older. Austin was thin and athletic, intelligent without being showy, and a natural with girls. Austin had thick black hair, which no one else in the family had. As a young boy, Robert was short and overweight with seemingly normal desires and aspirations. Unlike his brother, Robert was cautious. Robert observed the world rather than participated. He sat on the sidelines during most games, watched, and learned.

When Robert was ten, one of the boys in his swimming class gave Robert his nickname. Like most boys, Robert was very aware of the size of his still hairless penis. At ten, Robert's penis was smaller than average a fact made worse by Robert's weight problem. One day after swimming for an hour, one of the boys pointed to Robert's penis saying that his "wee wee" looked like a turtle. Looking down, Robert saw that his penis appeared to be sticking its head out from his testicles, looking much like a turtle. Embarrassed, Robert tried to hide his penis, which only made the situation worse, because several other boys starting taunting him, calling him 'Turtle'. By the next week, all of the boys in the swim class were calling Robert, 'the Turtle'.

Robert hated his nickname, because he knew its origin, but he also realized it fit him. Most nicknames are designed to hurt and humiliate the bearer, however they also make sense and often for the recipient, the nickname or how one receives a nickname becomes a favorite story. Mooch for example, is given to someone who is always begging. Whitey is the kid with the palest skin, and Little John, according to legend was the nickname given to the tallest man in the forest. Robert's older brother, for example, called himself Audie because his name was Austin and Audie Murphy, who he idolized, was the most decorated hero in World War II. Austin believed that one day he would be a hero too.

For Robert, the explanation of why he was called the Turtle was too painful to admit, even to his brothers, so the explanation became the fact that Robert was withdrawn and tended to be the last boy to be selected in every activity because he was the slowest. After a year of being called Turtle, no one could explain the nickname, but everyone, including Robert and his family, called him the Turtle, everyone except the family's maid, Chessie.

Chessie started with the family shortly after Austin was born. Caroline Cederberg, Robert's mother, quickly found that caring for a newborn baby boy and household chores was beyond her ability or temperament. In truth, Caroline Cederberg never was one for household chores, like cleaning, doing laundry, or cooking dinner, but the addition of a crying baby only made the situation worse. At first, Austin's grandparents, seeing that Caroline might endanger their grandchild, hired a Swedish nurse to take care of the new baby. Eventually the nurse declared that the child no longer needed a nurse, rather, she told the boy's father Eric Cederberg, the boy needed his mother. During this critical time, Eric was spending considerable time at the office teaching the newspaper business to his new secretary and he realized that if he did not get help for Caroline, he would be dragged back into the household. The solution came in the form of a wizened-old black woman Chessie Johnson who had already raised three children when Eric hired her.

Chessie Johnson grew up in the Deep South, Alabama. She was one of those African-Americans whose skin color was a dark chocolate black. Her palms and the soles of her feet were almost pink in contrast to her blackness. Chessie came to the Cederbergs during a time in Detroit when African-Americans were called Negros in polite conversations and Niggers everywhere else. When she started working for the Caroline Cederberg, she was forty-one and Caroline was twenty-three. Chessie knew more about the world and about raising children and taking care of a house than Caroline did, and she was hired because Caroline's mother could not be there every day to help and protect her grandchild.

Originally, Chessie cleaned the house two days a week, Tuesday and Fridays. After Robert was born, Chessie cleaned three days a week and when John and William arrived, Chessie ran the household, leaving Caroline to take on a career as an encyclopedia saleswoman, right at the time when television began to educate America's children. For all practical purposes, by 1963, Caroline and Eric were absent from the home most of the day, leaving Chessie to raise the boys.

Eric Cederberg was the only child of Ruth and Edward Cederberg. Born in Illinois, Eric father Edward moved the family to Grosse Pointe Michigan in 1930. In Grosse Pointe, Eric lived in a large house with a full time maid. In 1931, Edward purchased a summer cottage in Kingsville, Ontario. For the next ten years, the cottage became Ruth and Eric's summer home, with Edward spending his weekends with the family. In 1942, Eric and Caroline married and spent two weeks at the cottage. After the war, Eric, Caroline, and Austin started visiting on weekends in July and August. Eventually, Caroline and Austin were living at the cottage all summer and Ruth and Edward restricted their time to visit the cottage to weekends in September and October. When Edward died in 1957, Ruth bestowed the cottage upon Eric; a treasure he lost in less than ten years.

In June 1963, Caroline and the three youngest boys packed up the family station wagon and drove the forty-three miles from their home in Grosse Pointe to their cottage in Kingsville, Ontario. Austin, who had a summer job, spent some nights in Kingsville and some nights in Grosse Pointe. Eric Cederberg only spent the weekends at the cottage.

Saying she was overwhelmed, Caroline had insisted that Chessie lived at the cottage in Canada during the week, going home to Detroit on Friday. Chessie and her husband, "the Reverend," held a service on Sunday in their small church, the Church of the Everlasting Christ. Every Friday, Chessie would race about the cottage making it ready for the Cederberg family on the weekend. On Monday morning the Reverend would drive Chessie back to the cottage, leaving himself time to fish and still return home before dinner, which the Reverend ate with a widowed member of the congregation.

Mirroring the Reverend, Eric Cederberg often spent his Sunday's in Canada and drove to Detroit on Monday. Eric worked in downtown Detroit, and even though Kingsville was only twenty-nine miles from his office, he chose to live at home and stay in the city on weekdays, spending most of the weekend with his wife and family. For both men, the situation represented the perfect combination of bachelor and married life. For the Reverend, who painted houses for a lining, having Chessie working during summer, when her employers were on vacation represented extra income and with Chessie in Canada he was able to take under his wing members of his congregation, who sought out his spiritual and physical guidance. For Eric Cederberg, having Caroline living with the boys in Canada meant that Eric could spend more time at the thing he loved best, the Detroit News.

Robert got up early on Monday September 2, Labor Day. The family was scheduled to leave for home by two o'clock and Robert had a lot to do. Eric had the Monday off, so he stayed over so he could drive the family home to Grosse Pointe in the afternoon. Chessie was scheduled to arrive as usual at 8:00 a.m., so she could help Caroline and the boys pack for home. In general, Chessie's arrival on Monday would awaken the family. By the time Robert and Austin were out of bed, Chessie would have eggs, bacon, and English muffins on the table waiting for her boys. Caroline seldom emerged from her bedroom before 9:00 a.m., so she was treated to a second round of food. Today, Robert had much to do, so he planned to be out of the house before Chessie arrive. With luck, he would be back in time to join his parents for the second round of breakfast.

Carrying his tennis shoes, Robert tiptoed around the cottage. The last thing he wanted was to wake his parents. On his way out, Robert grabbed a blueberry muffin, two slices of wonder bread, and a peach. Robert did not really like peaches, the fuzz bothered him, but he was hungry and biting into the peach, he enjoyed the sweetness.

Robert listened at the front porch door for any sounds that his family was awake. Through the screen, the southern sky was still blue black. Two massive willow trees divided the large manicured yard, ending at a paved two lane coastal road overlooking Linden Beach and Lake Erie. The coast road ran east and west. For the locals, the Cederberg's end of Linden Beach was the eastern end or the 'near end,' meaning it was nearer to Kingsville. The narrowness of road at the eastern end prevented cars from parking along the side of the road.

Crossing the yard, Robert spent several minutes sitting in each of the wooden Adirondack chairs and the art deco metal lawn chairs. Robert was already hot, and the chairs were wet with dew, so the water soaking into his tee shirt felt wonderful. Having a dozen or so chairs out on the front yard was a sign that the family was still on vacation. The metal chairs were too hot to sit on during the day, so they formed a circle around the fire pit. The cedar Adirondack chairs pointed toward the morning sun just visible in the east. When friends from Detroit visited, the Adirondack chairs became a large sundial moving with the sun. Today, Chessie and the Reverend would move the chairs into the shuttered front porch.

From the edge of the road, Robert looked up and down the tarmac. The road ran west for two miles until it reached the store and gas station. In the afternoon, Robert liked to walk to the store to buy penny candy and soda from the machine in front of the gas station. At certain points along the road, the water came up to a break wall right beside the road. At other places, there was thirty feet of beach and the water was less than two feet below the road. Near the eastern end, the land rose thirty-five feet above the lake. For families like the

Cederbergs, living on these high cliffs, the path to the water usually involved a series of steps or stairs leading onto a long dock that pushed out past the muck and into the reeds.

The Cederberg cottage was the fourth house from the eastern end of the coast road. The cottage was a two-story Cape Cod style beach house with a screened-in front porch. In the Cederberg cottage, the living room, dining room, kitchen, master bedroom, and bathroom were all on the ground floor. Robert's parents slept downstairs with their door closed. Upstairs were two large bedrooms with dormer windows. In the summer, the ground floor rooms benefited from the occasional lake breeze and an array of fans. The second floor rooms never cooled below eighty degrees. In the fall, the sun pouring through windows in every room and a wall of screened windows on the porch heated the house. On cold nights, the family would light the oil furnace in the corner of living room. Locals described the house as a summer cottage, meaning the plumbing was off in the winter to prevent the pipes from freezing. Robert's father was useless when it came to home repairs and even worse, when it came to spending money to keep up the cottage. In less than five years, everything associated with the property was in need of repair. This summer it was the roof and the septic tank.

West of Robert's house was the O'Neal's house a nearly identical cottage built at the same time by a Detroiter related to the Hudson family. When he left Detroit, Tom and Sarah O'Neal and their seven children moved in. On the other side, Ian McGregor, a fourth generation Canadian, live in his year round one level farm home. According to Mister McGregor Americans were ruining Canada.

When Edward, Robert's grandfather bought the cottage, he built new stairs to the beach, with a landing half way down. Thirty years later, Eric begged his family to be careful when they used the stairs, walking slowly, listening to the creaks or cracks as the stairs swayed under their weight. Standing on the top step, Robert smelled the dark stagnant water below.

Robert knew that his father wanted the family to use one of the neighbors' stairs for fear that their stairs would collapse. Robert took great delight daring the fates by stomping his way down the steps. Looking at his new Timex watch, Robert saw it was six thirty. For his birthday, he asked for a BB gun, but his mother objected and his father, who never paid any attention, said he had seen the Timex on display in the drug store in his office building. He said it was "just the thing for a teenager." Robert planned to test the claim that it was waterproof.

Robert carried a beach towel and half inflated yellow raft down to the end of their dock. The raft was the kind used in pools. On Linden beach, people without boats used rafts to swim out the quarter of a mile from the shore to the line of waves breaking over a sandbar. In between the sand bar and the beach, the water was shallow and filled with reeds, and a bottom mucky. At high tide, the lake washed up its dead, leaving carp and catfish, perch and pickerel stranded in the rocks. At low tide, the tops of reeds were visible in sections, growing in the sun. On most days, an adult man could walk to the sand bar without having to swim. However, because of the mucky bottom and reeds, most people took a boat to the sand bar, or they paddled and floated to the sand bar on rubber life rafts. The Cederberg family had a rowboat and a large air force surplus life raft they used to haul kids, a cooler, and the three dogs out to the sand bar. Today, Robert was going out to the sand bar alone on a raft.

Looking back up the cliff face, Robert saw a pile of broken rocks leading to the road. On hot days, Robert liked to take one of the croquet mallets out of the rack by the front door and pound the rocks pretending he was already in prison, a place his brother said he was destined to go. From the road above, Robert heard a car racing down the coastal road, its engine whining, as the driver shifted. Robert was used to the sound of cars racing on the coastal highway at all times of the day and night, but most raced from east to west, speeding down the long straight a way to the beach store. This car was heading east and at high speed from the sound of the engine.

For young men anxious to drive fast and race their finely tuned hotrods, sports cars, and the occasional family station wagon, the coastal road was ideal, provided you raced west. Those racing east usually began breaking before the Cederberg cottage in order to make the turn. The driver of a red MGA roadster traveling at forty miles an hour or fifty-eight feet per second applied the brakes too late to make the turn, sliding past a hedge, the car slipped sideways between two of the smaller evergreen trees. Over reacting, the driver turned the steering wheel violently from the left to his right, hoping to correct the skid. For a moment, the car seemed like it might make the turn, except the front of the car had already left the cliff ledge flying over the rocks and trees heading towards the beach below.

Robert heard the screech of bakes and then sound of metal slamming into the trees at the edge of the cliff. It only took the car two seconds to land hard on the sand below, bounce two feet in the air, and land hard again. The rear tires dug into the soft sand, while the front right wire-wheel buried itself in the muck at the edge of the beach. For a moment, the car's horn sounded and its engine raced causing its headlights to peer out into the morning sky. Then, all was silent.

Running east along the beach Robert climbed over the last three docks before he came to the rock jetty that formed a natural border between his beach and the town beach a mile east. Beyond the wall was a small cove and then nothing except rock shore and farmland until the city beach. From experience, Robert knew one had to swim or walk in the water around the jetty to reach the cove beyond. At the McGregor dock, Robert ran to the end to see if he could see the car. Peering in the darkness, he was not sure whether the car was on the beach or buried in the trees above. For a moment, he considered running up the McGregor stairs to check, but he knew he would be yelled at, if old man McGregor caught him using his stairs.

Leaning out from the end of the McGregor dock, Robert could see the silver grill of the red sports car sitting half in and half out of the water. Robert considered leaving his tennis shoes on the dock, but he knew the mucky lake bottom could have glass or other sharp objects just waiting to cut his feet. Wearing his shoes in the water was safer, but it meant washing them in bleach later and letting them dry in the sun.

Climbing down the ladder at the end of the dock, Robert jumped onto his yellow rubber raft, and swam to the cove, careful to step down into the muck only at the last moment when he was near the edge of the sandy beach. Leaving the raft, Robert approached the car, like a soldier, wary, walking slowly watching out the corners of his eyes for other people on the beach. The driver was sitting in the car, weeping. When Robert walked up to the passenger side door, the man's face broke into a huge smile.

"Kid, thank God. Youse gota help me. Youse gota get help. I think my leg is broken. I need a doctor. I need an ambulance." The man spoke in a rush, he words understandable but slurred. "Kid, for God's sake, run home, and tell your parents to call for help. Do you understand? Parley vu English. Come on kid, do you speak English or not?"

Robert guessed the driver was over twenty-one years of age. He was tall and athletic with black hair, bushy eyebrows and dark eyes. He had a large hooked nose and super white teeth. The man sounded like he was an American, but not from Detroit. His accent was different, like that actor in *On the Waterfront.* He was wearing a white tee shirt and navy blue swimming trunks with white piping up the side. His left leg was pulled up near the steering wheel; his right leg looked twisted, caught beneath the steering wheel and red dashboard with all the silver dials and black switches. On the black leather passenger seat, Robert saw a pair of broken sunglasses and an half empty pint bottle of liquor. There were two Scottie dogs on the label. In between the two seats was a long knife, like a bayonet and a gun, a sleek silver metal pistol with black handgrips.

To Robert, the pistol looked like one of the guns German officers carried in war movies, not a Luger, a different gun. Without thinking, the Robert leaned into the car and picked up the gun immediately enjoying the weight and the feel of the silver metal. With his index finger, he pushed the safety on and off.

"Hey Kid," screamed the man. "Be careful with that gun it's loaded." Trapped by his broken leg, the man leaned across the passenger seat as far as he could and reached for the gun with his right hand. Instinctively, Robert stepped back, away from the car considering both the man and the gun.

"Really, Kid, I'm not kidding. That gun is dangerous, give it back to me and go get an adult, I'm bleeding, and I need a doctor." Again, the man tried to pull himself free of the car, at the same time reaching for Robert and the gun with his right hand.

Seeing he was out of reach, Robert held his ground at the edge of the water, moving the gun back and forth between his hands without touching the trigger. The gun was about as heavy as a sack of candy, but not as heavy as the baskets of wax beans he picked last week, perhaps a little over a pound. Robert had shot a BB gun before, and he had played with his grandfather's British Bulldog revolver from World War I, a gun with the firing pin filed off. This was the first time he held a loaded gun. For a kid growing up on war movies and police shows on television, the feel of an actual loaded gun was more exciting than Robert could imagine. He was at a loss for words at what he was feeling. It was like the excitement he felt when Cathy let him touch her bra only here he felt in control.

Looking up and down the beach, he thought how cool it would be to carry a gun like this in his official air force flight vest, the one from the Korean War, the one with the built in pistol holder, just like Robert Wagner in *The Hunters*. Refocusing on the man and the car, Robert saw how angry the man was becoming. Looking up and down the still empty beach, Robert wondered if he could take the gun home and not be caught. After all, his family was leaving this afternoon. Whatever he did, at least for the moment, the beautiful gun was his.

"Why do you have a gun?" asked Robert, speaking in a low quiet voice. Robert wondered why the man did not honk the horn.

"I am an American, like you. I am traveling alone in Canada. My dad gave me the gun for protection."

"Is it a Luger?"

"Smart kid. It is like a Luger," said the man trying to calm his voice.

"Was your dad a German soldier?"

"No, of course not. My dad took it off a dead German. It was made in Germany for German soldiers in the war. It is a Walther."

"Like James Bond has?"

"Very smart. Now, how about getting some help, kid?" The man tried again to free his leg, only to shout out in pain.

"Look kid, the booze is wearing off and I am in a lot of pain. Be a good kid. Go for help and I will pay you twenty bucks."

"Give it to me now," said Robert, excited by the prospect of twenty dollars, more than enough to buy that new Marksman BB gun he wanted, the one that looked like a Colt .45. "Let me see the money," said Robert.

"Look you fat motherfucker," the man said barely under his breath. "Don't be an asshole kid. I am hurt. Go get your parents." The man in the car looked around. To the south, the lake was still dark, the cliff above covered in trees, except for the hole through which the car had crashed. Pulling at the wallet in his shorts, he offered Robert a twenty from a roll of twenties. Robert saw the roll was thick and the man was trying not to show the entire roll.

When the driver offered Robert the twenty, Robert stepped around the car to the driver's side and reached out with his left hand to take the bill. As Robert reached in, the driver tried to grab the gun out of Robert's right hand. Pulling away, Robert grabbed the roll of money leaving the man with a crumpled twenty still in his out stretched right hand. Screaming, the man grabbed the MGA's wooden steering wheel with both hands, leaned back, and let out a loud cry for help that should have been heard for a block, except the cry that was muffled by the cove's rock walls and seemed to go nowhere. Without thinking, Robert closed the distance between himself and car door and placed the gun barrel against the man's head, and pulled the trigger, but with no effect except a click.

Robert was unaware that the gun had a double action, meaning that the first pull on the trigger cocked the weapon and a further pull fired the weapon. Had the gun's safety been on, pulling the trigger would have had no effect at all, and very likely, the day would have taken a different turn. In that instance, the man gave Robert a look that seemed to ask what he had done to deserve this end, but he could only say "Please," as Robert pulled the trigger for the second time, this time with an effect.

The Walther's report was sharp but most of the sound was muffled as the left side of the man's head absorbed the bullet and the right side of his head exploded out in a spray of blood and brains, coating the black leather passenger seat with small fragments of bone and a mist of blood. At the sound of the explosion and the sight of the blood, Robert experienced a level of excitement, a level of pleasure and sexual release that was so far beyond what he had experienced masturbating that Robert considered shooting the man again, even though he knew he was already dead.

Looking up to the road, Robert thought it unlikely anyone had heard the shot, but he knew his time alone with the dead man was ending. He was not sure why he had pulled the trigger, but he had and the man was dead. Looking at the man's burned and blistered temple with bits of bone and brains sticking out of the exit wound, Robert was struck by the fact the man was dead and nothing would change that or the fact that Robert had killed the man.

For a moment, Robert considered running up to the cottage to tell his mom and dad there had been an accident, but he knew they would be worthless. For a longer moment, he debated keeping the gun or leaving it. At first, the desire to keep the gun as a souvenir was overwhelming, but Robert knew Chessie or his brother Austin would find it eventually. He also knew if he kept the gun, he would have to kill again, if only to experience that delicious feeling when he pulled the trigger. Robert had seen enough episodes of *M-Squad* to know he had to wipe the gun clean and then place it in the man's left hand.

Afterwards, Robert swam out to the sandbar where he watched old man McGregor discover the car seven minutes later. Lying on the sand bar, he watched other neighbors arrive followed by the police and finally an ambulance. By noon, two wreckers dragged the car up to the road. For half the morning, Robert watched the investigation from the safety of a strip of sand five hundred yards out from the beach. Robert did not know about all the tests that might have led the crime scene investigators back to him, but fortunately by the time, the police arrived at the scene Ian McGregor and other cottage owners had touched the gun and the dead man making later tests inconclusive.

When Robert finally returned home, the police, the body, and the sports car were all gone. Only the broken tree limbs, footprints, and tire tracks on the beach, remained as evidence of what had happened. Entering the porch, Robert listened for his younger brother or mother, but instead, he heard Chessie calling from the kitchen.

"Where you been," she demanded. "I kept breakfast, biscuits and jelly. You momma and brothers are down at the McGregor's, there has been some kind of car accident."

"I went for a swim. I saw the wrecker from the sand bar. Pretty cool."

"Don't be saying that. Your brother said the driver died."

"Well, I am sorry I guess, but that car was pretty cool."

"You boys and your cars. I left a box of Sugar Pops out. You go ahead and finish it, so I have one less thing to pack." Chessie walked into the living room and gave Robert one of her long uncomfortable looks.

"When you are done, I expect you to take your good pants and church coat out of the closet and fold them and pack them neatly in the suit case I left on top of your bed."

"Chessie, can't you do that? This is my last day. I need to go see Tim and Chuck, and say good bye to Cathy."

"You stay away from that girl if you know what's good for you. You have spent eighty-five days following that girl around, chasing after her scent, and as near as I can tell, she has managed to keep you out of her room and out of her pants. And, don't give me that look, we both knows what I am talking about. And, I say you are lucky, at least for one more year."

"Come on Chessie, Cathy is nice."

"That girl is no good, and you and I both knows it, even if she doesn't yet. That girl is going to end up pregnant before she is out of school, and my little Turtle is not going to be the father, not if I have anything to say about what you do and where you go. So, go eat your breakfast and go pack. After that, we will see what trouble you can get into in one day." Chessie turned back into the living room, leaving Robert to consider all that she had said and the possibilities for the remainder of an already eventful day.

Around noon, a white police cruiser with Kingsville written in blue parked in the driveway behind the shed. Seeing the cruiser from the back dormer window, Robert raced downstairs creeping into the dining room where he pretended to be asleep on the daybed.

Robert held his breath, when the police officers asked Caroline whether anyone in the house had heard or seen anything related to the unfortunate accident on the beach. Caroline, who had watched the police drag the car up from the beach, said her family knew nothing about the dead man or the car on the beach. At which time Chessie entered the kitchen and said she was the only one up in the morning and that she had "heard nothing except the crows and redwing black birds out back."

Sitting on the day bed in the dining room, Robert said nothing and made no move to been seen or heard. He knew he should be hiding in a closet upstairs, but he wanted to listen. The problem was he knew in his heart, if he were questioned at that moment, he would make mistakes. He needed a day or two, time to master the lie. He just needed time to get over the excitement he felt. If he had to talk about this morning, saying that he had swam to the sand bar this morning would be easy because it was the truth. The problem was he knew the police would ask if he saw anything and they would wonder why he did not swim in to see what was happening. Strange behavior the officers would think. The actions of a killer, they would think, and then Robert would be taken away in handcuffs. Lying on the couch, he could see it all. From the kitchen, Robert heard one of the officers ask, "What about your boys, Aye? Did any of them hear or see anything, then?

"Are the boys in the house?" asked the second officer.

Robert looked about and considered whether he could get out of the front door without alerting Chessie. Then he wondered if there was a police officer stationed at the front waiting for him to run. Robert knew that the police in the *Naked City* always left a man at the back door in case the criminal ran. Which usually happened, and yet the bad guy often got away and had to be chased down on foot or shot fleeing the scene. Robert knew he was too fat to run, so he buried his body deeper in the day bed pillows and waited.

"Ask Chessie," said Caroline. "I haven't even seen the boys today. We are leaving this afternoon, and the boys are out saying their goodbyes. Surely, you know more about that poor man killing himself than my boys do. I was just saying to Chessie, what is the world coming to when a young man like that commits suicide."

"Our sergeant said just about the very same thing, except he wondered if that is really what happened, so he asked us to talk to you and your neighbors. Seeing as you are so close to the road there." Robert could not see into the kitchen, but he imagined the officer pointing out the side window to the bend in the road.

"Mr. McGregor said the boy tried to kill himself by driving off the cliff and when that didn't work, he shot himself."

"That could be right, but for now we have to consider other alternatives."

"Like what," asked Caroline more sharply than she intended.

"Like as someone came on the boy trapped in that car of his and shot him with his own pistol.

"Don't be silly," declared Robert's mother. "What do you think; old Mister McGregor walked down to the beach and finding a stranger on his property, shot him." Caroline laughed, but no one else found this funny. Robert wished his mother would shut up. She was clearly making the officers angry.

"Well, Mrs. Cederberg, if you do hear anything that would be useful to our investigation, please gives us a call. I've written the number for the station, just in case you want to take it back to America." Robert smiled at the way the police officer said America rather than Detroit, emphasizing that the Cederbergs were more than a family from another city vacationing at their lake cabin. He thought of the Cederbergs as foreigners invading his country. Robert imagined the officer and his partner going back to their police car and complaining about the 'fucking Americans'.

When the policemen left, Robert moved from the day bed to a wicker chair on the porch. The front porch ran the length of the house with screened windows on three sides. On the back wall were nautical maps and charts of Lake Erie and the other great lakes. Robert had spent hours examining these maps, wondering what all of the coves were like and what had happened to the various wrecks marked in red on the charts. Sitting in the green wicker chair, Robert picked up a

Hardy Boy book, *The House on the Cliff* from a side table. On the porch were stacks of books for reading, board games, and decks of cards. Robert and his brothers often played board games at night, or put together a puzzle. Caroline usual listened to TV or to music on the radio. On the weekends, his father played gin or pinochle with Mister O'Neal for hours, the two men only taking a break to refill their drinks. Holding the book on his lap, Robert pretended to read as he listened to his mom and Chessie talk about the police and the man on the beach.

"Where's Robert?" asked his mother. "He was up early. Did he say anything about the car and the man on the beach?"

"Robert's only thinking about that girl."

"That Mathews girl is no good. Did you know that Robert spent all his summer money on her at the fair last week? He used to be such a sweet boy. Always doing nice things for his mother, and now he is so moody. Always sulking around and talking about Cathy Mathews or that McKinsey girl.

"Robert had to come out of his shell eventually. All it took was that girl, with her white shirt and black bras."

"Now stop that," laughed Caroline.

"Robert knows I loves him as much as any child of mine, God rest their souls. He also knows when it is time to get out of the house!"

"Whatever are you talking about Chessie," asked Caroline, looking around the kitchen in confusion. On the porch, Robert did not wait to hear an answer. Chessie was telling him to get out of the house, so Robert set the book down and quietly stepped out of the house.

Outside it was hot and the waves on the lake shimmered in the midday sunlight. Most of the fishing boats had come in, leaving the ski boats and speedboats inside the sandbar. On the southern horizon, a lake freighter steamed towards Cleveland, Ohio. Four houses away, Robert saw Cathy Mathews and Chuck Zane standing on the Mathews dock. Below them in a rowboat tethered to the dock, Tommy McKinsey had his hand on the throttle of the boat's outboard engine, ten horsepower mercury that his dad rebuilt over the winter. Cathy had beach towels in her arms and Chuck had a cooler. They were probable going out to the sand bar, or waterskiing. The boat was wooden and heavy, and the Mercury engine was just powerful enough to get a kid on skis out of the water provided there were not too many in the boat. Robert very much wanted to get in the boat and watch Cathy water ski in her black one-piece bathing suit, but if Chuck Zane,

Cathy's third cousin were going, there would be no room for Robert, both literally and figuratively. As far as Robert could tell, Cathy and Chuck had decided they were kissing cousins some time after Robert's birthday party. For all of August, they were always together and always clinging to each other. Robert had come to hate Chuck, and now watching Cathy smiling at every move Chuck made, he realized if he had kept the gun, he would have shot Chuck too.

"I hate her," Robert said under his breath, knowing instantly what he felt was not hate. Walking slowly away from his house, Robert saw the police car at the O'Neal's next door. One of the officers was walking up to the O'Neal's back door, as the other officer crossed their lawn heading to the McKinsey's cottage. Standing behind one of the large willows, Robert watched the officer cross the lawn until he was out of sight. Leaving the willow, Robert ran to an even larger tree near the road. This tree has an iron bench around it that people sat on at parties and at night. Once he was around the tree, Robert sat down on the bench as if he was watching the road or the lake beyond. What he was really doing was waiting and hiding. Hiding from the police and waiting for them to leave.

Robert did not hear the squad car drive up and pull off the road right behind him. The officer who was driving waited in the car, as a second officer stepped slowly out of the car, taking a moment to adjust his belt, and gun, and put on his brown Monte hat.

"Excuse me son," said the officer, his voice deep and rough like the man at the gas station who smoked so much. "Do you live around here?" Robert considered his options. He could run, but where to? He could explain what happened, claiming that it was an accident, but he was too frightened to tell anyone, or he could lie, something at which he was not any good. For a moment, he did nothing, sitting frozen, saying nothing.

"Did you hear me boy," demanded the officer using a less friendly tone of voice. "I asked if you live around here." The officer was tall and thin with big hands. He wore black leather boots that came up to his knees. He stood very straight and looked down at Robert waiting. Robert said nothing, only nodded and pointed back towards his house.

"You live there, in the old Sullivan house?" Robert had never heard his home called anything other than the Cederberg house, so he said, "It is the Cederberg house, and I'm Robert Cederberg."

"Well, Robert, I am Sergeant MacArthur, and I want to ask you a few questions, do you think that will be alright."

"I am not supposed to," said Robert.

"You are not supposed to talk to policemen?" Asked the sergeant with some curiosity. "Why not."

"Strangers," said Robert, acting as if he was five years old and not thirteen.

"You're not supposed to talk to strangers. Very good rule, that, but you see it doesn't include policemen, besides, I have given you my name, so we aren't exactly strangers." The sergeant walked up to the bench and sat down next to Robert.

"Robert," he began, "did you see that car on the beach today."

"The red one that crashed over the cliff."

"That's the one. Did you see or hear the car go over the cliff?"

"No." Said Robert, understanding that saying less was good.

"Did you watch them bring the car from the beach?"

"I did. I watched from the sand bar."

"You were out at the bar. Did you see the car go over?"

"No, later."

"How much later? Were you there before the ambulance or the police cars?

"I heard them from the sand bar."

"So you were out on the bar before the police arrived but after the car crashed? From the bar, did you see the car on the beach?"

"Yes, but only after the sirens. Before that, I didn't notice the car. I didn't start from our dock; I started down by the McKinsey's."

"Were you in a boat or on a raft?"

"On my raft. I started from the McKinsey's because it's easier. The bottom is better."

"When you were paddling out or when you were on the bar, did you hear a gunshot; a loud bang?"

"A gunshot?"

"Yes, like a firecracker only louder. You know, like in the American westerns."

"No."

"Can you hear anything out at that sandbar?"

"In the morning you can hear the motors starting on boats, and once in a while you can hear people calling to one another, but mostly you hear the waves and the gulls."

"How about this morning, anything unusual?"

"No"

"No one calling for help? No tires screeching? No gunshot?"

"No just the gulls."

"Where were you on the bar? Can you point to where you had your raft?" asked the policeman, watching where Robert pointed.

"I watched the car from over there," said Robert pointing to a spot on the sand bar opposite the cove. "I landed my raft more like between there and there," again Robert pointed to a spot, this time a place further down the bar, opposite the McKinsey house, where he usually landed a raft. Robert looked at the officer out of the corner of his eye. So far, the questions had been easy, but Robert could feel the danger in the man sitting opposite him on the iron bench.

"Do you often go out to the sand bar alone Robert?"

"No I usually go with my brothers or friends."

"But this morning you were out there alone before seven thirty. Did your mom or dad know you were going to the sand bar all alone?"

"No I was alone. I went out to the bar alone."

"Did anyone see you go out?"

"Maybe, but I didn't see anyone."

"Why did you go out to the sand bar alone? Was something wrong? Did something bad happen? Were your parents fighting? Why did you go out to the sandbar alone?"

"You will laugh at me."

"No I won't son. I promise. Just tell me the truth."

"We are going home today. I got up early to the say good bye to the Mathews. When I got to their house, no one was up, so I paddled out to the sand bar."

"Look son, I understand these things. Tell me what happened this morning, because I know something happened that caused you to swim out to the bar, and it was not because no one was up. Tell me what happened."

"I can't it is bad, very bad."

"You saw something bad this morning."

"Yes."

"Was it the man in the car?"

"No." Robert debated telling a part of the story, but saying that he had found the man dead and then out of fear swam out to the sand bar. This was so far from the truth, that Robert was not sure he could pull off the lie.

"What did you see?"

"I looked in the window. Cathy's window. I shouldn't have. It was wrong. I have been told that I am never to look in a girl's window." This was the truth. What Robert did not say was he had been caught several times peeping into neighbor girls windows and his father had whipped him with a belt.

"I see. Well, this one time let's forget about what your dad said. You looked in the window. What did you see, huh boy. Did you see a little titty, boy? Is that it, Aye?" The officer laughed in spite of himself. "Did you see her naked? Is that it? Did she see you?"

"No, she didn't see me. But I saw her, and..." Robert hesitated. He never planned to tell this story, and now he was.

"And, what?" asked the policeman, sitting up.

"I saw her cousin Chuck. He was in the bed with her. They both were naked. I hate her," said Robert starting to cry.

"So you liked this girl, and then you found out that she is cheating on you, so you went out to the sand bar to be alone, and you saw nothing about this car until you were out at the sand bar?"

"Yes."

"Are you sure, because I may have to go to the Mathews house and ask a few questions. This boy Chuck, do you know he is a cousin?"

"Well, they call him cousin."

"And you saw him in bed with this girl?"

"Do you know old Cathy is?"

"She is fourteen."

"And, what about the lad? This Chuck, how old is he?"

"He is nineteen."

"Okay, now raise your right hand, and swear to me that you saw this Chuck naked in a bed with this girl Cathy."

"I swear," said Robert starting to cry. Robert turned away from the officer and looked down the beach towards the Mathews dock. The rowboat was just leaving the dock. Cathy sat wrapped in a beach towel with her head and bare shoulder leaning against Chuck's naked arm, just as if she had been the other morning.

Robert entered the cottage at 2:05 that afternoon. Robert's two younger brothers were watching afternoon cartoons in the living room on the portable television set with the large rabbit ears antenna. In the kitchen, Bobby Vinton was singing Blue Velvet on the radio. In Kingsville, they listened to CKLW and watched WXYZ.

Robert was hungry and wanted to go into the kitchen to make a sandwich but he could hear his parents in the kitchen arguing about who was going to drive the Sunbeam convertible home and who would drive the Ford station wagon. Robert had watched Austin, who was driving Grandma Ruth's 1958 Chevy leave with a trunk full of suitcases and boxes of food. Robert had expected to drive with Austin, but he left without even saying goodbye.

Starting up the stairs to his room Robert heard his father, call out, "Robert, where have you been?"

"Out."

"Did you see the car on the beach?"

"Yeah."

"How about the driver. Did you see the driver?"

"Only from the sand bar."

"You went to the sand bar alone!"

"Sure, why not."

"We talked about this Robert. You aren't supposed to go out there alone. You take too many risks. If you wanted to go out to the bar, you should have gone with your mother or Austin. You know we are worried about you son. Did you see the police?"

"I talked to one."

"You talked to a policeman, without your mom?"

"What would she know?"

"She knows enough not to talk to the police alone. Did you have something to do with what happen on the beach?"

"Of course not."

"How about what happened at the Mathews?"

"What happened?"

"Austin says the police came and took that boy Chuck away in a car. Did you have anything to do with that?"

"No."

"Robert, I am going to ask you again, and don't lie to me, because I have spoken to the police. Did you have anything to do with that boy being arrested?" Robert watched his father carefully for signs that he was lying. Already by thirteen Robert was good at detecting a lie when he heard it, especially out of his father's mouth. When his father lied, he tried to maintain eye contact, staring at you as if saying, trust me. Right now, he was watching Robert as carefully as Robert was watching him.

"I told the police what I saw. I told them the truth."

"What did you see?"

"I saw Chuck Zane in Cathy's room. They were naked."

"Robert, we have talked about peeping in windows before. Now they have arrested that boy, merely because Cathy Mathews is a little whore. And you are a snitch."

"She's not."

"She is," said Caroline sticking her head in from the bedroom. "She is a tramp, and that boy was doing nothing she did not let him do." Robert wanted to cry and at the same time scream and swear at his father, but he did neither, instead, he pulled back in his shell and ran up to his room. He hated boys like his brother Austin and Chuck Zane, boys who were successful and confident with girls, he hated his father and mother, and he hated the man on the beach for thinking he was nothing but a fat kid. Lying on his bed, he covered himself with his bedspread and prayed for the day when he would own a silver gun with black handgrips.

CHAPTER 2

THE TURTLE AND THE HAIR

For Christmas, Eric Cederberg finally gave Robert a BB gun. Robert had been talking about a gun for months and his father assumed he wanted a rifle, the popular Red Ryder Daisy air rifles that looked like the Winchester that John Wayne used in the movies. Seeing the air rifle, on Christmas morning, Robert was at first disappointed, he wanted a pistol, but he realized his father had gone against his mother in buying the rifle. Besides, a BB gun, even a rifle, was one-step closer to owning a real gun.

The lever action rifle proved to be an accurate if underpowered weapon. Robert practiced with the rifle nearly every day in their basement, shooting at paper targets held by a paper clip in a red three-sided metal shooting trap. At first, he fired the gun from five feet away. When he was routinely hitting the center of the target, he moved to ten feet. Eventually, he had to move outside and still he was shooting bull eyes even at the limit of the gun's range.

Naturally, as his shooting skill improved he sought out other targets, tin cans, bottles, and boxes. For the longest time he kept from shooting a living thing but eventually while he was practicing in his back yard, he shot at a robin. To Robert's way of thinking, Robins were a common bird, and rather ugly, not like cardinals or blue jays, yet when he hit the robin and it took a step or two and then died, he was overwhelmed at what he had done, killed a defenseless bird, a thing that could fly. Seeing the dead bird, Robert considered the difference between his two killings. With the robin, there was no sign of blood no exit wound, no bits of flesh and bone. The bird was simply dead, almost like it was asleep. This type of quiet death bothered Robert. It was too easy. One minute the bird is hopping around looking for worms and the next it is lying on its side with a microscopic puncture wound, dead because something bigger than it wanted to practice his marksmanship.

All of this seemed wrong to Robert. Birds, even dumb robins were beautiful, and he had no right taking their lives. Standing in the back yard with the dead Robin at his feet, Robert wondered whether he would have felt the same if, he had killed a squirrel or one of the annoying cats that used his yard as a little box. Thinking about it, Robert realized that while he felt no guilt about what happened on the beach, he regretting killing the man and the robin, and he would probably regret killing a neighbor's pet. Confused by the mixture of thoughts and emotions he was feeling, Robert placed the robin under a shrub, packed up his red metal target, and went inside to watch television.

In 1964, three things changed the course of Robert's life. First, in April, Eric explained he was selling the family's summer home of thirty year because he could not pay the taxes on the cottage. He did not mention the taxes were only eight hundred dollars. Less than the amount of money still hidden in the iron bed at the cottage.

The second announcement was the family was moving to Grosse Pointe Woods in June. Eric and Caroline did not explain to the boys why the family was moving or that they were using the cottage tax money as down payment on the new house. Privately, Austin speculated that the house on Cadieux needed a new roof, and rather than replace the roof, the family was moving. Whatever the real reason, moving provided Robert with a new neighborhood, a new school, and a new group of kids who had never called Robert "the Turtle."

Robert spent many days and nights that summer hanging out with a group of neighbor kids who seems to do little more than roam the streets. On his new street alone, there were dozen boys and girls around Robert's age. Immediately, across the street, Neil Morgan was the same age as Robert and born only a week before Robert. Neil was an only child. His dad had married his secretary. When Neil was born, her parents moved in and never left, except for the month they spent each summer at the their cottage.

For Robert, Neil Morgan took the place of all of Robert's old friends. Neil introduced Robert to cigarettes, bowling, and poker. Riding their bikes, Robert and Neil would race to the Grosse Point Woods Lanes, where for less than a dollar you could rent bowling shoes, buy a pack of cigarettes, and bowl three games.

One of the reasons the boys bowled at Woods Lanes was the cigarette machine located in the exit way, between the double doors, halfway outside the bowling alley. By placing the cigarette machine out of view and technically outside the bowling alley, the owner did not feel the need to enforce or supervise Michigan's law that you had to be eighteen to buy cigarettes. Neil Morgan had identified at least five local businesses where he could purchase cigarette. In general, the boys purchased one pack and divided the twenty cigarettes, so that each boy could smoke cigarettes while he bowled and still have some for later.

At night, the boys would play dodge ball or flashlight tag, or they would simply sit on someone's front porch drinking soda, smoking cigarettes, and listening to top 40 hits on a portable radio. On weekends, they would go to the park to swim or just ride their bikes around the neighborhood looking for excitement.

In July, using the money his grandmother Cederberg gave him for his fourteenth birthday Robert purchased a Crossman BB pistol. The Crossman air pistol looked like a Colt model 1911. The all-metal gun fired .17 cal BBs, pellets, or darts. The gun was a single shot spring loaded air pistol that required the shooter to pull a bolt back to cock a spring and chamber a BB. The gun only had an effective range of fifty feet, but it looked and felt like the real Colt automatic soldiers carried in World War II. Perhaps just as important to Robert, it looked like the gun Lee Marvin carried on M-squad.

For days after buying the new gun, Robert ran around the neighborhood shooting at trees, lampposts and stop signs. Dressed in shorts and a tee shirt, Robert took to carrying the gun in his surplus air force vest the one with the built in pistol holster. Even though his outfit drew jeers from the older kids, Robert loved carrying his pistol everywhere he went until one day, he heard Neil Morgan describe Robert as the 'gun nut.' Something about this title made Robert uncomfortable, so he packed up his air force vest and Crossman air pistol in a suitcase in his closet, and tried to act like all the other boys, interested in poker, muscle cars, and girls. An act that was not difficult.

Robert started ninth grade at a new Junior High, Parcells. At school, he met several other boys with whom he started to hanging out. Carl Thompson and Richard Logan lived near Robert, Kurt Lea lived in Harper Woods; close enough on a bike to visit. Carl and Richard also had BB pistols, and eventually the three boys conceived of a game where they would wear army clothes, helmets, and sunglasses and hunt each other in back yards and basements. In the summer before he learned to drive, Robert and his three best friends Neil Morgan, Richard Logan, and Carl Thompson, expanded their hunting game to a nearby wood where seven to ten boys played using their bikes to expand the range of the game.

On Saturday mornings, the boys played their simulated war game at the site of the future high school. The large lot had a series of bike and footpaths that divided the existing woods from the excavation site. At the start of a game, the boys would divide into two or three teams. In general, the new players, the boys who did not know Robert did not pick Robert as a teammate because he was overweight and wearing real glasses.

Being the last boy picked did not bothered Robert, he was use to it. He was confident that whatever team he was on, he would be an individual winner more often than not. Robert was without question the best shot in the group, but he was also too fat to hide and so clumsy walking in the woods, he could be heard a block away. On his bike, Robert was more of a threat. Robert was stronger than he looked and fully able to ride his bike as fast as any other boy, at least over short distances. Because his bike leveled the playing field, Robert tended to volunteer to serve as scout, riding ahead on this bike and then quickly returning to his team to advise them on the enemy. On most Saturdays, two teams would start from one end of the woods with the goal of reaching a finishing line on the other side.

Over time, Carl Thompson, Neil Morgan, Richard Logan, and Robert Cederberg became the team to beat. The four boys hung out together at school and after school. Like Robert, Carl had both a pistol and a rifle. Neil only had a Marksman pistol, and Richard only had a Daisy rifle. In some games, Robert's younger brother John would join Robert's team, other times John would fight on team of boys his age. When they fought against one another, the two brothers spent most of their time hunting each other. John, who could wait in ambush for hours, seemed to take great delight shooting Robert in the face, hand, or ankle, places where the BB really hurt.

On some games, the contest became a race to the finish line, with no shots fired until the two teams were within sight of the finish. Then the fight became close combat firing from tree to tree until one team had no players left alive. On some days, the two teams hunted each other, hiding in the woods and staying away from the finish line. When a team used this strategy, the other team might race to the finish line and then have to come looking for their opponent. The last way of playing the game happened when each kid started from a different spot and they raced to the finish line or hunted as individuals, one winner, and winner take all. Robert had won more of these contests than any other boy. Given his size and clumsiness, winning was a testament to his patience and ability to find a good place for an ambush and stay quiet.

On Saturday October 3 1964, Robert got up early to clean his guns before breakfast. Robert's older brother Austin was away for his first year at college. Temporarily, Robert had the large upstairs bedroom all on his own. His two other brothers, John and William had their own rooms at the back of the house next to his parents. This morning Robert awoke before 6:00 a.m. His parents had been up late drinking and on Saturday, they slept with their shades down. Pulling on jean shorts and a tee shirt, Robert crept out of his room stepping one foot in front of the other down the stairs into the kitchen. On the large yellow kitchen clock, it read 6:06 a.m. Using the small bathroom off the kitchen, Robert washed his face and brushed his teeth.

Taking down a box of Sugar Crisp, Robert filled a bowl to the brim with cereal while he hummed the jingle, "Can't get enough of those sugar crisps." Taking two donuts from a box of Kroger nutty Donuts in the breadbox, Robert was very aware that if Chessie was here, he would be eating the toast and skim milk the doctor had prescribed for his weight condition. Robert recognized that he needed to lose weight, but the donuts were his favorites, frosted nutty donuts and he was excited about the game they had planned for the morning. *If everyone showed up there would be twelve kids playing in today's game, enough for three teams or enough for the greatest winner take all game in history,* thought Robert.

After breakfast, Robert walked quietly down the steps into the basement. In the back room by the furnace, there were two workbenches. On one bench were all sorts of tools his father had used; screwdrivers, pliers, black tape, and nails left scatter across the top of the workbench. Robert hated the clutter on his father's bench, but that was his dad's workspace. To the right of the workbench was Robert's gun table. The table was an old card table with its plastic top cut and torn. On the table were Robert's own set of pliers, screwdrivers, packs of BBs, his BB gun oil, and cleaning kit. Behind the table, Robert's tools hung on hooks attached to a pegboard. His worktable was clear of all clutter on his dad's table. Above the table, Robert's Daisy Rifle and Pistol hung from their own hooks.

Robert took down the Daisy rifle and looked down the barrel, already knowing it was clean and ready for use. Taking down the

Marksman pistol, he experienced the joy of having the pistol in his hand. Some of the other boys were using the new semi automatic pistols with CO2 canisters, but Robert was happy to use his spring action single shot. In the comics, Sgt. Rock carried a Colt .45 as his sidearm, because one shot from the Colt was enough to stop a crazed German in his tracks. In Robert's war, what mattered was accuracy and leaving a mark when you hit another boy. Kids ignored hits on their clothes, hits that did not hurt. However, a well placed hit on the cheek or hand would leave a mark that would be visible for twenty minutes. Some of the boys had started wearing gloves and hats to protect more of their bodies, leaving only smaller patches of skin as targets. For Robert, this is what made the game exciting. Robert had a tendency to overheat, so he chose to wear his summer warrior garb, shorts, tee shirt, and pilot's vest even in the fall. If another player hit him, Robert wanted to know it.

Checking the action on his Marksman, he wondered if he would need to replace the spring at some point or purchase a new pistol. Putting his pistol in his vest holster, Robert wrapped his rifle in a blanket. The rifle came with a western style gun holder, like the ones cowboys tied to a horse. The holder was actually ideal for transporting a rifle, but the older boys made fun of Robert, calling him Sugar Foot. In addition, ever since a man with a rifle had killed President Kennedy, Robert was very aware of the looks he received riding through the village on his bike, with a BB rifle across the handlebars. Now he covered the gun in a blanket and stuck it in the wire book basket attached to the back of his bike.

Robert left the house at a quarter to eight, two hours early, so he could select several places to hide. Outside, the air was crisp with the hint of fall. In the front of the yard, the big maple was already starting to change a little of its color. The building site where they played was a mile and a half away by car, less by bike. Robert rode first to the shell station where he purchased an orange soda that he would drink later. In his saddlebags, he had a Cub Scout canteen of water, two donuts, and four Clark bars. Before he started, he ate another donut and half of one of the Clark bars.

Robert wasn't sure when he first learned about the new school building site, but every boy within a ten block radius became aware of all that was happening in Hanson's Woods. Before the board of education selected the site for the new High School, Hanson's Woods was a dense forest with bike paths and walking trails. Once digging began, huge mounds of earth piled up around the foundation. In a cityscape that averaged less than fifteen feet about Lake St. Clair, the mounts of earth piled high by the builders represented the highest hills for five miles in any direction, and all unsupervised.

Robert entered the woods peddling fast into the still dark wood. Out of the sun, the sweat on Robert's forehead cooled. Robert had been on this path many times before. To the west, the path led to the center of the woods, a place where the various bike paths crossed. Off the path to his right were high uncut grasses; to his left, thorn bushes, oak and maple trees, and large moss covered boulders. Scanning the area for other early arrivals, Robert decided to create one of his ambush spots here among the boulders. Dragging dead branches, he covered over the open gap between two boulders half way up the hill. In front of the space, he placed more branches and a pile of leaves. Working quickly he created a shooting blind, that had space enough inside to hide him and was not obvious from the paths. All that Robert needed was enough time to ride ahead of the others, hide his bike and enter the blind. From it, he could shoot any person on any one of the five paths without necessarily revealing his position.

Satisfied with his work, Robert left his rifle in the blind. If anyone found the rifle, he was free to use it for the game, but honor dictated he return the rifle to its owner at the end of the game. Riding to a second and third spot, Robert built new blinds where he might hide if the game lasted long enough. Robert believed in planning, yet early on Robert learned the importance of varying what he did and taking advantage of the situation. Today, he had several options including blinds in two new spots, and one tried and true.

At 10:15 they met at the south eastern entrance to the woods, twelve boys dress in jeans and tee-shirts and covered over by various forms of surplus army clothes, vests, shoulder pads, helmets, gloves and sun glasses; two boy even wore athletic protectors. For today's game it was agreed it would be 'winner take all', meaning that the last boy standing was the winner. Straddling their bikes, the boys discussed the rules of the game. They agreed that teams were fair, but everyone understood that eventually teammates would have to turn on one another. Among the group, there were two boys who had never played before. They were friends of Dave Kennedy and like Dave; each boy had a rifle. Because they were new, they rode ahead with Dave so he could show them the tree at the north end of the woods that would the goal. Watching Dave and his friends leave, Robert considered what

Dave might be planning. Robert guessed that Dave was going to use the new boys as bate, as targets. He would sacrifice them to a frontal attack, while he shot the attackers from behind. Watching the three boys ride ahead, Robert looked at his teammates, Carl Thompson, Neil Morgan, and Richard Logan. All three understood and loved the game as much as Robert, but Richard did not seem to be paying any attention, which was a surprise. Richard was as competitive as a boy could be, even though he was a terrible shot.

"What's up Richard," Robert asked moving his bike closer to the crew cut warrior.

"What?" Richard turned away and wiped his face.

"Come 'on man. What's up?"

"We are moving." Richard sat on a full-sized ten-speed bike, dangerous on paths but very fast on surface streets.

"Moving where?" asked Robert. He spent more time with Neil because they lived across the street, but he liked Richard better, and he liked Richard sister, Karen more than he could explain. The idea the Logan's were moving was awful news.

"We are moving to Colorado. My dad has a new job and we are moving in a month. We are moving to fucking Denver."

"A month, holy shit man, what about school? What about drivers training?"

"It will be all fucked up, you can count on that. My mom says I will probably skip school for a month and then start in January."

"What about Karen?"

"Same thing, she will finish her senior year in Denver. All she cares about is that asshole Bill Arnold. She keeps talking about how she cannot leave her fucking boyfriend. My guess is they are already doing it, so if anyone should be angry it's fucking Bill Arnold." Richard cared about his older sister and he thought her choice of boyfriend was stupid at best. Secretly, he thought moving to Denver was exciting and would be good for Karen.

"You know I was really looking forward to this game, but right now it all seems so meaningless. I am thinking about just going home, and starting to pack. Fucking Colorado. You know that means we will never see each other again. The Turtle and the Hair." Richard brushed his hand along the top of his crew cut, and all four boys laughed. Like every boy in America in 1964, the boys had started letting their hair grow out, in an attempt to look like John or Paul in the Beatles. At the point Richard had begun to resemble George Harrison, his father, an ex-air force officer, took Richard personally to barber shop in the village and instructed the barber to give his son a genuine marine crew cut. In his father's words, 'not a letterman or Kingston trio crew cut, or a fancy Princeton, but an honest to goodness military hair cut'. When the barber finished, and turned Richard around to face the mirror he proclaimed, "now that is good looking hair." Hoping to restore some father son relationship, Richard's father took Richard for an ice cream Sunday at Sanders, but all Richard could do was look at his reflection in the store mirrors, and say "my hair, my hair." Ultimately, the other boys had taken to calling Richard "My Hair," shortened eventually to "Hair" or "Richard Hair," which led to Robert and Richard privately calling each other the Turtle and the Hair, as a not so clever play on words. For their part, both boys enjoyed the shared nickname.

Robert sat on his old heavy duty Schwinn watching several boys disappear down a path bordering the western side of the woods.

"Richard, you can't go home," said Robert. "You have to play. This might be your last game. You have to go in there and kill as many of those assholes as you can. You know you have the skill."

"Sure, then you will kill me from one of your ambushes and win the game."

"No, in fact, I will guard your back, if that is what it takes to get you in the game."

"You know the game has already started. If I wanted to, I could shoot you right now. We could have a duel."

No, we will duel when everyone else is dead. You and me, face to face, Pistols at ten paces, no protection."

"That I would like to see that," said Carl to Neil standing next to him. The two boys had waited for their friends, understanding that this was a personal moment for the Turtle and the Hair. Carl was the tallest boy in the group, standing nearly six feet. He was not a very good shot, but he was fearless on his bike, riding it at full speed through the rutted paths. Every combat squad needed a Carl; he was the guy who would eventually dive on the enemy grenade. Looking at Carl and Neil, Robert wondered how he could use Carl and Neil to make sure Richard and he finished the day in a duel that he would lose.

"Neil, what do you say, shall we fight together as a team and then whoever is alive at the end, we fight it out in individual duels."

"Right now, I have my marksman aimed at your heart," said Neil in his very precise German voice. "I could take you and Richard out right now and the game could be mine." Robert saw the barrel of the .45 sticking out of Neil' army coat. Robert assumed Neil was waiting for a sign that one of his friends was going to betray him. He looked over at Richard and smiled. Richard was pointing his Daisy target pistol at Neil. Carl was standing guard over his friends, unconcerned that one of them might shoot him, while they sorted out their own game plan.

"So here is what we do," said Robert. "We use Carl as the point man and as the bait. My guess is Dave is hiding near the goal and his two friends are hiding with him. Jerry and that pal of his,"

"Adam," offered Neil.

"Yea, Adam. John and Tim will be together and that leaves Bob Anderson, Tommy Hammond, and Bill Patterson. They will all be on their own.

"I think that our first objective is to get to the crossroads. Richard and I will go on foot. Carl you and Neil will wait five minutes and then will ride your bikes on the central path to the crossroad. Neil you are Carl's wingman. You make sure no one walks away if he goes down. If both of you are hit go to the goal tree and wait. Richard and I are going to try to get in place ahead of you and hide. If you make it to the crossroads unharmed, take cover there and we will ambush anyone who enters the cross roads." Under Carl's insistence, they shook hands and then Richard and Robert, the Turtle and the Hair took off on the run, both carrying a pistol in his right hand, Richard with a rifle slung over his back.

The builders divided the site into three sections. The excavation was fenced off from the original forest park. The dirt from the foundation formed a series of hills. For the most part, the hills had bike and footpaths, with tall grass and bushes on both side and only a few large trees. The forest was just that, a Midwest forest with maples, oaks, elms, evergreens, pines and low thorn bushes. At first, Robert and Richard walked along bike path into the center of the hills. At a point of Robert's choosing, they left the path and made their way through the high grass to the edge of the forest were Robert stepped onto a deer path leading into the center of the forest. The two boys walked without speaking. Through several games, and with the benefit of the Cub Scout manual, they had developed a form of combat sign language. Signally to halt, Robert crouched as he and Richard listened for the sounds of battle. On the wind, Robert heard a boy shout "Your Dead," and then another shout "I got you." Dave Kennedy he thought. Someone got one of Dave's friends and then Dave took him out.

"That was Dave," Richard whispered in Robert's ear. Robert nodded, and pointed for them to get moving. The two boys followed the narrow deer path between trees, some so close together Robert had to remove his pack. After walking for several minutes, the path began to climb. Near the top of a hill, Robert got down and began crawling. When the two boys reached the top, they could see down into the forest below. They were on the hill above the crossroads. Robert could see his hidden blind. Beside him, Richard, pointed to Carl straddling his bike, an open target. Robert could have easily hit Carl if he had his rifle, but a boy would have to get a lot closer to hit Carl with a pistol. Robert knew that Neil was in hiding near Carl, but he had yet to pick him out, when he heard the zing of a BB shot and saw Carl hit the dirt, using his bike as a shield.

From behind a large oak, John Bridgewater came charging out with a pistol in his hand intent in shooting Carl. Behind him, Tim Lancaster followed more slowly, watching for other shooters. Beside him, Richard put his rifle to his cheek and took aim at John as Robert fired his pistol at Tim. Before John had crossed half the distance to Carl, he was shot twice, once by Richard and once by Neil, who had stepped out from behind a different oak. Behind him, Tim stood rubbing his right hand with his left, trying to take the sting out of the hit.

"You are both dead said Carl standing up with his bike. Go wait at the goal, and try to keep it fair, don't tell anyone where we are."

"You are playing as a team," said John.

"You cannot do that, this is winner take all," wined Tim. "You can't play as a team, it isn't fair."

"Look asshole, if you whine anymore about the rules I am going to punch you. We are a team, and that is that, now head for the goal and say nothing if you want to avoid a punch in gym on Monday," said Carl, meaning every word. As the boys ran off, Neil melted back behind his tree and Carl knelt back down behind his bike as if he was fixing his chain. In all, the fight had taken less than five minutes during which Richard and Robert had remained in hiding as they moved to different positions.

Carl, who was not very good at play-acting and even less effective at waiting, actually began resetting the chain on his bike. So involved in his task, he took his eye off the paths and the woods, and really focused on getting the chain on each sprocket. When the first bb hit him in the back, he did not even notice. When a second BB hit him in the face, Carl continued fixing his bike. He never expected to make it out of this ambush; he just wanted to give Richard a chance. From behind a tree, Tommy Hammond came running down the path.

"Good shot, Tommy."

"Are you alright Carl, I didn't hurt you?"

"Did you want too?"

"No I was aiming for your chest, but the shot when high."

"No problem, said Carl standing up. I was trying to get my chain back on and I didn't hear you.

"Well, you are dead, so remember, no helping your friends." Tommy heard Neil behind him, but three BBs hit him at nearly the same time.

"Motherfucker," screamed Tommy. "That isn't fair. Nobody said anything about teams today."

"Yes, well, you and Carl are dead so go to the goal and leave the fighting to the living," yelled Neil before slipping back into the trees. Tommy had not seen Robert or Richard, but he knew the pain in his right nut was Robert's way of payback for hitting Carl in the face. By the time Tommy turned back, Neil was invisible.

When the Tommy and Carl had disappeared from sight, Neil stepped out from his oak into the clearing. He walked his bike to the middle of the path and announced to the forest, "I am going to take Carl's place. Let's see if we can get Patterson or Anderson, before we go after Dave." Neil was not concerned when the forest did not answer back. He knew Robert and Richard were close.

With his back to the hill, Neil knelt behind his bike and pretended to work on the chain. The large Schwinn offered little protection and Neil had his pistol cocked and ready. In the distance, he heard boys laughing, no doubt John and Tim laughing at Tommy and Carl. Unlike Carl, Neil did not enjoy being the bait. He would have liked to be the last man standing, but Robert wanted this to be Richard's day, and Neil knew when to let Robert have his way. Still, that did not mean he enjoyed being a tethered goat. Neil lay down on the ground and pulled the heavy bike over his feet and legs, making it seem like he had fallen off the bike and was hurt. Reaching out with his right hand, he slid his pistol under a pile of leaves, pointing the barrel at the nearest path.

Neil had seen this move in all kinds of movies, and TV shows, but he had never tried it in backyard combat. Perhaps, I can get one more, he thought. For Neil, it mattered how many you killed not whether you were the winner. For Richard and Robert, it was all about winning.

Focused on the path in front of him, Neil did not hear Jim Anderson coming over the hill behind him, until Jim, stepped on a tree limb and shouted "Shit" as the limb broke and twisted his ankle in the bargain. Rather, he saw Bill Patterson creeping towards him from one of the northern paths. Guessing where Jim must be, from the stream of swear words, Neil assumed that Bill was the real threat, so when he was close enough to chance a shot, Neil fired missing Bill by inches. Taking aim, Bill shot back at Neil who was already diving behind a tree. Bill was sure he hit Neil on the foot, but he knew he would have make a second kill shot before Neil Morgan would admit he was dead, so Bill ran to take cover behind an elm., at once exposing his back to Jim Anderson, Robert, and Richard. Before Bill could correct his mistake, he was hit by a shot from Jim Anderson, standing not five feet from Bill, and then Jim was shot once in his leg and two more times in his back.

"Son of a bitch," swore Bill. "You pricks are fighting as a team."

"So what," said Neil stepping out from behind his tree? "You two are dead and that is all that counts. So head out, and don't say anything to Dave or his buddies." Neil pointed his pistol at the two, like a sheriff in a western. As he stood there, Richard Logan stepped out from a large boulder and walked down the hill to joint Neil.

"You're dead too, Neil."

"What do you mean, I am dead." Neil started to point his pistol at Richard, when a BB hit him in the chest.

"Jim hit you in the back. I saw it and so did Bill, so now Robert and I have decided the issue."

"But I am on your side. We are a team."

"And, you are a great teammate, and you probably have the most kills, and you fought with bravery and cleverness, but fair is fair, and dead is dead. Besides, this game has to end with Robert and me in a duel. Be cool and go to the goal and make sure no one say's anything about Robert and me playing as a team."

"Ok, but, wherever you are Robert," shouted Neil, "I don't think that was fair, and I am not going to invite you over when the

Lang sisters visit, so say good bye to feeling any tit for a while, because you are cut off, you asshole." Before leaving, Neil smiled at Richard. Both boys knew that Neil was not mad at Robert and that Neil and Robert would be making out with the Lang twins in Neil's basement regardless of what Neil said today.

Robert smiled at Neil' protest and at the prospects of seeing Jan Lang again. In the day light, Jan and her sister Jane were no beauties, but in the basement, with the lights out, and the Beatles playing, the sisters were everything a teenage boy could desire. Jan loved kissing and her sister went even further. When Neil was gone, Robert stepped out from his blind, not four feet from where Richard was standing.

"Robert," said Richard, "That only leaves Dave and his friends."

"I know. What do you want to do?"

"I am going to work my way to the goal. If I can take out Dave and his friend, you and I can have our duel. If they get me, I will leave it to you to win." Robert realized that Richard wanted to win on his own, and he hoped Robert would understand and simply have his back. Robert was going to miss Richard. There was something solid about him. Richard was probably the only boy in their school who knew the meaning of Robert's nickname, the Turtle.

In ninth grade, when Robert and Richard met, Robert had matured, and his penis, while not as large as Richard's was certainly as large as Neil or Dave. One day after gym, Robert said he wished he had a penis as big as Richard's. That was when Richard told Robert that Karen said it did not matter. She said that girls knew it wasn't the size that mattered it was how much you loved the girl that mattered." Robert had to think about that statement for a minute. In his heart, he hoped that Karen was still a virgin, but he also was excited by the idea that size did not matter, because that meant there was a chance for Robert with Karen. Confused by it all, Robert explained to Richard when he was younger he thought his penis was too small, always hiding like a turtle, Robert said without thinking.

"Is that why you are called Turtle," asked Richard later that day.

"Yes."

"Well don't worry man; you are no different than half the guys in gym class, no turtle anymore.

"But I like being called the Turtle and the Hair."

"Sure, sure, but the reason has changed. You are the tortoise, slow and steady you get it done. I am the hair, fast and slick." Richard ran his hand along the top of his crew cut. "Friends forever," he said offering his hand. Robert never forgot that day. Now, he had to see if he could make this a day to remember for Richard.

When Richard was out of site, Robert entered the blind that he had made that morning. If Dave shot Richard, Robert would wait for him here. If Richard were the survivor, they would fight their duel here. Robert would have like to followed Richard and help him take out Dave and his friend, but that was not what Richard wanted. Sitting down behind the pile of branches, Robert relaxed and closed his eyes, falling asleep.

Robert awoke with a start. The forest seemed alive with sound, there were birds flying and cawing, Robert heard kids screaming. Not the friendly I got you screams, not the 'all you, all you in come free' scream, but screams of terror. Something was wrong, and Robert did not know what it was because he had been asleep. He did not even know how long he had been asleep until he looked at his Timex and saw it was five minutes after twelve. Picking up his pistol and slinging his rifle over his right shoulder, he rode his bike to the north end of the park, towards the goal tree. Because he was unsure what was happening, he had to assume the game was still on so he approached the goal with the greatest of care, which meant leaving the path and his bike and walking across country.

Climbing a slight rise, Robert saw the large oak they used as the goal in the distance, but the tree's large canopy was too thick for Robert to see down to the ground. Walking off the path, Robert continued to hear Kids screaming or crying and then a new sound, a siren, a police car or fire engine. "That cuts it," thought Robert. After all these weeks, someone had reported them to the police, or one of the new kids had started a fire, and now they would have the fire department on their case. Either way," thought Robert, "we will not get to play here again anytime soon."

Robert made his way to a point where he could look down on the place they set as the goal. Sitting out the ground were Carl and Neil. They had their legs crossed and it looked like they were crying. Standing over them was a police officer. Beyond them, Jim Anderson, with Tim and Bill were talking to another police officer. Dave's friends Jerry and Adam were sitting in a police car parked on the lawn near the oak tree that served as goal.

An emergency fire truck pulled up and two firemen jumped out running into the forest carrying a stretcher. When they stopped, Robert saw there were two boys lying on the ground near the base of the oak, Richard and Dave Kennedy. Dave was sitting against the tree and when the firemen reached him, one of them started talking to Dave while he did something to him. The other fireman turned and knelt beside Richard, picking up Richard's hand and then feeling at his neck. For a moment, the two men talked, and then the fireman called to one of the policemen who walked to his car and then returned with a blanket, which he handed to the fireman. Robert tried to create some different explanation for what was happening, but he knew before the fireman covered the body with a blanket, that Richard was dead.

Walking into the clearing, none of the adults, the policemen, the firemen, the neighbors who had begun to crowd around the scene, no one noticed Robert as he knelt down beside Richard, pulling back the blanket, to stare at his friend's face already a gray color, his eyes open and glassed over. On the right side of his head was a small black hole, no bigger than a fingertip. On the other side, Robert saw the larger hole that he knew would be there, with bits of bone and brain, and a pool of blood, drained from his body like water from Robert's boy scout canteen All necessary parts of his friend Richard, once alive, now dead.

"The kid said he did not know there was any difference between a BB gun and his dad's pistol. He says his dad calls it a pellet gun and he knew these kids play this game using BB and pellet guns, so he brought his dad's pellet pistol," said one fireman to the other.

"Yea, the only problem is it was a .22."

Where once, Robert had been excited by the sight of death, now an intense sense of loss and grief racked his body, until he cried out and wept. One of the policemen, crossed from where he was keeping a small crowd back, and taking Robert by the shoulders helped him stand and walk away from his friend's body.

"This is going to be tough son. Try to remember your friend when he was alive. Is this your first time seeing a body?"

"Yes lied," Robert

"Believe me, it is never easy. You want to forget about what you have seen and only think about your friend when he was alive. Focus on the last time you were together. Think about a joke you shared," said the policeman, showing no obvious signs that he was bothered by seeing a dead teenager.

"I should have been with him. I should have had his back."

"Look kid. The game you are playing is crazy. Even with BB guns, it was dangerous, and now you see what has happened. An accident like this could have been avoided if your fathers had taught you properly about gun ownership and use. Now we have a dead boy because one kid did not know the difference between a .17 cal gun and a .22 caliber gun. Now the anti gun nuts will say we need to lock our guns." The officer stopped; embarrassed he was lecturing a kid.

"Look kid, I am really sorry about your friend. How about I drive you home?"

"No I have a bike; I left it near the south entrance."

"Ok, you and I will go get your bike."

The officer, whose name as Sergeant Thomas Wilson, carried the bike and put it along with Robert's rifle and pistol in the trunk. Driving to Robert's house, Sergeant Wilson asked about Richard's family. He didn't say it but he would be the one to visit the family right after dropping Robert at his home. Tom Wilson had worked with troubled kids and he could tell Robert was one of the quiet ones, he just wasn't sure if Robert as the dangerous type of quiet or the good type.

Robert found riding in the police car very exciting. He found the shotgun in a rack between him and Officer Wilson fascinating.

"Does your dad have a real gun Robert? Any real guns in your house, or maybe your uncle or grandpa have a real gun, something from the war."

"No sir. I don't have uncles and my grandfathers are dead."

"And, you have two BB guns."

"Yes."

"You like guns don't you. I can see how interested you are in that shot gun."

"I would like to learn how to hunt, but my mother said 'no'.

"Have you ever shot a real gun? You know not a BB gun. But a real gun."

"No," lied Robert thinking if he had a gun, he might kill Adam.

"Have you ever attended a class on guns, a class where they show you how to properly handle a gun?"

"No."

"I think maybe all you boys need to attend a class like that, before use you BB guns again. If I arrange a class at your school will you make sure all the boys with BB guns attend?"

"Will you show us how to shoot real guns?"

"Not at that class. I may shoot a gun so everyone understands what it can do to a person. However, this isn't a class to teach you how to use a gun. It is sort of the opposite.

"I want to learn how to shoot a real gun."

"Ok, I'll tell you what. If you promise me you will never shoot anyone with a BB gun again, and you get your friends to attend my class, I will take you to a gun range and teach you to shoot. Is it a deal. Do you promise you will never shoot at a person again?"

"Sure, I promise." said Robert, knowing he was lying.

In the aftermath of that day, Dave recovered from the trauma of seeing Richard killed, but he was never the same and neither were any of the boys who played that day. Robert, Carl, and Neil stayed friends, but the other boys stopped playing together.

In the fall when Robert entered high school, his world revolved around smoking cigarettes, making it on time to classes, and trying to talk to girls. Richard's death made Robert more aware of his loneliness and isolation, aware of his difference. Rather than take the bus, Robert rode his bike to school on those days when he could in an effort to lose weight. Starting in a new school, he wanted to fit in, he wanted to have a girl friend and live a normal life.

Unfortunately, nearly everything Robert did made him made him a member of the out-crowd. He sat at a table of guys at lunch; un-cool guys who rode bikes not motorcycles, guys without girl friends. In cool classes, like English Lit, he stayed in his shell said nothing. In the un-cool classes, like math, he raised his hand all the time because he was smarter than most of the other boys. In his crowd of guys, all anyone ever talked about was girls and sex. Secretly, all Robert wanted was to own a Walther PPK.

CHAPTER 3

THE BULLSEYE GUN CLUB

Robert visited the Bullseye Gun Club for the first time with Tom Wilson. Officer Wilson told Robert that he liked to visit the club on Saturday morning because Saturday was a popular day among policemen. On their way to the club, Tom Wilson explained that Evert Yale owned the club and the land around it. He bought the buildings and the land for the club using his GI pay. It was right after leaving the Army. Evert started the Club and competed on weekends. He named the club after the Bulls Eye Pistol shooting completion in Camp Perry Ohio. In his time, before his eyes gave out, Evert won dozens of local and regional events. For Evert, his life's achievement was winning two national competitions.

Located on the northern side of Eleven Mile Road between Belleair and Chippendale in Roseville, the main building started out as a cinderblock warehouse with a loading dock and back parking lot. Getting out of Tom Wilson's red corvette, Robert saw what looked like a rundown warehouse. The cinderblock building was a patchwork of pealing white and red paint. The front door had a large hand printed sign that said "Open." Robert saw noting on the outside identifying the club. Inside there was a lobby with side tables and chairs and old gun magazines on the tables. At the far end of the lobby was a reception desk with a man in oil-covered coveralls. It looked to Robert like the old man only had his underwear on underneath the coveralls.

"How's it going Joe," said Wilson addressing the man in the overalls. Wilson was wearing khakis pants, an Izod shirt and a tennis sweater. For early in October the weather was cool. Robert was dressed in his usual shorts, tee shirt, and Jack Parcel tennis shoes. Robert had wanted to wear his air force vest, but his mother would not allow it.

"Mister Tom, so who is this?" asked the old man pointing a screwdriver at Robert.

"Joe Kaminski, meet Robert Cederberg. Robert doesn't know it yet, but he wants to be a Bullseye Champ. I'd like you and Evert to check him out, and teach him the right way to shoot. I have a feeling one day he might even beat Evert in target shooting. "

"Well, I can teach him the right way, but it is up to God to say whether he will be any good," said Joe Kaminski. Joe was from Poland, and everyone in the club called him Joe, everyone except Evert Yale and Jozef himself. Jozef came to America as a teenager in 1935. By the time the United States was in the war, Joe could speak English and had joined the Marines. Decorated in battles on two different pacific islands, Joe came back to Detroit and got a job at the Bullseye cleaning the gun ranges. Overtime, Joe became the club's gunsmith and second best target shooter in the club. Standing with Mister Kaminski, Robert noticed by how each club member said hello to Kaminski and Wilson and shook their hands.

"Robert, said Wilson, pointing to the double door just beyond the reception desk. "That is the locker room. Will you go in there and wait for me; I have to talk to Mister Kaminski for a minute." Robert did what he was asked, feeling immediately embarrassed that he might have to undress in front of mister Wilson and other men until he discovered that the locker room turned out to be a large room with guns in locked cabinets. Inside the room was a second smaller room with a workbench. On the bench were gun parts and ammunition. Standing by the door to the lobby, Robert heard Wilson say 'accident' and '.22.' He also heard Wilson describe Robert as 'a natural.' Not wanting to be accused of eavesdropping, Robert walked to the door on the opposite side of the locker room and looked out. Facing Robert were five cages that looked like batting cages. Robert knew this was where men practiced shooting, because two of the cages had men shooting with pistols. Robert could tell that one man was shooting a .38 revolver. The man wore earphones and given the loudness of the explosions, Robert wished he had some cotton. Standing in the doorway Robert did not hear Wilson and Jozef Kaminski approach from behind him.

"Mister Tom, you are a police man, so I don't tell you anything, but he is under age," said Kaminski putting his hand on Robert's shoulder. Robert hated being touched, but he resisted flinching. He knew this old man held the key to his learning to shoot.

"If you or any of your friends reported that we were letting a minor use the range, it could mean Mister Evert's license."

"Look, I do not want the boy shooting a .38 when there are other club members here, he can practice with his BB gun. In fact, if he is as good as I believe, the Club might sponsor him in the Michigan 4-H shooting competition.

"How old are you Robert?"

"I will be sixteen in July."

"He could be competing in senior boys," said Kaminski. "Tough competition to start."

"Look Joe, I want him to be so comfortable around a gun that he never feels that burning desire that some boys get for a gun. Do you know what I mean?"

"Of course I do." Both men looked at one another and then at Robert. Robert realized Mister Wilson was worried about Robert's fascination with guns.

"Robert," said Tom Wilson, "Joe is going to show you around and then he is going to explain the rules of the club. Joe is the club's gunsmith. He is a certified NRA gun instructor. Next to Mister Yale, there is no better teacher in Michigan. I am going to take some practice shots with my service revolver, so I will leave you with Joe. Is that OK?"

"Ok," said Robert watching Tom Wilson opening one of tall the lockers. Inside Robert saw a rifle and shotgun. Turning back to the old man, Robert put his feet together, arms at his side, and waited.

"Robert," said Kaminski, "let's start with the difference between a rifle, a shotgun, and a pistol." Taking Robert into his workroom, Kaminski handed Robert four bullets, a 30/30 shotgun shell, a .30 cal rifle bullet, a .22 cal pistol bullet, and the bullet for a .38. Putting the bullets in Robert's hands, he said, "Robert, tell me what you see."

"Four bullets, one is for a shot gun, one is a .22 cal another is marked .38 so I assume it is for a pistol. This one," said Robert picking out the .30, "is probably a rifle bullet, but I have never seen one like it before." Kaminski took the four bullets and opened each using pliers, separating the shell from the power and the slug. Taking the shotgun shell, he poured the content into Roberts's hands.

What are these?"

"They look like BBs."

"They are Robert. They are Buckshot, or Bird Shot, BBs. Smaller, but like what you use in your BB gun. Alone when you shoot one at a time, they can certainly hurt a person and they can easily kill a bird or a squirrel, but when they are packed together like this, they are very lethal, a single load of buck shot could easily kill a man. So, Robert that is your first lesson. Can you explain it back to me?" Kaminski watched the overweight boy, as he pulled his head in his collar looking as if he wanted to hide.

"I am not really sure."

"Then, I have nothing more to teach you."

"But, I want to…"

"I know what you want; I can see it in your eyes. You are dying to shoot a gun. However, not before you learn the right way. So tell me what is the lesson of the bullets?"

"Separately the parts of the bullets are not dangerous, but any bullet, even the BB can kill."

"Robert, you are smarter than you look. I think you and Jozef will be friends."

"Who is Jozef?"

"Why, that is me. In my country we say Jozef, but you can call me Joe." Opening a gun case behind the workbench, Kaminski took out a shotgun. Checking that the gun was unloaded, he handed Robert the gun.

"Robert, this is a single barrel pump action shot gun and that was your second lesson. Can you explain it to me?"

Enjoying the feel of the gun, the question surprised Robert. The shotgun looked like the one in Tom Wilson's police car. At first, Robert was going to asked Mister Kaminski to repeat the question, but looking at the old man, he knew that would be a mistake. He knew from this point forward everything would be a test.

"The lesson was check that a gun is unloaded before giving it to a person."

"Good enough. That is a rule of the Club. We never hand a loaded gun to another person. Only the person firing the gun may load it." Kaminski took out an over and under double-barreled shotgun. Breaking the breech he showed Robert the gun was unloaded, then he loaded it with two shells, and then removing the shells, he handed the gun to Robert. "Now you try. Load the gun but do not close the breach." Robert took the two shells and slipped one into each barrel.

"If you are going to shoot birds, there is nothing like the gun in your hand, a long barreled side by side. However, if you plan to compete, if you are going to shoot skeet, I say you cannot beat the first gun I showed you."

"How about Walther," asked Robert? "Do they make shot guns?"

"Walther," said Joe Kaminski. You have been reading too many spy novels, Robert. Walther makes pistols for the military and the police in Europe. A lot of the Nazi officers carried some type of Walther, the bastards." Joe spat on the floor and crossed himself for what he was thinking. "If you are going to buy a shotgun, you go Italian or English. They make great shotguns."

"What about pistols?" asked Robert?

"Let's save pistols for another day. How about we shoot this shotgun," said Kaminski standing up. Carrying the gun out to the back ranges, Joe placed a box of shotgun shells along with a pair of inexpensive shooting glasses on a table behind one of the empty shooting stalls. For the next hour, Joe Kaminski taught Robert every aspect of the Winchester pump action shot gun, invented by Browning. During that time, Kaminski explained all of the commands used in rifle and pistol shooting. Standing at a firing stand, with an unloaded shotgun, Robert practiced without using real shells. When he was satisfied Robert understood how to safely handle the shotgun, he called to Tom Wilson and told him he was talking Robert outside to the fenced in skeet range.

Outside the day had turned warm and sunny. Shading his eyes, Joe took a double-barreled Ithaca cracking the breech and checking that the gun was unloaded, he handed the gun to Robert. Following a marked path in the grass, Kaminski explained how to walk in a field, with your gun unloaded, breech open barrel pointed down. Given Robert's height, the barrel of the gun nearly touched the ground. At one point, they stopped and Kaminski pointed to the mud-covered barrel. Using direct but gentle words, he explained what happed when you shot a gun with a blocked barrel. Joe described what happened to Marines with sand and water in their barrels.

"Robert, I watched a good marine, one of my best friends blind himself with one careless shot from a fouled weapon. If you are going to learn to shoot a gun, you have to remember, check your safety, check your load, and check you barrel. Joe Kaminski handed Robert a cloth and made the boy clean the barrel of his gun.

"Can we shoot out here?" asked Robert.

"Not today," said Joe. "Today we are just enjoying the Indian summer. A walk in the sun."

"Isn't that a war movie?"

"Yes, I think it is," said Kaminski. "You like war movies and guns don't you, Robert? I did too when I was your age. When the war started, I was excited to fight. I wanted to shoot a gun and kill the enemy. You see, my family moved to the United States in nineteen-twenty nine, when I was ten. Before that, we lived in Warsaw. In Poland, my father sold hats and my mother cooked and cared for me and my brother Eli. She raised us as Catholics and not as Jews like her grandmother. One summer day my father announced the family was moving to Hamtramck Michigan. A year later, when we in Michigan, father explained that one day soon it would be dangerous to be a Jew in Europe. When the war broke out, my father took great pride in how smart he had been to move us where it was safe. When the United States entered the war, my father was prouder still that his two sons were going off to fight the Nazi, even though I fought the Japanese in the pacific, and Eli died in Sicily fighting the Italians.

"Did you kill Japs?"

"A few. I killed several Japanese soldiers. Boys, just like me, fighting for their home and families."

"Did you like killing them?" When he asked the question, Robert was afraid he had gone too far. Turning away, he asked, "Did you feel guilty or bad."

"I didn't feel guilty. They were trying to kill me, and luckily, I killed them. However, I didn't enjoy it. Some men do. They like killing. For me, the killing started to bother me. War is not a game. There are very few rules. You kill or you die. It is nothing like shooting BBs in the woods." For a moment, Joe looked angry and then he looked away.

"Look Robert, I heard about your game in the woods and your friend. Now you know shooting at another person is no game."

"Sometime I have nightmares," said Robert admitting something to Joe that he had never revealed before.

"Sometimes I do too. When I got back from the war, I talked to a doctor about how I was feeling. Most men need to talk to someone, but they never do."

"The men who like killing, is that why they hunt?"

"It may be a reason for some men," said Joe Kaminski, "However, it is complicated. Some men like the chase, they like spending a day in the woods trying to find a deer. For them they love the hunt. For others, hunting is a way of putting meat on the table. It is a job. There are men who love killing. They get pleasure out of taking the life of another living creature, whether deer or man, these men love how they feel taking a life.

"There are criminals like that," added Wilson joining the pair. "They kill people just for the thrill. We have started calling these men serial killers. The psychiatrists say they had problems when they were children. Even as little kids, they were different.

"Like me? Different like me?"

"No, son, I don't think so. Anyway, I hope not." Wilson stopped to consider the overweight boy. "A lot of boys your age, love war movies, and love guns. That doesn't make you different; it makes you like a lot of other boys."

"But, I…" Robert hesitated; he was close to telling his secret.

"But what Robert?" asked Kaminski, giving Robert a chance to collect his thoughts.

"Is there something you want to tell me Robert?" asked Wilson giving Joe Kaminski a hard look. "Something about your friend Richard? Something about your Dad? Something you did?" Wilson knew a troubled boy when he met one, and this boy was troubled by something. Studying the boy, he wondered again if he should look deeper into Robert's past.

For a moment, Robert became a turtle, pulling back in his shell. He was unsure if he was becoming a serial killer or something else, but he knew he could never tell the truth to a policeman, even to Tom Wilson. Right now, Robert could tell that Mister Wilson, as nice as he was, could not be trusted. He had the same look Robert's father got when he explained why he had to go out at night. In TV shows, Robert knew the police were always lying to the crooks and then throwing them in jail. Robert was not going to jail. On the other hand, Joe Kaminski seemed different. All he wanted was to teach Robert the right way to shoot a gun.

"What is it Robert. What is bothering you?"

"A gun killed my best friend. But, I still want a gun. There must be something wrong with me." Robert lied.

"It is like I said Robert. It is complicated. I hated killing other men in Korea, yet I am a police officer and I carry a gun. I like hunting, but I don't really like killing animals."

"So what is the answer? What should I do?"

"Have you ever killed an animal? Be honest with me."

"I killed a bird once, a robin."

"Did you like it?"

"No, I hated seeing that bird dead. All I wanted to do was hit it. It was a hard shot and I was proud of the shot until the bird didn't get up."

"You want to learn the right way to shoot a gun," said Tom Wilson. "That is why I introduced you to Joe here." Wilson put his arm on Kaminski's shoulders and Robert could see the old man did not like it anymore than Robert did.

"Joe is the best gun instructor in Detroit. And, this is a great club, even though it could use some new magazines and some soap and toilet paper in the bathroom." Wilson gave Kaminski a direct look.

"Robert, I have arranged it with Joe. You can come here and practice with you BB gun. If you are good enough, he will eventually teach you to shoot with a real gun. After that when you are old enough, if you want, you can compete, you can target shoot against other boys and men. You can prove what a good shot you are, without having to kill anyone or anything." The two men and Robert were standing by the first gun cage. Before leaving Tom introduced Robert to Evert Yale, the owner and he made arrangements for ten hours of instruction with Joe.

* * *

Over the course of the next year, Joe Kaminski taught Robert how to shoot a shotgun and rifle and he learned to shoot with a revolver and automatic pistol. Old Joe as Robert called him, turned out to be a great teacher. He was also a racist, a devote catholic, and a lonely old man in search of a woman he did not have to pay.

On most Saturdays and some Sundays, Robert rode his bike the six miles up Kelly Road to Club and hung out with old Joe. If a member showed up and was willing to have Robert as his guest, Robert was allowed to shoot on the range. Because Tom Wilson sponsored Robert, Evert Yale rented Robert a locker where he stored his targets, his glasses, his BB guns, and his gun cleaning equipment. On days when he did not shoot with a club member, he set targets on the ranges and cleaned the meeting room and bathroom.

Some days Robert sat with Jozef Kaminski loading ammunition for sale. During their days together, Jozef told stories about his time as a Marine and he complained about how President Johnson and the democrats were ruining America. In his free time, Robert practiced with his BB gun. According to Joe Kaminski, Robert was a natural, meaning that he was relaxed and he saw the shot. When Tom Wilson was in the club, he and Robert would practice with his Winchester 70 and his .38 revolver. As Robert became a fixture at the club, other men would sit with Robert talking about their favorite gun. Robert carried a notebook in which he would write down the name of each gun he fired, describing the gun and its ammunition in detail. For the rifles, and shotguns Robert even recorded the type of wood used in the stock and the type of loading and firing mechanism. Robert's devotion to learning everything about guns made him a favorite among the members.

Over time, and under Joe and Evert's coaching, Robert became an expert marksman. Comfortable with both, rifle and pistol, Robert came to realize that many pistol owners were different from rifle owners. Some were men like Tom Wilson, men who loved all type of guns, and owned pistols, rifles, and shotguns too. Some of the rifle owners only saw the rifle as a tool for hunting. If rifles were illegal, they would hunt with a bow, and in fact, many hunted during both seasons. Then, there were the club members who only owned pistols. These were the club member who most interested Robert.

CHAPTER 4

PRIVATE LESSONS

Among the pistol owners, perhaps the most unusual club member was Susan Kay. Miss Kay owned a women's clothing shop on the Hill in Grosse Pointe. She purchased a pistol and obtained a private carry permit after begin robbed in her store. Ever since, she practiced once a week, on Sunday at 9:45 before attending the noon catholic services. Susan had auburn hair, blue eyes and a cheerful smile. Standing next to Robert, she was two inches taller, but sitting in one of the metal folding chairs, they had at the club she seemed smaller and very petite compared to Robert's bulky frame.

On entering high school, Robert made a commitment to lose fifty pounds and to get a girl friend. After owning a Walther PPK, more than anything else, Robert wanted to break out of his shell; he wanted to be liked. Robert met Susan Kay in the spring of 1966, when he was still fifteen. By then, he had added two inches in height and because of riding to the Club three days a week he had lost twenty-five pounds. While still short, Robert no longer seemed fat, just slightly overweight for his height.

In talking with Miss Kay, what excited Robert even more than the occasional sight of her bare breasts beneath her white V-neck sweater was the gun that she brought to the Club, a .32 caliber Walther PPK, the very gun that James Bond carried. According to Miss Kay, once you got use to the recoil it was a very accurate pistol.

Unlike the other club members, Susan Kay did not use her locker to store the gun. She carried the Walther in her purse and used the locker to store her protective glasses, earplugs, and spare ammunition. According to rumors, a burglar robbed, and some said raped, Susan in her store. After that, she purchased a Walther and joined the club where she learned gun safety and combat shooting, quick shooting without aiming. According to Evert, Joe actually taught her to shoot, but Tom Wilson who became her boyfriend for a time, acted like he was her personal instructor until the same man tried to rob her a second time. As Evert described it, the man raped her and after, she shot the man in the head. When Robert asked Joe Kaminski about her, he said she was a very nice lady, perfect for Tom, but after she killed the robber, she and Tom stopped seeing one another. "Now she practices alone on Sundays before church."

On the second Sunday in May, when Susan Kay arrived at 9:30 a.m., Robert was there to let her in. As was his habit, Robert was dressed in khaki pants and a dark green tee shirt with a left front pocket for cigarettes. Robert came in early on Sunday to clean the lobby and gun ranges. This morning he had washed his face and brushed his teeth. Working at the club on Sunday allowed him to avoid going to church with his family. Alone in the club, Robert had his transistor radio tuned to CKLW. On the radio, the Lovin' Spoonful were singing about the *Summer in the City*.

Noticing that Miss Kay was carrying her gun case, Robert immediately volunteered to set her up in one of the pistol ranges. After setting a target at twenty-five feet, Miss Kay asked if he would like to spot her. Normally Joe would stand behind her and spot her shots meaning he would call out where she hit the target. However, Joe called in saying he and Evert would be late. Standing in the pistol range together, Robert was very aware of how aroused he was standing so close to the young woman.

"Are you ready?" asked Robert seeing that she was waiting in front of the shooters box.

"Ready," said laughing at the formality.

"Then you can enter the box and take your position."

Stepping into the shooters box, Susan sighted the Walther using a straight-arm stance and said, "Ready to fire."

"Fire away," said Robert, as she fired the entire eight round clip at the target twenty-five feet away. She was a good shot and hit the target four out of eight shots.

"Good shooting, Miss Kay," said Robert. "You hit a five and a nine."

"But, four misses," she said.

"You shot too fast. Try taking a breath between each shot."

"I'll try again." She stepped down and went through the process of unloading a clip and reloading. She followed the steps Joe taught exactly, making Robert smile at the thought of old Joe alone with this beautiful young woman.

After three clips, Susan Kay was hitting the target on five out eight shots and scoring bulls eyes on two or three of the shots. According to Susan, the real target should be about eight or ten feet away, because that is where he would be in her store. When they moved the target to ten feet, Susan tore the center out of the target.

By the time, Miss Kay was finished shooting, Joe and Evert had arrived, and after she left, Evert and Joe joked with Robert about his new girl friend. Robert only smiled at their jokes, but privately he very attracted to the older woman and her Walther PPK.

After that, Robert told Joe he would be glad to come in early on Sunday so he could let Miss Kay in the club. Smiling at Robert's offer, Joe took to arriving at 10:30 a.m. after church.

On the first Sunday in June, while they were still alone, Susan asked if Robert would like to shoot her Walther.

"I am not allowed."

"But no one is here, why not have a try?"

"Joe will find out and he would not like it."

"How would he find out?"

"I'd have to tell him. I tell him everything."

"Everything."

"Nearly."

"So you have some secrets."

"One or two."

"Good for you, so do I. Look you go back to your chores, and when Joe comes in I will talk to him about letting you try the Walther."

Sweeping the floor, Robert did not see Joe approach. It was 10:45 and the club was still empty except for Susan Kay. Joe had on his coveralls over his Sunday suit.

"Miss Kay wants see you shoot. Did you put her up to this?"

"No, I just helped her with her stance and her breathing.

"Do you want shoot?"

"I better not; Mister Yale will not like it."

"Bullshit, Robert. Evert never comes in this early and you know it. Go get your glasses and earplugs. Let's see how you do. How far do you want the target?"

"Fifty feet."

"Trying to impress the pretty lady?" asked Joe smiling. Robert said nothing, as he walked to the gunroom to fetch his equipment.

Robert had shot a rifle at further targets, but fifty feet was the distance he used with his BB pistol. At that distance, the paper target looked small, let alone the black center. Taking a shooting stance, Robert tried to calm his thoughts. He wanted to impress Miss Kay and the Joe but he knew shooting successfully at this distance took a lot of practice. Clicking the safety off, he announced he was ready to fire. After checking his stall and the other ranges, Joe said "fire away." Holding his breath, Robert cocked the gun and sighted the target. Squeezing the trigger, he fired and waited. "In the circle," he heard Susan shout out. Holding his breath again, he fired three more shots.

"One in the center, two in the circle," Susan whispered. She was standing right behind Robert with her hand on his back, as if she wanted to pat him on the back.

"Close the circle," she said, and I will treat you to lunch."

"I think that is enough. I have to meet Mister Wilson in a half an hour and I need to go to the bathroom." Robert stepped out of the shooters box, put the gun on safe, ejected the round in the chamber and pulled the clip from the gun. Handing the gun to Susan, he said, "If you will excuse me, I'll be right back." Racing to the men's washroom, Robert knocked, and then entered the bathroom, locking the door behind him. He knew he had ejaculated, he just wasn't sure if the front of his khaki pants were stained. Thankfully, he was saved from that embarrassment. After urinating twice, he washed himself off and put paper toweling in his underpants. In the mirror he was embarrassed and ashamed, but he was also, excited, shooting those bulls eyes in front of Miss Kay was the was the second best experience in his life. When he exited the washroom, Joe Kaminski and Susan Kay were both waiting.

"Are you alright?" asked Susan Kay smiling.

"I am fine."

"That was very good shooting Robert. I think he is ready. Don't you Miss Susan?"

"Ready for what?"

"Ready to shoot in competition. The Club is going to sponsor him in the 4-H competition once he turns sixteen."

"How old are you now Robert?"

"I'll be sixteen in July," said Robert hating how he must seem like a boy to this older woman. "How old are you?"

"Robert, a man never asks a lady her age, but I am twenty two."

"Same as my brother," said Robert.

"Right, we could be brother and sister. Do you have any sisters Robert?"

"No, only brothers." Robert liked talking to Miss Kay. He wished Joe would leave.

"Well, Robert, I am hungry. How about I treat you to a Hamburger?"

"I have my bike, and I am supposed to meet Mister Wilson later today.

"Well, let me take you for a burger, and then I can bring you back in time to meet Tom. Anyone who shoots as good as you do deserves a cheeseburger and ice cream at Sanders."

"Is it OK Joe?" asked Robert.

"Of course, take the afternoon off," said Joe with a smile.

Robert had so little experience with girls, that he accepted Miss Kay's invitation to lunch without another thought. He was hungry and having a hamburger with an attractive woman like Miss Kay was a new adventure. In the parking lot, Susan Kay climbed into a white mustang convertible. Seeing her car, Robert thought for a moment he must be dreaming. Firing 007's gun and now a car almost like the one in *Goldfinger.* Getting into the passenger seat, Robert was impressed that the car was an automatic.

"Better fasten your seat belt Robert; I have a tendency to drive a little fast." Susan started the car and pulled out of the lot onto Eleven Mile road. Driving east towards the lake, they talked about the mustang and Robert's drivers ED class. It was June and Robert would get his license in July.

"I have a learners permit," he announced, "but my parents never let me drive."

"Could you drive this car," Susan asked.

"Of course, I could," said Robert, "but I would not want to take the chance. If anything bad happened, my parents would ground me." The idea of driving the mustang was very tempting, but a voice of caution sounded in Robert's head.

"Ok, well another time, after you get your license, perhaps." They drove along the lake into Grosse Pointe Farms. Turning up Fisher Road, they reached the Hill and Susan turned into the alleyway behind a row of shops on Kercheval. At the fourth store, she parked the car in a space behind the back of a store.

"Have you ever seen my store?" she asked.

"Not really," he lied. He did not want Miss Kay to know he had ridden his bike to the Hill so he could watch her working in her store at night. One night he watched her until she closed the store.

"Come in, while I lock the gun in the store. We can go out the front and walk to Saunders for lunch." She got out of the car, unlocked the rear door to her store and disarmed an alarm.

"I keep the gun under the register. Want to see?" asked Susan walking with certainty in the darkened store. The front windows had drawn shades but enough light shown in that she was able to walk down an aisle without knocking anything off a shelf. Following her Robert had a harder time, taking care to put the blouses back he knocked over. Behind the counter, Susan opened her purse and put the gun in a black silk bag. When she put the bag away, Robert could see down her sweater, at her small breasts.

"How old are you Robert?"

"Like I said, I'll be sixteen in a month."

"I you ever been with a girl Robert?"

"I've kissed a girl, if that is what you mean."

"Anything else? Do you have a girl friend right now?"

"No." Robert wondered why she was asking such personal questions. He wondered if she had some cousin she wanted him to go out with on a blind date.

"I have a feeling you like girls, Robert, because I noticed at the gun club that you seemed pretty excited? Was that because of shooting the gun or because I was there in the box with you?"

"Both I suppose," said Robert, looking backward toward the rear door. Susan reached under the counter and put the gun bag on the counter. The butt of the gun stuck out and Robert noticed the clip was back in the gun.

"Would you like to hold my gun again Robert? Would you like to touch my gun, feel my gun?" Susan pulled the gun out of the bag and placed the gun against her face and then against his cheek. "It feels good doesn't? Cool and dangerous, even exciting. I could tell you were excited at the range. I was too. I was excited seeing you shoot, you may not know it, but when you shoot you have this calm look that makes you look dangerous. When you shoot, you are no longer a boy. You are a dangerous man. I find that very attractive." Susan handed the gun to Robert, and placed her right hand behind his back as she reach into the front of his pants, running her hand up and down his pants. Instantly he was aroused and without thinking, he kissed her as she pulled him to the floor.

In his first attempt, he came the moment he was inside her, but she did not laugh and she never stopped kissing and touching him. In seconds, it seemed he was aroused again, and this time she controlled what he did, keeping him from coming long enough that she had an orgasm while she was on top of him. When he came the second time, he was thankful that he had ejected the clip from the gun because he pulled the trigger repeatedly as he spewed into and onto Susan Kay.

Lying on the floor exhausted, with her skirt still on but her sweater and panties in a corner, she stroked his limp cock as he traced her breasts with the Walther. Looking down his cock was shriveled and small, but he realized he had fucked Miss Kay two times, and somehow, he touched a place inside her that caused her to shutter in pleasure. While she played with his cock, she encouraged him to explore her and look at her. When he put three fingers in her vagina, she pulled him close. When he rubbed her clitoris with the barrel of the gun, she shuttered with an orgasm. "Try that with your tongue," she said, and setting the gun aside, he tasted pussy for the first time.

After riding him a third time, she announced that she was hungry and they should wash and then get some lunch. Watching Susan stand up and walk naked to the bathroom, Robert wondered whether his body was capable of getting aroused another time. When she turned at the bathroom door and gestured for him, he knew he could. After washing herself, she soaped a towel and gently washed his chest and penis.

"When people have sex like we just had," she explained, "they smell of sex and other people can smell it on them. If you went home right now, your mother would know you had sex. If you go to the gun club, Joe and Tom Wilson will know for sure. We will get some food from a deli, and go eat our lunch in the park. After an hour or so in the sun, it will be OK to go home, but this afternoon, before dinner, you should take a shower. Robert, I know you will want to talk with your friends about what happened this afternoon, but I would really appreciate it if you do not tell anyone. Do you think you can keep this a secret? Our secret."

"I can keep anything a secret."

"You see, the thing is, you are under age, and I could get in trouble if your parents or Tom Wilson learned about what happened today. Can you keep this a secret from your parents and Tom, from Officer Wilson?"

"I know I can."

"How about old Joe?"

"I have never lied to Joe, but I can keep a secret."

"I believe you."

"Would you like to do this again?"

"I would." Robert want to shout, to scream 'yes'.

"I would too, but only if it will be our secret. You see, Tom and I use to go out, but then we stopped and he was very angry about it when I told him I didn't want to see him anymore. I said he was too old, and I did not want to have sex with him. If he found out that I was having sex with you, with a boy, he would get very angry. He might hurt me or have me arrested and he might even hurt you, even though you are great pals. Tom really likes you and I don't want to come between you two. It is just that I am lonely and I like you. You are like me. You have secrets and I do too. We are hiding who we are. Do you understand?"

"I think so. We are like turtles, hiding inside our shell."

"Robert, you may not understand this but I did not choose you because of your age. The reason we had sex isn't that I like young boys. I chose you because you are like me, hard on the outside and vulnerable on the inside. Today I realized how much you needed a girl. I realized that if you are going to compete and win against other boys your age, you need the confidence that comes from having a girlfriend."

"Are you going to be my girlfriend?"

"When we are alone, but not in public. In public, I will be your big sister. You teacher, like Joe. I am going to teach you about girls and women. I am going to teach you about being a man. When I am done, when you are ready, you will find a girl your own age. Until then, we will have sex, we will shoot my gun, and we will talk. What do you think?"

Robert did not know what to think. He already wanted to have sex again and the thought of talking to Miss Kay was even more exciting. Robert desperately wanted to understand about girls. His mother refused to talk about girls, and his older brother only talked about blowjobs and big tits.

"When do we start?" asked Robert, not knowing what else to say.

"Let's go have some food, and then I will take you back to get your bike. I don't think we can meet any more on Sundays. If old Joe sees us together, after this, he will guess what is going on. I know you will want to keep working at the range, so I will just stop going for a while, and instead we can meet at my house. You can tell you parents you are cutting my lawn on Sundays. How will that be?"

"Can it be on Saturdays?"

"No it will have to be on Sunday. It is the only day the store isn't open."

"And, will I actually have to cut your lawn?"

"Yes, but I have a power mower and it is a little lawn, which you already know because you rode by my house several times just this week, didn't you?"

"Will I get paid?"

"I'll pay you for cutting my lawn." she stopped and laughed.

"I did not mean you would pay me for this." For the first time Robert looked at Susan Kay seeing her as an equal, someone he could talk with honestly. There is one thing." He added watching how she reacted.

"What?"

"When I have saved enough money, will you buy me a Walther like yours so we can go somewhere private and shoot together?" Robert had been thinking about this ever since she touched him with the gun. He wanted a Walther of his own and Susan Kay might be a way to get one.

* * *

Over the next year, Robert cut Susan Kay's lawn, raked leaves, and shoveled snow every Sunday. On most Sundays, he would ride his bike and stay all morning and sometimes part of the afternoon. At first, they had sex in her bedroom, then they had sex in every room, and then they went back to having sex in her bedroom.

One week when Susan was having her period, they watched baseball, and talked about what was happening in their very different daily lives. Susan talked about the store and new fashions. Robert talked about school, the gun club, and competitions. He and Tom Wilson still talked and occasionally practiced together, but Tom's work schedule moved him to nights and Robert stopped seeing him.

On the second Sunday in September, Susan announced that she wanted to drive into the woods so they could shoot the Walther at tin cans. After asking twice, Robert had stopped asking for his own gun. Susan had made it clear that it was not only illegal but also irresponsible for her to give him a handgun. She promised, when he was eighteen, she would give him a gun for his birthday, but not before.

Since obtaining his driver's license in July, Robert had driven Susan's Ford Mustang on several occasions, but the trip into the country was the first time he drove the car on a highway. Following Susan's directions, they drove up Interstate 94. Existing in Port Huron, they drove on back lanes toward Imlay City for more than three hours, finally arriving at a forest park with a closed sign on the gate.

"Don't mind it, said Susan. It is always closed, but I use it anyway. Drive on. I'll tell you when to stop." When they reach a turn around on the road, they pulled off, and unpacked the car. From the look of the road, no one had been on the road in months. At the top of a hill, Robert set down their cooler and a blanket beside a tall oak. For a moment, Robert was back knelling next to Richard, but then Susan pulled her tee shirt off and Robert returned to the present.

When they finished, they lay with the blanket wrapped around them, sleeping in the warm September sun. When Robert awoke, Susan was dressed and eating a leg of chicken, from a paper plate on her lap. The filled plate had chicken, coleslaw, and a Parker House roll. Beside her Robert spied the silk gun bag.

"Where is my plate?" he asked sitting up and looking around. Below them, a creek sparked in the afternoon sun. Robert saw cowbirds and sparrows. On a tall blade of grass, a red-winged black bird guarded his territory.

"I'll make you a plate, but first, how about a little target practice. See if you can hit that can I placed by the river." Susan pointed to a can more than a hundred feet away.

"That is pretty far. I am not sure."

"Don't give me that Davy, pull old Betsy out, and fire away." She handed him the silk bag.

Opening the bag, he pulled out the gun, realizing it was not her black Walther with the black grip. Rather it was a black Walther with a brown wooden grip.

"It's beautiful," he said, removing the clip, he checked the bullets, jacking one out and then reloading it, he slid the clip home and jacked in a round, admiring the pull of the action. "It is really beautiful, I love it, and I can't tell you how beautiful it is, almost as beautiful as you." Robert was disappointed it did not have the silver finish, but when he aimed the gun at a can, steadied his breathing, and shot. The gun felt perfect in its balance. The report echoed in the woods as the can leaped off the rock it sat on, while it was still in the air, Robert shot it from a combat stance, no aiming.

"God, that was a good shot, you have improved."

"It's the gun. It is fabulous. I cannot thank you enough."

"Oh, Robert, wait, you misunderstand. Remember what we agreed on. This gun is for the other store. I bought it for the other store. I thought you and I could practice with it, get used to it. Ultimately, it is for Amy."

"For the other store," he said turning to face her. "For Amy! After everything I have done for you, you'd give this to Amy. The one thing you know I want. You'd give this to that bitch Amy." Secretly Robert liked Amy and found her attractive in a mannish way, but her hold on Susan had become an issue.

"Robert, don't call her that. You know I don't like that. You know how important Amy is to my business. You know how important she is to me."

"I know how possessive she is. I know she is sleeping with you. What do you call it when you do it with a woman? What is it now, three nights a week? Nearly every night except Saturday, because that might interfere with fucking me." He was on the brink of crying. All he wanted to do was crawl in his shell.

"If you know all that, why didn't you say something before this?"

"Because my day is Sunday. Just like Tom Wilson's day was Saturday. What you do on the other days has always been your business, except, how could you give this gun to Amy."

Robert looked down at the Walther in his hand. "I have never asked you for anything, except a gun like this," said Robert starting to cry.

"Robert, put the gun away, and make a plate of chicken." Susan put her plate down and pushed the hamper across the blanket to Robert. "Before you get crazy and say or do something you will regret, look in the hamper. Please."

Robert hesitated looking at the hamper. He knew Susan was considering opening a second store and she talked a lot about Amy becoming the manager of the new store. Taking the hamper in his left hand, Robert turned reaching out with his right hand, extending it until the barrel of the gun was inches from Susan's head. Looking around for any witnesses, he cocked the hammer manually.

Seeing the look on his face, Susan opened the hamper and pointed to a silk bag in the hamper. "Robert, please, before you do something that will change your life forever, take a look in the bag. I beg you to look in the bag." Keeping the Walther in his right hand, Robert pulled out a silver silk bag, and removed a second Walther, this one a silver PPK with a black grip, unquestionably, the most attractive Walther in the line. Seeing the other Walther, Robert set down the gun in his right hand and picked up the silver gun.

"Beautiful," he whispered.

"This one is for you Robert, it is used," said Susan picking up the other Walther. "I brought the new one for the store and so we could shoot together. But, now I think we should go home before there is an accident." Susan set the first gun down and started to cry.

"That gun was going to be your birthday present. Now, I am afraid it is a farewell gift." I do not think we can see each other anymore."

"Because of a gun?" Robert set the silver Walther on the blanket. Susan picked up the silver gun.

"I asked Tom Wilson to buy me a second gun for the store and I asked him to be on the lookout for a gun like this. Apparently, Tom purchased both guns at a police auction. When I saw the silver gun, I knew it was perfect, just what you wanted. So, I bought both guns. Unfortunately, I pulled out the wrong gun out of the hamper." Susan put the Walther beside her cheek feeling the metal. Robert was not sure if she was going to shoot herself or him.

"Robert, you have your gun, and I…"

"You have Amy."

"Robert, do you remember when we first had sex?"

"In the store."

"Right and you know what happened to me in that store?"

"Of course, you were being robbed and you killed the robber."

"As simple as that. Is that what you believe? Is that why you never asked?"

"No, I know it wasn't as simple as that."

"When that bastard robbed me the first time he beat me and raped me, he would have killed me, except someone knocked on the front door, and he ran out the back. When he came back, he was just going to rob me, but I laughed at him, I made fun of his manhood, I forced him to raped me again, and while he was on me, grunting away, his limp penis trying to force its way in, I reached under the counter and found the Walther, just where I had left it, and I put the gun barrel against his head and pulled the trigger, I pulled it once and he heard the hammer and I said, finally, a hard cock, and I shot him. Shot him in the temple, and then when I got up, I shot him again. I left him there with his pants down, and him pathetic little cock. I left him on the floor and called the police, and Tom Wilson arrived

"So we had sex behind the very same counter. How could you do that?"

"Come on Robert, can't you guess?"

"Did you plan to kill me too?"

"Perhaps, you were such a strange boy. All you seemed to think about was guns, and Tom Wilson told me why you are called the Turtle. When I saw how aroused you were shooting my gun, I wondered what you might do if you had me alone."

"Why didn't you shoot me? You could have easily made it look like the other man."

"Robert, really, how can you ask that? You were wonderful, that was the best sex I ever had, and there was certainly nothing wrong with your cock." Robert smiled as he picked up the silver Walther. The gun barrel sparkled in the sun. Robert loved Susan with all his being, but at the moment he considered shooting her and himself, except the weight of the gun felt wrong, it wasn't' loaded.

"So what now," Robert asked standing over Susan.

"Take these empty cans down by the creek, and we will have a competition, winner takes all."

"And, after that."

"After that you can eat some chicken or you can shoot me, your choice."

"Can we have sex instead?"

CHAPTER 5

NUMBER 23

The breakup with Susan Kay was relatively easy at first. At Susan's house, they kissed goodbye and Robert rode his bike home. At home, when his mother asked about cutting Miss Kay's lawn, Robert explained that she was using a lawn service. At the Club, Susan left a letter for Robert explaining that she would always love Robert, but she decided she was going to keep the Walther. After that, Susan stopped coming to the gun club and when Joe asked Robert what happened to Miss Susan, Robert explained that she had gotten over her fear of being robbed.

In the days that followed, Robert at first retreated into his shell, staying in his room and staying away from the club. For a sixteen year-old boy, achieving sexual release required little more than a worn copy of playboy hidden under his bed. The problem was after having sex, Susan and Robert actually talked; they talked about adult things, the race riots, politics, about the Kennedys. When they were alone, they acted like boyfriend and girlfriend; they shared secrets. They did things together. Sitting in his room, Robert missed talking to Susan, he missed having sex, and most of all he missed shooting her pistol. In the end, the need to shoot brought him back to the Bullseye.

Walking into Evert Yale's office, Robert asked Evert for a part time job. Knowing how Yale thought, Robert explained that he wanted to compete in major tournaments and he needed to earn money for college. In august of 1967, Robert attended his first Bullseye competition in Ohio. For the competition, Joe Kaminski and Evert Yale drove Robert to Camp Perry and paid for his motel room. As a past competition winner, Evert was a bit of a celebrity and even signed autographs. For Robert this was his first major competition with three different pistols. In the end, Robert's scores were respectable, but he needed more experience with each of the three guns used in the match.

After the competition in Ohio, Joe mapped out a series of competitions, matches in the Midwest in which Robert competed during his junior, and senior year of high school. As Joe predicted, Robert was a natural with a Colt 1911 and eventually Robert started winning. Most of the competitors were boys and most of the audience was men, but there were enough women and girls are the matches that Robert realized that if he was going to ever have a real girlfriend, a girl his age, someone to do things with, he was going to have to make some significant changes in his life. First he would have to lose another twenty-five pounds and second, he have to meet a girl who loved guns.

Robert was at a competition in Harper Woods when he ran into Tom Wilson. Robert had not seen Tom in more than a year so he was surprised when Wilson asked Robert if he had seen Susan Kay. When Robert said, "No why would I?" Wilson laughed and said, "What was it, were you too young or too old?" To which Robert angrily replied, "Wrong gender."

"Ah," said Wilson, "Amy. Too bad really, Susan is a good woman, and eventually she will want a real man again, but by then all the good ones will be in college or living in Florida." Robert and Tom Wilson never spoke about Susan Kay again, and in fact, they hardly talked or saw each other again before Wilson moved to take a job with the Coral Gables Police Department in Florida.

After graduating from High School, Robert spent the summer working at the club and competing on weekends. In the fall of 1968, he enrolled in classes at Wayne State University. Robert wanted to go away for college but his father said after putting Austin through school, that he could not afford another four years. Eric agreed to pay for Robert's tuition, but Robert would have to live at home and work after school to pay for books.

Robert liked college and applied himself to his studies. He also continued to compete and he joined Wayne State's Collegiate Pistol and rifle club. Ultimately, he hoped he would represent the school in competitions, but the government had other ideas.

Robert was in his second year at Wayne State when his lottery number was drawn, number 23. That year the draft made it to number 195 and Robert was called in for his physical. Standing in line in his underwear, it was apparent that Robert was too short, five foot eight inches and too overweight at one hundred and ninety pounds but the doctor who examined him had a different playbook and failed to notice any of these shortcomings. After making Robert look to his right and cough, he stamped 1A on Robert's form and sent him into the room with the other inductees. A month later, Robert was receiving his Army basic training. Near the end of his training, Robert received a note from Joe saying that Susan Kay had died of cancer. Robert spent a year in Vietnam.

Being in Vietnam, forced Robert out of his shell and turned him into a soldier. In Saigon, he and his squad members drank together, fucked prostitutes together, and smoked dope together. The men in his platoon and squad were brothers. Compared to the other draftees, Robert was without question the Company's best shot and he was fearless in a firefight.

When Robert finally made it home in the winter of 1972, he found an indifferent America and a family that was falling apart. Walking through Detroit Metro Airport several hippies gave Robert the peace sign and one gave him the finger. On the ride home, Eric kept saying Robert looked good and asking 'what next?'

At home, perhaps the hardest thing to adjust to was learning that Chessie had died of cancer in November, and no one thought to tell Robert. At the dinner table that first night, John, Robert's younger brother came to the table smelling of marijuana and Robert learned that William his youngest brother had been in some kind of trouble that the family would not talk about at the table. The next day, Robert visited his older brother Austin and his wife Kathy at their apartment in Detroit. Kathy was pregnant when they married, and because of the baby, Austin had received a deferment. Three year into their marriage, Austin was awkward around the baby, and he and Kathy openly fought while Robert drank beer and watched.

When Robert visited the Bullseye Rifle and Pistol Club, he was amazed at how little had changed in the club, and yet how much had changed inside Robert. When club members greeted him and asked, "How was it?" He usually said how lucky he was and how glad he was to be back. The truth was he missed the heat and the smells, the whores and the danger in Vietnam; he missed the feeling he got killing someone two feet away who was equally intent on killing him.

For a while, Robert wore his uniform, but he quickly learned that America didn't care that he had killed men for his country. In fact, many of the kids his age stared at his crew cut and called him "baby killer," or gave him the peace sign as if he was a vampire they were warding off with a cross. In the army, Robert was a hero. Back at home, he was that fat kid who had lost weight in the army, along with what little soul he had when he left.

Late one afternoon, Robert was sitting in the club's meeting room reading old articles on guns and ammo, when Evert Yale and Joe Kaminski came in and sat on either side of Robert. To Robert, Evert Yale looked the same, perhaps less hair on top, but sitting down he looked older.

"I am tired, Robby, said Yale. Tired of the club and tired of Detroit. I need someone to take over. To run the business. "

"What about Joe?" asked Robert."

"Joe is too busy repairing guns and going to church. Lately, he has been talking about all the ladies at church. I think he is dying his hair."

"Do you have a woman?" asked Robert looking at the old gunsmith.

"I might one day soon," said Joe being serious.

"So Robert," said Yale, bringing the conversation back. "What now?"

Robert didn't have an answer. At his parents' home, he felt like a stranger. He didn't fit in and he didn't care about his family, in fact, the only people he really cared about Chessie and Susan Kay were both dead from cancer. Sitting at the worn club table, with the sound of gunshots and the smell of cordite and gun oil in the air, Robert realized that only the gun club felt like home.

"I am not sure. Of course, I want to join the club, but beyond that, I am not sure."

"So, Robert," said Jozef, "did you ever get that Walther I sent you? The one poor Miss Susan left you?" He pushed away a small tear.

"I have it right here," said Robert taking a cardboard box out of his rucksack. Inside the box, the gun was in a silver bag. "Funny thing is I never use it."

"Beautiful gun like that, I don't blame you."

"Yes, well," said Jozef sitting down the small gun, "my guess is that new pistol the Army issued had a lot more stopping power. I mean, when I was on Tarawa, one shot from a .45 and most men go down." Robert knew Joe had joined the Marines three days after Pearl Harbor. He spoke often about hitting the beach on Tarawa. They had twenty feet of blood soaked sand and then the jungle. Making it off the beach was easy compared to fighting their way through the jungle to the airfield. Joe was part of a machine gun team, loading .50 caliber ammo belts with his .45 at his side. Before he could reload the gun, Joe had to kill two Japs with his .45 pistol. Joe talked about the fierceness, the intensity and anger on one Jap's face when the .45 dropped him to his knees. Willing himself to stand, he made it up on one leg before blood erupted from his mouth and he fell forward.

"Yea, that Colt was a life saver, and yet I remember one NVA who took three shots to go down. The first shot was a chest shot, from my M1, a center kill, it sent him to his knees, and then he stands up and comes at me again. Bang, I hit him again right in the center but he is still moving, when I drop him with a head shot from my forty-five. Funny thing was his momentum kept him moving and he knocked me over. Probably saved my life because the guy right next to me was hit."

"Sometimes they just don't know they are already dead," said Evert Yale. "I remember a nip on Tappan who took five shots to kill.

"Was it like that a lot?" asked Jozef, "I mean was it close combat like that, hand-to-hand?"

"A couple of times, but most of the time I was on a base and the only danger was mortar attacks. Now those can scare the shit out of a guy." All three men nodded at that thought.

"You know Robert, if you need a job while you sort things out I would be glad to have you work here. Hell you know more about guns than I do, and next to Joe, there isn't a person I trust more. I mean, to say, the fact is I haven't been coming in as much as I use to an I have been thinking of making Joe the manager, but he isn't getting any younger either, and so, if you want, I mean you could manage the place for me. You could even start competing, and if you win a few tournaments maybe I could even spend the winter in Florida."

"Gosh, Mister Yale, the thing is I had been thinking I would go back to school in the fall."

"And, so you should," said Every Yale patting Robert on the back. "That is what the GI bill is all about, but how about running the club until you go back to school, or better still, run the club and go to Wayne State in the evenings. In five years I will be retired in Florida and you will be a lawyer."

"What do you say Joe?" asked Robert.

"I think it is a great idea. You know I am no good with bills, keeping track of figures and bank accounts. I can't even manage a rented room. No offense to Evert, but this place needs a manager who can win competitions and it does not hurt if he is war hero.

"So, is it a deal? Or, maybe, you should take a couple of days, and then we will talk about hours and salary."

"I don't need a couple of days. I can start tomorrow."

The next day, Robert arrive dressed in penny loafers, Khakis pants, and a blue Izod shirt, over which he wore his only sport coat, a blue blazer. He did not intend to keep the blazer on but he wanted Mister Yale to think he was serious about managing the club.

When he knocked on the locked front door, Evert Yale was dressed in blue jeans and a tee shirt that said Big Boy on it and Jozef Kaminski was dressed in his usual mechanic coveralls with a tee shirt showing underneath. Close up, Jozef smelled of sweat and sausages.

"See Evert, already the place looks better."

"Perhaps I should go home and change," laughed Yale.

"How about I put on this pair of coveralls, and clean the heads, and mop this floor, and then you can show me something about the business I don't already know, like doing the books, or sending out the bills. Next week, if you will buy the paint, I will paint the place."

In less than a week, Evert had Robert opening the store and working behind the front counter, while he attended to errands that took most of his time. For Robert, the club was a safe haven, where he could shoot his guns and be around men who like to shoot too. Men, many of whom shared the experience with Robert of killing other men. What the club could not offer, Robert quickly found after talking to a few of the younger police officers.

In the fall of 1972, Robert enrolled in a psychology class at Macomb community college and he picked up an application to join the Grosse Pointe Woods police force. Spending time with Evert Yale, Robert repeatedly heard about Evert winning the .45 competition at Camp Perry in Ohio in 1947. For a pistol shooter, the NRA conventional pistol completion in Ohio in July offered every form of competition with a handgun.

As the two men talked about the competition, Robert was certain that he could compete in the six and eight inch competitions using a .45, but he wasn't at all sure about the other events. Robert had very little experience with a .22 rimfire pistol and no experience in slow fire competitions, where a shooter had ten minutes to take ten shots. Robert thought that he might do well in the rapid-fire competition, but where he really hoped to excel was in the new combat or action pistol shooting competitions.

On days when Robert competed, he would leave the club to Joe and he would go early so he could set up a booth. Before the competition, Robert worked hard talking with gun enthusiasts about the guns the Club had for sale and if they lived in Detroit, he would play up the advantages of being a member of the Bulls Eye Gun Club. After a competition, especially if he won, selling memberships was easy.

Robert was not surprised when Evert Yale announced that he planned to spend January to April, in Florida, leaving Robert and Jozef Kaminski to run the club during the winter months. When Evert returned in April, he stayed two weeks coming in late and on some days not coming in at all. Most gun clubs make money offering classes and issuing permits. The Bullseye offered classes in basic firearms, home protection, competition shooting, and skeet shooting. Besides issuing licenses for basic firearms ownership, the club offered a class in owning concealed weapons, which resulted in a permit. Once he was officially the manager, Robert proved to be a better instructor than Evert and he quickly took over all the classes. Realizing the Club did better when he was gone; Evert announced he was going back to Florida early. Before leaving in May, Evert confided to Joe that he believed he had found the Club's future owner, Robert Cederberg.

CHAPTER 6

INTEGRATION

As Manager, Robert was anxious to improve the club. In addition to painting and remodeling the club, he wanted to expand the membership and attract younger members. He was hoping the membership might consist of more than cops and hunters. He wanted to see women in the club and minorities.

On a Friday in October, a party of four men walked into the club at 2:20 in the afternoon. No one was in the club and Jozef and Robert were in the back dueling with a pair of Robert's air guns. The afternoon was hot, Indian Summer. Robert had two rotating fans on in the lobby to move the stale air. Finding no one in the lobby, Eddie Farkas the only Club member in the group, started yelling loud enough for Robert and Jozef to emerge from the back.

As usual Robert was sporting a recent army style crew cut and wearing khaki pants and a short sleeve cotton shirt with a pocket on the left side. Because he had been in the back, Robert was wearing his khaki gun vest. Standing opposite the men, Robert adopted a balanced stance. He was the shortest man in the room but he had no doubt about his ability to handle Eddie Farkas.

Farkas was a heavyset Lebanese man with a beak for a nose, and long jet back hair greased back with barber products. Standing directly opposite Robert he was five inches taller and one hundred pounds heavier. Around the club, it was rumored Eddie had connections with several bookies on the east side. The three other men were unknown to Robert, but one man, an average height black man stood out because of his fierce glance, and his tailored sharkskin suit. The black man was actually coffee colored and looked like he could have been a Mexican or Puerto Rican until he spoke, and then he was all Detroit. Looking at the right side of the black man's suit, Robert was sure he was carrying.

It was obvious to Robert that Eddie and the two white men were drunk. Slurring his words, Eddie explained he wanted to arrange a private party. Knowing that Jozef had a strict rule about alcohol, Robert decided to delay the impending confrontation by asking Joe to go to the office and check on Mister Farkas' membership status, while he waited in the lobby with the four men. When Jozef returned with the membership ledger, he announced to all four men, that Eddie had not paid his dues in two years.

"Sorry Eddie," said Joe setting the ledger down, "but you are no longer a paid member in good standing. I am afraid we will not be able to accommodate your group's request." Hearing Joe, who was always polite with members, call Mister Farkas, Eddie told Robert what Joe thought about the situation.

"Come on, old man. Cut me some," said Eddie turning to smile at his friends. "I don't have that much bread, but I'll write a check. Bring me up to date, and I add something for you and the kid."

"Sorry, cash only. Those are the rules," said Jozef hoping that would end it. Joe did not mention that he had a gun in his pocket, but Robert could see he did. Evert and Jozef both kept guns in the desk in the office. Had Farkas been sober, Robert might have offered to renew his membership, but he said nothing.

"Look," said black man, "I'll pay Eddie's dues, and the cost of a private session on the range." Before the man could say more, Robert held up his hand.

"I am very sorry gentlemen, but guns and alcohol don't mix at this club. Come back early some morning, or book a Sunday and I will personally set you up, but not today," said Robert.

"Suppose all of us join," asked the black man. In his hand, he had a roll of twenty-dollar bills.

"Not today Sammy," said Jozef using his tough Marine tone.

"Did you call me Sammy, motherfucker? No Niggars allowed in your club, is that it Tom. Do you know who I am?"

"Sir," said Robert stepping between Jozef and the black man. "Mister Kaminski meant no offense. He is a great fan of Sammy Davis Jr., and Martin Luther King. The problem is sometimes Joe forgets." Robert was very aware of the racism that Jozef harbored but personally, after fighting with dozens of fearless black men, Robert was in favor of civil rights and would like to see the club integrated, he just wondered if this was the moment, and this was the right man to be the first black member.

"Look, kid, maybe you don't know who this is," said Farkas, trying to sound tough. "This is Guy Jackson. He owns a lot of real estate in Detroit and he is thinking of buying here in the St Clair Shores."

"Mr. Jackson, on another day I would be very pleased to have your party shoot at the club, but these men have been drinking and alcohol and target shooting don't mix."

"Ok, then, sign Mister Jackson up, you little punk. He ain't drunk, he only drank tea." Farkas was angry and embarrassed; his words were spit at Robert.

"Mr. Farkas, your friend is welcome to join the club. He can even use that gun he is carrying, provided he can show me his license for the gun and his permit to carry a concealed weapon." Robert's eyes never left the black man, even though he was addressing Farkas.

"What if I left my permits at home?" The black man acted as if he was checking his pockets when he again held up his money roll.

"Sir, half the members of this club are police officers, and the rules of this club are very strict. You can of course purchase a rifle or shotgun or rent a gun, if you really desire some practice. In fact, I will even let your friends watch, provided they behave. But, I should warn you, if there are any problems from you or your friends Mister Kaminski over there is likely to use the gun he has in his pocket." At this, Jackson looked over at Jozef and reached for the button on his suit coat. The three white men stepped back, from the smaller black man, but one also touched his coat. Before the black man could undo the button on his jacket, Robert had his wrist.

"Mister Jackson, let's be smart about all this. I do not need a gun to kill you, and even if your friend pulls his gun, when the police arrive, you all will have guns in your dead hands. All dead, killed by Mister Kaminski in an apparent robbery gone bad. So, you see, I am not going to let you or anyone else come into the club or go behind the lobby carrying an illegal weapon. For that, we can lose our license.

"Tough talk, when all you have is that old man behind you, kid," said the overweight white man who had also reached for his belt.

"Mister, I don't know you at all. You might be a very tough guy, someone's muscle. Perhaps you have killed a man or two, but I have killed dozens. Perhaps you like shooting men, or maybe you want to show these other men you are tough, impress the boss. It doesn't really matter, because, I like killing. I like getting close up and pulling the trigger, I like breaking a man's neck with one blow. Unfortunately,

I don't get the opportunity anymore, and I don't think you want to give me the chance right now." Robert let go of Jackson's wrist.

"So, what do you say, Mr. Jackson, do you want to become the club's first black member? If you do, you can all come back on Sunday for a private shoot or better still, if you want to shoot today, I'll put some coffee, while you and your friends go out and leaved your coats in your cars. If you do that, I'll get you a great gun to try."

"And, if I say, I am cold and want to keep my coat on?"

"Then it will be the Algiers Motel all over again, if you dig what I'm saying." Robert smiled and then Jackson smiled back.

"What's your name?"

"Robert, Robert Cederberg."

"I like you Robert. You are like me. Small but tough, a real hard case, like the kind you meet in the slammer. Tough, yet respectful. I admire that you showed some respect for a brother, unlike that old Pollack there." Robert held up his hand to Jozef and then leaned in to whisper to Jackson.

"One of the rules of the club is member respect one another. In here there are no Jews, spicks, wops, pollacks, or niggers; in here we are gun owners." That old man is the best gunsmith in Detroit. If you need a gun repaired or you need something special, Jozef Kaminski is the man. If you can be nice to him, club membership is only a signature away. Besides, when we were having our little talk, I think I heard him cock the pistol he has aimed at you.

"I see. A good motherfucker to have on your side."

"Right on, brother."

"Mr. K," said the black man raising his hands in a sign of surrender. "I would appreciate it if you accepted my apology for Eddie and my boys. Now, I think Robert mentioned coffee. That would be very nice. I am going to put my coat in the car. While I do, how about getting four application forms, and I'll need a pen, and the boys will want pencils."

That was the day the Robert integrated the Bullseye and Robert let Guy Jackson practiced with a new Beretta 92. Once the three white men were safely drinking coffee in the trophy room, Robert joined Joe watching Jackson taking shots in the first shooting stand.

"What do you think?"

"I think his wrist is too loose."

"Yes, I can see that, but, what about making him a member."

"He has money and he likes guns, you can see that. But he is a nigger, and I don't trust him. He is a criminal, a low life. Put a gun in the hand of a nigger like that, and sooner or later he is gonna shoot you."

"I don't think so, Joe. I really don't. In Vietnam, I knew guys like him. Sure maybe he does a little wheeling and dealing, but when the shit hits the fan he is a guy you want covering your back. I think he is a small time criminal who desperately wants to be a business man. He wants to live in Grosse Pointe and be a member at Lochmore.

"He'll need more than a gun to get in there," laughed Jozef.

Later, after the men were gone, Robert joined Joe drinking coffee in the office. Robert had his feet up on the desk, a practice Joe shared.

"Robby, you were real solid today, and maybe a little foolish. That nigger, Jackson, he is a criminal and so are his friends, including that Arab, Eddie Farkas. Mister Yale would never have let niggers in the club. He would have shot Jackson the moment he reached for his gun, and I might have too. I know these are different times, and the niggers are integrated, but not here, not in this club." Joe sipped his coffee. Robert smiled at the old man. To Robert, Guy Jackson was a black businessman, who liked guns. Certainly, Jackson, had underworld friends, perhaps he had illegal gambling houses and houses of prostitution, but Robert knew he owned pieces of three bars and four high raise apartment buildings. Robert had even read in the Free Press that Guy Jackson had invested money in a program for single mothers in inner city Detroit. That afternoon, all Robert could say to Joe was "Inside the club we are all just gun owners, nothing else." Later when they closed up, Jozef wished Robert "good night," but as Jozef walked to his truck, Robert was aware of how divided the two were over this issue.

When he got home, Robert spent a half hour on the phone explaining to Evert happened and what he did and why. Jozef and he did not talk about it for another month, but Robert spent an hour in a private meeting with several of the club members the next morning.

* * *

Guy Jackson became a regular at the pistol range and he and Robert spent considerable time together, on both the range and sitting in Robert's office drinking coffee and tea. Guy was four years older than Robert. He had been in the air force, stationed in Germany for a year. He liked to talk about fucking German girls, and about all the money that could be made selling drugs and guns. Without saying more, Jackson liked to add that Robert could be making a lot more money than he did as Manager. In Vietnam, Robert had smoked marijuana and he knew of guys who bought and sold guns. He also knew from Jozef and Evert that many guns stores and gun dealers, not to mention gun clubs sold guns illegally at a huge profit, but none of that interested Robert. Robert was happy with what he had, a place to shoot a gun without anyone shooting back.

Jackson had an office on Van Dyke in Detroit, but he got his hair cut every Thursday at a barber located less than a mile from the Bullseye. Typically, Jackson came to the club after his haircut to practice for a half an hour. One Thursday afternoon after shooting for an hour, Jackson stuck his head in Robert's office and asked Robert if he wanted to share a coke.

Sitting on Robert's desk, Jackson handed Robert a coke along with his targets. While they drank their cokes, one of Jackson's associates waited outside in Jackson's car.

"Good shooting Guy," said Robert adding up Jacksons points. "Robert, have you ever thought about starting a club just for black gun owners?"

"I have, but frankly I rather see this club integrated."

"What else would you like to see?"

"Oh you know, more women members," said Robert. "The problem is Evert Yale. He would never approve. What I need is to buy the Club."

"What you need is a partner."

"I have a partner, Joe Kaminski. Without Joe, the place doesn't work."

"Yea, but Joe's an old man," said Jackson. "I bet he doesn't have a penny saved. If he is important to the club, he can always work here, but why make him a partner. What you need is a partner with some ready cash and ideas for a future Detroit."

"Like you."

"Why not me? I have the cash, I like the place, and despite what people say about me, I do not have a criminal record."

"Guy, if Joe wants in he is in, but no one else, not even you. If you want to talk about a second club, the Bullseye Too, a club that you and I own, well, that is a different story."

"Why can't I be your partner in this place? I gots the cash. Is it the color of my money?"

"No, of course not. You know me better than that. It is just that this place is special to me. This is my club. I have worked here since I was a kid. If you were my partner, I'd always feel that I had to ask you to make changes in the club. I'd never feel like I was the boss."

"What about Joe?"

"Joe is different. He gets to be a partner if he wants because without him I'd be something else. I own him. Besides Joe, is like a silent partner, we think alike, and he will let me be in charge. You are different. You have to run everything, no offense."

"Your right about that kid. If I want something done right, I do it myself." Jackson sipped his coke and considered Robert.

"What if I just loan you the money. No partnership, just a loan paid back with interest and your help starting a new club. One designed for Black members."

'I'd like that. But first I have to own the Bullseye."

"Ok, I'll tell you what, put some numbers together. What does it cost to run this place, how much does it earn, what do you think it will cost to buy out Evert. Then figure out what it will cost to start a second club, include everything, the license, the equipment, the guns, the staff, everything."

"Including Joe?"

"Including Joe. If the numbers work for me in the second club, I will loan you the money to buy this club."

"Sounds great. I should have everything you want by the time you get your next haircut."

* * *

When Robert talked to Jozef about buying the club and about the possibility of Jackson being a silent partner, Jozef made it clear he did not want to be any part of any deal involving Jackson. They were sitting behind the counter in the lobby drinking coffee. It was morning and the first reservation was not due for an hour. When Robert finished explaining about the numbers, Jozef put down his coffee cup, the one that said, 'Bullseye' on the side, and sat for a moment saying nothing. Robert had explained that it would cost seven thousand to buy the assets of the company. What was unclear was how much to offer Evert based on the revenue and profit of the company. In 1974, even though Evert had only been in the store a total of two weeks, he earned a salary of thirty five thousand dollars and the company made a profit of two thousand dollars. In talking with Evert on the phone, it was clear to Robert that Evert expected to earn a salary until he died. When Robert asked about selling outright, Evert immediately said he would consider $100,000 in cash and a ten-year earn out of 30% of the profits.

The next day, when Robert asked Jozef what he thought, Jozef said, "Look Robert, Evert has it easy. He will never sell the club, and even if he did, you and I do not have the cash to buy the club."

"How about we start our own club in a new location?"

"Robert," said Jozef, "I owe Evert very much. Besides," he added, "I could never be partners with that nigger, Guy Jackson."

After talking with Jozef, Robert considered starting a club without him. Robert was convinced that once he had a new club up and running, he could get the old man to come along. From Robert's perspective, it would be cheaper to start a new club, but he wanted Joe and he needed the money Guy Jackson was offering.

Taking a different tactic, Robert called Evert on a Wednesday afternoon. He was just coming back from playing golf. After discussing the weather and Evert's golf game, Robert made his pitch. "Mister Yale, I know I owe you everything, but I want to own my own club. I plan on leaving the Bullseye and starting a new club in Grosse Pointe. If I leave, what will you have? A building no one will buy and seven thousand in guns and ammo. Instead, I can offer you $100,000 for the club. That is three years of profit. You and I both know that is a good offer. Take some time to think it over. If you decide, you cannot sell, I will give you a month to find someone else to run the club, but you should be aware I plan to take Joe with me." Robert drank a glass of water waiting for the old man to react.

"Robert, life in Florida is not as cheap as people make out," said Yale. "Wonder Bread cost the same here as it does there. Look Robert, when I go, I will make it easy for Joe and you to buy the place, but now, I need the money, and don't think you can hold a gun to my head. I won't sell."

"I'm not, I am just being honest. I want my own club."

"Robert, listen, what if I sell you and Joe forty nine percent right now for the $100,000, but I retain ownership for five years. That way I get half the profits and the income from leasing the building, and you get started in business. You become an owner."

"Let me talk to Joe," said Robert thinking if he could get the purchase price down he would make the deal.

"I already talked to Joe about this. Only thing Robert, and Joe and I agree on this, no Guy Jackson in the deal. We don't want no nigger owning the club."

"Mister Yale, we talked about this. Having black members has increased our revenue by forty grand."

"Members are OK, but not partners, not owners. Do you understand me?"

"I understand. I am just not sure Guy Jackson will understand."

* * *

Guy Jackson had a storefront office on Harper and Van Dyke in Detroit. On the front window, it read "Jackson Enterprises." Inside was a rundown looking reception desk behind which sat the best-looking black woman Robert had ever seen. She was tall, thin, and dressed in a tight black slacks and a white silk blouse. When she showed Robert into Guy Jackson's office, Robert got a good view of coffee colored breasts with dark nipples under her open silk blouse.

"Darlene, get Robert here some coffee will ya, Sugar. And better button up your blouse or Robert will want some cream with that coffee." The black man laughed as Robert blushed. Jackson's inner office was a distinct contrast from the outer office. Inside, it was painted in a linen color and decorated with expensive furniture. Underfoot was a thick new carpet. Sitting in a chair that looked three sizes too small was a large black man with massive hands and a nose that had been broken several times. Rather than wearing an Afro, which was the current hairstyle, he was bald.

"Robert this is my younger brother Raymond. Sugar Ray is a fighter. I am working on his next fight. I'll send you tickets once it is scheduled." Jackson was smoking an unfiltered camel.

"So, Robert, what did Evert say?"

"To be honest, Mister Jackson, you are not going to like what he said."

"Robert, if we are going to be partners, you have to call me Guy."

"That is just it Guy, I am not sure we can be partners."

"Evert said he would sell me and Joe forty nine percent, but he said he would not sell to you."

"Is that what he said Robert, or did he say he would sell to no nigger, is that it. Well, fuck that snowbird cracker," said Jackson his cheeks flushed with anger. "I'll start my own club and take the black members with me. In fact, you can take me off the member roll today."

"Look, Guy, this isn't what I want. I don't feel that way about you, or any black person. I'm not a racist. I have nothing against you or any black person. I grew up with a Negro maid who was more mother to me than my own. The problem is Evert, Mister Yale. He is just one of those Detroiters who doesn't like Negros, I guess Joe is pretty much that way too."

"Robert, I understand bigoted assholes like Evert Yale. However, you are something else. I thought you were some badass guy. A guy who could get things done, but you are just like that old Pollock. At your core, you fear the black man and will always try to keep him down. Listen to you talking about your Aunt Jemima maid. Yes sir master. All you Grosse Pointers make me sick. Hiring black women to cook your food and clean your kid's asses. You think because you had a maid that you understand black people. You think you were friends."

"We were."

"Bullshit. Your family owned her. In the South, the whites had slaves. In Grosse Pointe, you had servants. Same thing."

"It is not. I loved her."

"Robert all you love are guns and that crummy club. People aren't a part of your world. You are all cold inside."

"So what about our partnership?" asked Robert seeing the truth in Jackson's statement. Robert looked over at Sugar Ray. He was sitting up, watching Robert. Looking back, Guy Jackson's face had lost all its humor.

"Robert, I want that club now. If you can't deliver, you are of no use to me. I don't need any partner who can't deliver, I have plenty of employees like that, and I don't need another.

"What about opening a club together? I thought we were friends."

"Robert, my friends are winners. I thought you might be a winner that you might see the opportunity and go for it, but I guess you just another white trash loser. Our friendship ended five minutes ago." Jackson stood up from his desk. "Sugar Ray, will you escort this motherfucker out of my sight. And, understand this Robert. When I open up my own club, I will drive the Bullseye out of business and take you and that old Pollack with it."

"But, Guy,"

"That is Mister Jackson to you motherfucker. Sugar, get this worthless asshole out of my sight." Guy stood back and made like he was shoeing flies. His brother stood and put a hand on Robert's back. Robert had an instance to decide whether violence would prove any point. He knew he couldn't fight Ray, but he could drop him at any moment, with a killing punch, the problem was he still liked Guy and admired Ray for staying in the ring and fighting when other would have taken a dive. Putting up his hands, Robert marched out of the office and past Darlene who was still making his coffee. "Perhaps I can get that from you later," said Robert giving Darlene a half smile.

CHAPTER 7

LUCY AND RICKI

Over the next few months, Jozef and Robert spoke less and less about owning the club. Robert ran the front, taught classes, and interacted with members. Joe sold supplies, repaired guns, and supervised shooters on the range. True to his word, Guy Jackson stopped coming and so did seven of the other black members. Three black police officers from Roseville remained as members.

For Robert, the entire event was confusing. Thinking about it, Robert realized he did not really care if Evert owned the Club provided he stayed in Florida and let Robert run the Club. Robert was happy being manager and apprentice gunsmith to Joe. In hindsight, the idea of buying the Club had come from Guy Jackson.

In the spring of 1973, Eric Cederberg announced that he and Caroline were moving to Florida. At the time, John was in college, and William, who had just turned nineteen, was living at home and working on the line at Chrysler. When Robert's parents explained about the move, they made it clear there would be a room for any boy when he visited, but they also assumed their sons would live on your own. In their 'retirement' plan, they were moving to Florida without the boys. For Robert, the news that his parents were leaving Grosse Pointe, the news that he would have to live on his own was welcome news. Robert hated living in their attic bedroom, always hot in summer and cold in winter. In May, he loaded his single bed, two bookcases, and a few other selected pieces of furniture, along with some keepsakes from his room, his clothes and records, and moved into a two-bedroom house on Oxford north of Mack in Grosse Pointe. Robert should have rented a house closer to the Club in Roseville, but he was comfortable to Grosse Pointe.

Before Eric and Caroline left for Florida, Robert invited them to tour the Bullseye. In all the years Robert had worked at the

Bullseye, his parents had never set foot in the place. Over the winter, Robert had spent considerable time and sweat, cleaning, repairing, painting and decorating the gun club. Now the magazines on the wooden tables were new and the wooden tables clean and polished. In addition to new paint, Robert had purchased new signs for each room in the club. He traded his time instructing for a discount on the signs. To promote the club, he purchased an old high school trophy case and in it, he displayed Evert and Joe's trophies in addition to his own. In his new house, Robert applied the same energy, new paint in all the rooms. In terms of decorating, except for the few selected items from the house on Renaud, everything else was new. In touring the club, Eric said nothing and Caroline only mentioned how loud the guns were and how the place smelled. After the tour, Robert took his parents back to his house. Caroline and Eric seemed more at ease, and once they had a cocktail, they relaxed and Robert and his parents spent the evening reminiscing about living in Grosse Pointe and their summers at the cottage.

When Eric and Caroline finally moved, they left four sons in Michigan. Austin was divorced and living downtown. John was at school and for a month, William lived with Robert, until he moved in with his girl friend. For Robert's three brothers having parents living in Florida meant a place to go on vacation and a warm destination for Christmas. Surprisingly, Robert felt more alone, more isolated. His life became a cycle of going to work, working for ten hours, going home, eating, sleeping, and starting all over again. Except for shooting tournaments and fishing with Joe, Robert's life was empty, at least until Joe met Lucy Meadows.

* * *

Joe was off on Monday's, so Robert was surprised when Joe came into the club and asked Robert and Dave the clean up boy if they could help him move some furniture after work.

"What's up," asked Robert.

"I bought a house. A house on Anita in Grosse Pointe, just like you. We are neighbors." Joe lived in three rented rooms in Roseville.

"You bought a house in Grosse Pointe without telling me?"

"Yes," Jozef announced, "with three bedrooms. I even have a room for you if you want stay over."

"What was wrong with your apartment? Why buy a home now, and in Grosse Pointe?"

"At my age you mean."

"Well."

"My apartment was a dump. I wanted a place I could entertain. A decent place, and place a woman would like," laughed Jozef.

"Are you seeing a woman? Is that it?

"A lady from church."

"That explains the suit on Sundays," laughed Robert.

"I am a good Catholic."

"So you met a Catholic widow."

"Her name is Lucy Meadows," Joe explained, "She was in line behind me at Sunday coffee, and I heard her speaking Polish under her breath. She was swearing about how slow the man in front of me was. I turned to her and laughed, and then I scolded her in Polish for being so uncharitable at church. After, we sat together drinking coffee."

"Had you seen her before?"

"No she just started coming to this church, it was her first Sunday, her first coffee, and I lucked out. She has just moved here. She used to live for a time in Grosse Pointe and in Birmingham. Her husband died five years ago. Since then she has lived with her daughter in Birmingham. A month ago, her daughter moved to Florida for a job. Rather than move there, she is living in a rented a house in Grosse Pointe over by the church. She is German, but she grew up on the Polish border. She is forty-nine and very attractive. She wants to live in Grosse Pointe."

"And she likes you? You have been on dates." Robert was kidding, but he also was amazed that Joe, who smelled of gun oil, sour kraut and brats, a man who never shaved, and barley spoke English could attract a younger woman. He also wondered why Joe had not mentioned Lucy before. The two men nearly shared everything, now Joe had a secret.

"I know, it is unbelievable. After our coffee together, she asked if I would be at coffee next week, and when I said yes, she said it was a date. Since then we have had coffee three times together and last week I took her to Sunday brunch at the Pancake House."

"Sounds like you are dating. Sounds like you have a lady friend."

"I hope so."

"I hope so too, because buying a house it a pretty big step."

"I know, but when Lucy saw the house she said it was perfect."

"The two of you went house hunting?"

"Two weeks ago on my day off, she want to look for a house and I went along. When she saw this house, she said it was perfect. So I bought it."

Lucy was right, the little house on Anita was perfect, moving Joe's few belongings, and old furniture, Robert was amazed at the change in Joe. Joe practically hummed as he carried in tables and lamps. Seeing Joe so happy, Robert felt great for his old friend, with the possibility of a woman in his life; on the other hand, he worried how this would change their relationship.

The next Sunday, Jozef came to work twenty minutes late. Robert was coaching a new club member on different shooting positions when Jozef came strolling in smiling as if he had won the Irish Sweeps States. Robert was struck by the fact Joe was still wearing his only suit, a blue all wool suit that he purchased in 1964 when his brother died. That meant Joe had come straight from church.

Closing the manager's office door, Joe took a hanger off a hook on the back of the door. Sitting in Evert's swivel chair he untied his black dress shoes, removed his coat and then his white shirt and pants. Carefully Jozef hung the suit and his one good white shirt and the maroon tie Evert had given him for his 60th birthday on the wooden hanger, placing the clothes behind the office door.

"This is the suit I will be buried in," Jozef said to Robert when he walked in the office.

"Let's hope you own a few more suits before that."

"What would a man do with two suits?" Standing in his underwear, Jozef pulled on his coveralls and then laced up a pair of steel-toed work boots. When he finished dressing, Joe walked out of the office whistling "*That Old Black Magic.*"

Following Joe into the repair room Robert said, "What's up Joe? You seem in a good mood. Hear a good joke at church?"

"No, No, Robby better than that. I got a date with Lucy for this Friday. Dinner and a movie and then back to my house."

"That is great. Where are you taking her?"

"She mentioned she wanted to see that new Peter Seller's movie, the Return of the Pink Panther. Personally, I rather go home and watch TV, or see that Western, the one with Gene Hackman, Bite the Bullet, but an early dinner at Stouffers and then we see a funny movie at the Woods Theater, and later, maybe home for a night cap."

"Sounds like a plan," laugh Robert as he put several extra targets back in the cabinet. "There is just one thing. When I helped you move, I noticed that all your furniture is second hand, and the sheets on your bed, they looked like they had been issued to you in the pacific. And, then there…"

"There is what?"

"Well, I have just seen you with you coveralls off. I think you and I need to drive over to Hudson's and spend a little cash in the Men's department, not to mention buying some new linens and towels. I remember a woman told me the sign that a man cares about a women is how he leaves the bathroom. Take it from me, if you want that widow to think you care, buy a new couch, put fresh towels in the bathroom, and empty the beer cans from the kitchen.

"Is that all?"

"Well," laughed Robert, "If you really feel lucky, you might spring for a new mattress."

"Next you'll have me cooking her dinner."

"That's not such a bad idea; except I've seen you burn canned soup."

"That's why I looking for a companion."

"That isn't the only reason and you and I know it.

"What about you, Robby, you are young and not bad looking. I mean, why pay for it when you can get it for free."

"Where would I meet a decent girl?"

"Well, how about at my church. Come with me on Sunday, I think there is a coffee for young singles after the 12:00 service."

"No, you know I don't believe."

"How come you don't believe, I mean doesn't it make you feel a little lonely?"

"One day in the Nam, I asked God for his help. I told him I would pledge my life to spreading his word, if he would help me keep this eighteen year old kid with a chest wound alive long enough to make it to a chopper, but he said he wasn't interested. The kid died, so I told God to get fucked, him and his religion too."

"Robby, you shouldn't speak like this. God is listening, maybe not that day in Vietnam, but he is listening and watching."

"Sorry Joe. But I don't buy it. God, Church, the Priest thing, they are all out. Finding a girl at church is out. I think I'd have better chances at that dance club the Hideout or at Kelly's bar."

"Robby, bars are great places to find a certain kind of woman when you are in the service. However, they are no place to find a decent woman, a wife. Maybe you should try the Cadieux Café."

"Maybe I should start hanging out that the Library or Farmer Jacks. I hear a grocery store is a great place to meet women."

"Sure, but you'd have to know how to talk to a woman. I know how to talk to women. What would you say to a nice girl if you met one? All you talk about is guns and ammo, and this club. One day you are going to meet a nice girl, the she'll ask you about church and family, and you'll ask if she has ever fired a Walther. Take my word for it Robby; you need a woman to keep you straight, to keep you sane. You can't spend your whole life here." Joe pointed to the office. "You need a woman to go home to. Otherwise,"

"Otherwise what?"

"Otherwise one day you'll find yourself sitting in a chair with a gun in your mouth, wondering if anyone will care."

"I have already been in that chair."

"Yea, Robby, so have I."

"So what kept you from going through with it?"

"Because life is God's gift, and only God can take it. It is a sin to take your life. Besides you have everything to live for, your life is still in front of you."

"Joe, I know you really believe that, and I am glad it kept you from it, because you're the best friend I ever had, and I'd sure miss you around this place, but that isn't enough for me. Frankly, the only thing that kept me from it was…"

"Was what? What kept you from eating a bullet?"

"I thought about that kid with the chest wound, and how hard he fought to stay alive, how much he wanted to live, and I felt like a coward. There I was, sitting with the gun Miss Kay gave me, Susan who fought so hard to overcome her fears, who died fighting cancer, and there I was sitting in a chair, perfectly healthy, a guy with a job, with a great friend, and I was thinking about ending it. I felt like a coward, so I put the gun away, and promised myself I would never take it out again, at least not for that reason."

"I think that is good enough for now. I don't worry about you and you don't worry about me. We are both survivors."

* * *

In the winter months, the club was open Monday through Fridays 10:00 a.m. to 6:00 p.m. On the weekends, the club opened early on Saturday 8:00 a.m. and closed at 6:00 p.m. On Sunday, the club opened at 12:00 noon and closed at 5:00 p.m. During the summer, the Robert and Joe decided that on Fridays, the club would open at noon and stay open until 8:00 p.m., a schedule allowing Robert and Jozef to go fishing on Friday mornings.

Joe had a twelve-foot aluminum skiff with ten horsepower mercury on a trailer. On Fridays, Robert would meet Joe at the Woods Park boat-launch and take the skiff out for three hours of fishing just off Ford's Cove on Lake St. Clair. For these outings, Robert would bring a thermos of coffee and some type of pastries, bagels, or muffins. When he brought bagels, Robert included a jar of Jiffy Peanut Butter; he loved peanut butter, often eating it right out of the jar for breakfast.

Whenever they caught perch, they would go to one or the others house and have a complete Friday fish fry dinner, with tartar sauce, cold slaw, green beans and new potatoes. Robert had grown up eating fresh perch or whitefish on Friday, so his fish dinners with Joe were like family dinners, except there was beer and less arguing. For Joe, fish on Friday was part of obligation for being Catholic. Nevertheless, he looked forward to their day on the water. On days when they caught nothing, they would eat the extra fish stored in Joe's freezer.

Robert's and Josef's Friday fish fry changed after Lucy Meadows became a part of Josef's life. Lucy took over Robert's role in the kitchen, making tartar sauce, cold slaw, and German potato salad all from scratch. In general, Robert liked Lucy and appreciated the changes she had brought about, including Joe smiling more and talking less about the past and more about the present. Lucy said she was forty-nine. Robert thought she looked was over fifty, but her dyed red hair, ample bust, trim waist on bird legs made her seem younger.

Lucy and Jozef were cleaning up the kitchen dishes after a Friday fish fry, when Lucy mentioned that an old friend of hers had a very nice daughter, Fredericka who was Robert's age.

"Liebchen, she said, to Jozef. "Tell Robert she is a very nice girl. Make him ask her out."

"Myszka, said Jozef, "He is a grown man. What can I do? You invite him and her to dinner. We will have dinner together." Joe had taken to calling Lucy, Myszka his little mouse.

All the next week, Jozef begged Robert to go out with the daughter of Lucy's friend, Fredericka Williams.

"Robert, you have to do this. Everyday Lucy is asking me when her little Schildkröte is going to call this girl, Fredericka. What should I tell her? You are afraid? You do not like girls. Only Whores." They were sitting in the repair room loading ammunition. Robert had a difficult time explaining to Joe why he did not want to go out. The more Lucy pushed, the harder Robert pushed back.

"You know I don't want to go out with a twenty four year old unmarried daughter named Fredericka," said Robert cleaning his area of the worktable. The new cleanup kid, Dave Livingston was manning the desk in the lobby.

"But, Robby, Lucy says she is nice, very nice."

"Joe, you know that nice means homely, I'm telling you, she is a dog, she barks, and I am not going to waste my Saturday on a dog."

"Robby, please for me. Lucy is very important to me. I want her to be happy, and she will not stop until you and Fredericka are sitting across a table. She can be very determined, very German. Besides, it isn't like you have something else to do." In the end, Robert agreed so Lucy would stop talking about Fredericka Williams.

Robert and Jozef did so many things together that double dating sounded like it would be easy, but it was uncomfortable for both men right from the start. Jozef and Lucy had a way of being together, talking in Polish and German using pet names, a secret life, a life separate from Robert and the gun club. Robert understood this, still at times he felt like an intruder.

On Friday evening, after a morning of successful fishing, Robert showed up at Joe's house for his date. The original plan was dinner at the pickle barrel and then a movie. However, meeting Robert at the door, Joe announced, "We are eating here, Lucy insisted on cooking the perch." Stepping into the front living room, Jozef pushed Robert ahead saying "Robert, please to meet Miss Fredericka Williams."

"Please, call me Ricki," said the blond girl standing up from the couch.

"Ricky," said Robert. The girl had curly blond hair, she wore brown glasses, had apple cheeks, and a large toothy smile. She was small, five foot five with a lean boyish figure. Less than one hundred and five pounds, thought Robert who always assessed a person's weight relative to his own. Robert noticed the palms of her hands were rough and red as if they were chapped.

"That's Ricki with two "i"s. I never call myself Fredericka.

"Lucy and Ricki," laughed Robert. "Well, I am Robert, not Bob or Rob, or Robby, although I can't get this guy to stop calling me Robby. That's Robby with a y," he laughed.

"Robert," said Jozef. "You talk to Miss Ricki, and I get Lucy." Sitting in Joe's living room Robert didn't know what to talk to about, and he had no idea what Lucy and Jozef were talking about in the kitchen, as they whispered in German and Polish. For his date, Robert was wearing a pair of khaki and a blue Izod shirt. Before leaving home, he shined his brown penny loafers. Ricki wore a paisley print dress with a starched shirtfront like a man's shirt. Her dress was too short and when she reached for a glass of tea that Jozef gave her without asking, Robert noticed she had very good-looking legs. A thought that made him slightly aroused.

All throughout their perch dinner, Lucy talked a lot and she and Jozef smiled at one another and at the younger couple who said very little. Robert for the most part, drank beer and laughed when he supposed he should. When dinner was over, Lucy pushed Ricki and Robert out of the kitchen into the living room.

Schildkröte, said Lucy addressing Robert, "talk to this girl," before ducking back into the kitchen.

"Turtle, did she call you turtle?"

"You speak German?"

"A little, my mother is German; I grew up with German and English spoken in the house."

"Where did you grow up, because that isn't a Detroit accent?"

"I have lived all over I guess. My mother lives in Ohio. Lucy says you were in Vietnam, but you won't talk about it."

"It isn't that I won't talk about it, it is just that you can't talk about being in combat, unless you are talking to another veteran. If you have never experienced a mortar barrage, there is no way to explain the sound and the fear. Then everyone wants to know if you killed someone. Why does everyone ask that?"

"I killed someone."

"What?"

"I had just turned twenty one. I had been drinking with friends. I was drunk. I hit another car. It was a fender bender, but the other driver wasn't wearing a seat belt and she died four days later from a head injury." Ricki, turned away to wipe tears. Robert noticed she did not drink.

"Look, I'm sorry," started Robert. "I didn't mean for you. Oh look, I have bad stories in my life too. I guess everyone has stories they don't want to tell. It sounds like you have a bad story too, so, let agree, only good stories. Like our maid Chessie use to say, if you can't saying anything good…"

"Wait, you had a maid named Chessie. Now that seems like a story."

"Yes, and a good one," said Robert as he embarked on several funny stories about when he was young and Chessie would catch him being bad. Like telling people about Joe, Robert loved talking about the Chessie. When Robert finished one story, he explained how Chessie died while he was in Vietnam, which brought him to the brink of teas, before he told about the day Chessie caught him kissing Jill McCullah in his bedroom with her shirt off. For a moment, Ricki looked rather put out, and then she asked in all seriousness "You mean Chessie had her shirt off?" Laughing, Robert knew he liked this woman.

When Jozef and Lucy emerged from the kitchen, Lucy asked if Ricki minded if Robert takes her home, and she said she was hoping he would. Driving through Grosse Pointe, Robert mentioned several times what a good time he had, hoping Ricki would say she did too giving him some opening to ask her out again. When he pulled up in front of her house, he again said he enjoyed meeting Ricki.

"Oh Robert," she laughed, "don't you know I enjoyed myself and that I like you?" She gave him a fierce kiss. "Look, I'd ask you in, but I can't, at least not tonight. Why don't I make you dinner on Friday, say at 6:00 and we can go from there."

"I'd like that," said Robert enjoying the intensity of her kiss.

"Good," she said, kissing him again, this time a sweet gentle kiss. "Do you like Chinese? No wait, how about Italian, spaghetti."

"Good again."

"Ok, Robby now go home and think about what stories you will tell me on for Friday night."

"Please don't call me that."

"What should I call you, Schildkröte like Lucy does.

"Turtle is better than Robby, but I stopped being the turtle years ago and now I prefer Robert."

* * *

In the week that followed, Robert and Joe ran the club, talking about everything except Robert's upcoming date. Friday morning, Robert was so anxious that he cancelled fishing and had his haircut. That night, he arrived at 5:45 p.m. carrying a loaf of garlic bread and some flowers from the bushes beside his house. After showing him, the house, Ricki, parked him on a kitchen chair. On the stove, a pot of sauce shimmered, filling the room with the smell of cooked tomato, onion, and garlic.

"I really like cooking at home, said Ricki with Robert watching her from the chair. She who wore a white apron. My mom is a great cook, and so was my grandmother, my Nana Kleist. How about your mom, is she a good cook?"

"Awful, if you want the truth," said Robert watching her move about the kitchen. Under the apron, she had on bell-bottom jeans and a peasant blouse, with sandals.

"My mom was always trying new dishes, with foreign spices. Once she liked a spice, she used it in everything. I remember a month where everything had dill weed in it. I mean everything, hamburgers, potatoes, macaroni and cheese; I think she even added dill to my frosted flakes.

"Is that why you had a maid?"

"I never really asked; we just always had one. I think it started with having a nurse maid for each baby."

"A nurse maid?"

"Yes, as I understand it, my mom had this German lady, Kultie help her with my older brother Austin when he was a week old. Something about my mom going into a depression after a baby is born and not having any milk. As I understand it, after I was born, Kultie wasn't available so we hired Chessie. I guess when I think about it, my mom was a terrible homemaker and a worse cook. Maybe having a maid was the only way Dad would stay married to my mom. My brother believes we moved out of our house on Cadieux and moved to Renaud, because it was easier to move than to clean and repair the old house.

"And, when your parents moved to Florida, you stayed here, why, because of the club or because you…you hate your parents?"

"In part, I guess. Joe and Evert were my real fathers for the last ten years. When I got back from Vietnam Evert offered me a job and I took it."

"But isn't there more you want to be, more you could be?" They had moved to the kitchen table. Ricki handed Robert a plate of spaghetti, with a meatball on top and a piece of garlic bread. On a separate plate, she had a green salad.

"I love guns, said Robert between bites. "They are all I know. One day I expect to be famous because of a gun."

"John Dillinger was famous too, and not just because of his huge thing," laughed Ricki, expecting Robert to laugh but he did not.

"All I am saying," she continue, "is look at me. I have a high school degree and a two-year college degree. All that education and I am working at Jacobson's selling sweaters. Someday, I plan to get a better job, one that uses more of my hidden talents. I think you are the same. You have hidden talents."

"What are you hidden talents?"

"You will have to discover those on your own. Right now, we are talking about you. How about explaining the deal with the guns, what it is about men and guns?"

"Guns are black and white for me. A gun is either loaded or empty, either you hit the target or you did not. They are precision machines that require tremendous skill to get it right."

"How about all the sex and power, all the James Bond stuff you guys like."

"There is that at times. Shooting a gun can feel sexual, and a gun can make a person feel powerful or at the end of a leash." Robert had moved to a couch in her front room. He still had half a glass of wine and he was feeling full and happy from the meal, very satisfied and safe. Ricki sat down beside him with a glass of water. She slipped off her sandals.

"Will you teach me to shoot?"

"I will if you really want to, but don't feel you have to because I like shooting. I'll teach you to shoot so you can feel what I am talking about, but then I want you to promise if you don't enjoy it to be honest and tell me, because when we are together, as far as I am concerned we never have to talk about guns or the club or selling sweaters."

"Gee, what is left? We have talked about families and food that only leaves religion, politics, and sex." She smiled and kissed him on the mouth. "I have been warned to stay away from religion, and the elections are too far off, so that leaves sex." This time she kissed him hard, as he kissed her and pushed her back on the couch.

"Look," she said stopping him from biting her ear. "I am a liberated woman. We have ice cream for dessert, which we can have before or after sex, but personally, I like my sex in a bed with no clothes and all the lights on, so unless you want to take the ice cream upstairs with us, I suggest we leave the couch and go to my bedroom right now."

Robert realized Ricki wasn't kidding about being liberal and when she had him naked, she took every advantage of his firm manhood and his anxious body. After they finished, she kissed his chest, and then move down to kiss his penis. When they finished a second time, he slept while she lay beside him with her breasts under the sheets.

"That was nice," This wasn't your first time," she kidded, but he looked away. "Bad story?" she asked.

"Just for a moment," he said. "Right now," he said feeling the heat and wetness between her legs, "what I would really like is some ice cream; right here in bed. Do you think if I used the bathroom, you could get us some ice cream?"

"Do you need it to cool down?"

"No to restore my strength.

"I will get the ice cream, but, only if you turn on some music. I like music with my ice cream."

When Ricki returned, they sat in bed eating ice cream and kissing. In between bites of dessert, they talked about favorite music, what TV they liked, the best movies ever, and about their families. At some point Ricki talked about what she wanted out of life, a career, marriage, a family, but mostly a man who would be companion through life.

"We didn't get into this before, but I have been with enough men that I am tired of experimenting. I like sex, but I can go without a man for that. Lately I have been lonely. I want to settle down with a man. A man I love and one who loves me. Shit, I didn't mean that the way it sounded. I like you Robert, otherwise, no spaghetti dinner and dessert. Having sex doesn't mean I am in love with you and I am sure it doesn't mean that you are in love with me. I like you, and if you like me and want to see me, that is enough for now. Later we can see what happens when we peel the onion back." Ricki looked closely at Robert as he ate ice cream.

"Robert, if you want to put your pants on and go, I will understand. The only thing is if you leave now, and come back later, well, I might offer you dessert, but there will be no more dinners."

Robert realized he had no idea what he wanted in life other than to win the Bullseye competition in Ohio. He had no answer to how he felt as he ate more ice cream He was not in habit of spending the night after sex. "I would like to stay the night, if you want me to, but I have to be at the club early because it is Saturday, so I have three questions."

"What are they?"

"Do you have a toothbrush I can use?"

"Yes, and it is in a wrapper. What is question number two?"

"Can I make coffee before I leave?"

"I will make us both coffees. What is the third question?"

"Which side do you like to sleep on, because it doesn't matter to me?" After switching sides, she kissed him and touched his back when he turned over. When he was asleep, she got up and brushed her teeth and hair, sprayed on a little deodorant, put on her robe and went down to the kitchen to set the clock radio and get the coffee ready to go. Back up stairs, she folded his clothes and then slipped in the bed beside him.

A week later Robert and Ricki went to a movie on Saturday night and then Robert spent the night at her house. That next morning, Robert took Ricki to see the club. When they arrived, it was 9:35 in the morning, Robert who had been up since 5:30 had already had four cups of coffee, but Ricki had slept in and was working on her first coffee which she brought in the car in a extra large mug that she use to warm her hands.

Parking in the back, Robert saw Dave Langston's Ford Maverick. Dave was the boy who mopped the floors and cleaned the rooms and ranges. Walking in through the back door, Robert reached up to stop the bell above the door from ringing. He wanted to see if Dave was actually working. Asking Ricki to wait in the back by the pistol range, Robert crept through the club, checking Joe's workroom first and then his office, the locker room, and then quietly entering the clubs main room, the members meeting room. So far, no Dave. When Robert reached the lobby and the reception counter, he found Dave drinking coffee and eating a donut. Beside him was a pail of water and the mop.

"I hope you have more donuts to share," said Robert in his Drill Instructors voice.

"Jesus, Mr. Cederberg, you just about scared me to death. What are you doing here so early?"

"I am giving a tour. It is a good thing you weren't asleep, because you'd be out of a job. But, now, I think your coffee break is over."

"Right, of course, and thanks."

"Oh, and Dave."

"Yes, sir."

"Do you have any more donuts?"

"No, sorry."

"Well, go over to that Drunken Donuts and get a dozen." Robert handed the boy a five dollar bill."

"Certainly, you bet, a dozen, any kind?"

"Plain, cinnamon sugar, those peanut ones are great, but no chocolate. And Dave, take your time. I will be in the back."

He found Ricki sitting in one of the folding chairs people used when they were waiting for a range. Taking her hand, he took her into the gunroom where he planned to select a pistol for her to try. Before turning on the lights, he pulled her to him and they kissed, several times, even though they had exhausting sex the night before. Feeling himself getting aroused, he gently pushed her away.

On the wall facing the outdoor ranges were two display cases, one with guns for sale and one with guns for rent. Normally, for a private session Robert would have selected a gun from the rental case. Instead, he went to his own locker and after taking a minute to find a key from a ring of keys, he opened the double door steel locker. On one side were three rifles, on the other, were four shelves with pistols. The last shelf was three feet off the base and below that shelf hung shooting vests and Roberts coveralls. On the top shelf was a silver gun box. On the second shelf, there were three pistols in their own cases. The third and fourth shelf had built-in drawers. From the third drawer, Robert took out a box of bullets, handing these to Ricki, he took two of the gun cases form the second shelf, and then directed her out the door to the ranges.

The club had two long open ranges for rifle shooting and two open ranges for pistol or shotgun practice, and then an enclosed range just for pistol shooting. Outdoors, behind the ranges they had a skeet range that they offered twice a week, on Saturday and Thursday afternoons. The skeet range required three people, so it was only offered when Robert, Joe, and one or both of the clean up boys, Dave or Garret were present. For their first practice, Robert decided to use the closed range. Going into Joe's workroom, he grabbed two sets of ear covers and earplugs. At the front of the range was a firing stand with a box. The range was constructed of cinder blocks five feet by eight feet high and one hundred and fifty feet long. On the shooting stand, Robert placed a .38 caliber Smith and Wesson, and a Colt .45 1911. With Ricki standing back from the guns, Robert began his general speech about guns and target shooting.

"In target shooting, there are four basic safety concepts. First is the shooter's responsibility. Then we talk about understanding the course of fire, understanding the idea of a 'cold range', and finally gun handling. On a cold range, all handguns are always to be holstered or in a case, unloaded with the magazine removed, and hammer down on an empty chamber." Robert picked up the police special.

"This is a .38 caliber revolver. The bullets, six of them, go in here." Robert showed the empty chamber. "This is the hammer. On a cold range the gun is unloaded, and the hammer is down, not cocked," He demonstrated both putting the hammer down on the empty chamber. "In a cold range, no handling of firearms is ever permitted, except in the safe handling area. The reason we run a cold range and never handle our guns behind the firing line is for safety. It is our most important rule."

"When you are ready, I will say 'Eyes and ears on. The range is going hot!' I will then ask, 'Do you understand the course of fire?' You will say 'Yes I understand the course of fire," and then I will say 'The shooter understands the course of fire. The range is clear. Shooter, load and make ready!' On that command, you step up to the firing stand, and draw your pistol, insert a magazine or load the cylinders, charge the chamber, make safe, remove that magazine and stow it in a back pocket, and replace it with a fully loaded one. Then, you verify that the pistol is safe on the stand. Once your pistol is loaded and safe, I will ask, "Is the shooter ready?" A verbal "Yes" or nod will bring the next command, "Shooter ready…Standby!" The signal to start will be a tap on the shoulder. Once you have the start signal, you can fire the weapon at the target in the agreed on course of firing, meaning one shot at a time or multiple shots." Robert walked up to the line and picked up the Colt.

"In firing on a range, there are several commands or rules you must follow. One is the finger command. Any time an instructor shouts 'finger,' you must immediately responds by placing you trigger finger back to where it always belongs when not actively engaging a target: straight alongside the frame outside the trigger guard." Robert demonstrated safely holding both the automatic and the revolver, with his index finger outside the trigger guard.

"If you hear the word 'Muzzle!' shouted, you must instantly, turn the muzzle of the gun downrange"

"When you hear 'Unload and show clear,' you are to show clear, slide the hammer down, and place the safe weapon in its box or holster. With any semiautomatic, when you hear the command to 'Unload and show clear,' you first drop the magazine and stow it in a pocket, then eject the round from the chamber and let it fall to the ground. Next, you lock the slide to the rear, all the while keeping you pistol pointed safely straight downrange. The instructor will visually inspect the chamber and magazine to verify the weapon is completely unloaded. When I say 'Slide down' you will drop the slide on an empty chamber. The instructor will then issue the command 'Hammer down,' which means pull the trigger and dry fire straight and level into the backstop to prove the pistol is unloaded. If something goes bang instead of click, we have a problem. The last command is to 'Holster a safe weapon.' meaning it is time to holster the pistol or in this case, place in its box. Finally, I will say 'The range is safe you may go downrange to score, reset your targets.' One last command, the word 'Freeze!' The command to 'Freeze!' means just that, to instantly stop whatever you are doing in your tracks, point your pistol safely downrange with your finger out of the trigger guard and wait for further instructions." Robert could see that Ricki was a bit overwhelmed.

"Honey," he said, "We will go over each step slowly, but I always start this way to give the trainee the whole picture. Now, let's practice loading and unloading the revolver and then we will try a few shots. In less than a half an hour he had her hitting the eight inch target from ten feet using the revolver in a two handed stance. After clearing and safely storing the gun, they took a break for coffee and donuts, Robert eating a peanut covered donut, Ricki eating two cinnamon sugar donuts. When Robert asked if she had enough, Ricki smiled and thought about it long enough that Robert knew she was weighing her answer.

"I'd like to try the other gun; I really would, but only if we can go home and make love right after, because shooting made me horny."

"Maybe we should strike while the gun is hot, if you know what I mean, because I have class at noon. And there is always next Sunday." Robert laughed like he was joking but they both knew he wasn't and they immediately packed up and left, with Robert telling Dave to tell Joe, he might be late.

CHAPTER 8

JOZEF

By the time snow was falling, Robert was sleeping at Ricki's three nights a week, and Joe and Lucy were practically living together. At work, the two men worked as usual, but both smiled and laughed more and each man talked about getting married in the future. For Robert, having a woman like Ricki care about him, made him more human. He could open up and talk about what was bothering him, he could talk about his parents and his brothers. He expressed emotions and feelings that only Joe knew he felt. As Robert and Ricki's relationship grew, Robert felt himself less connected to the Club and to Joe. In part, the same was happening to Joe. Joe arrived late on some days and he left the moment the Club closed. In December, Jozef started leaving at five thirty, an hour early, explaining the Lucy like to eat dinner at six o'clock.

Two weeks before Christmas, Joe told Robert he was taking a week vacation starting the Monday before Christmas and returning the Tuesday after Christmas. When Robert asked what was going on, Jozef said he and Lucy were going to Florida over the holiday. When Robert asked Joe if he was planning to see Evert Yale or Tom Wilson, Joe said he was not sure, and Robert could tell he did not want to talk about it.

Normally Robert and Joe went to church on Christmas Eve to listen to the carols and on Christmas day, the two would see a movie. This year, when Joe announced that he was taking his first vacation in ten years, Robert was disappointed until he thought about Ricki and him spending Christmas Eve and day together. When he told Ricki about Joe and asked what she wanted to do on Christmas Eve, she explained that she was going to stay with her mother in Ohio for the holiday. At first, Robert said nothing, but eventually he asked if she would like him to go with her to or to visit after Christmas. Kissing him, she explained that her mom was not ready for Robert and she wanted a little time alone.

On Christmas Eve, Ricki called Robert saying she missed him and wanted him. Robert replied that he missed and wanted her too, but the depth of his loneness and need for her was more than he could talk about on the phone. In the end, he begged her to come back early, but she said he would have to wait until Monday.

Finding himself without his oldest friend and without Ricki, he spent Christmas Eve at the movies watching The Godfather Part II and on Christmas day, he made a fire and read a new Ed McBain novel. On the following Sunday morning, Robert found a voice message on the Club's new answering machine. It was Joe calling to say he would be in the club on Tuesday, on Robert's day off. After hemming and hawing, Joe added, "Robert, we need to talk, see you on Wednesday."

On Monday night at 9:00, Ricki called saying she had just gotten back, and she was lonely. Robert raced over to Ricki's house, where he was treated to Ricki modeling the new clothes she received for Christmas, with considerable time spent out of those clothes. On Tuesday, Ricki and Robert left early for a winter's day in the country, driving to Yates Cider Mill to buy frozen donuts and frozen cider from their outlet store. That afternoon they went to see Roger Moore in the Man with the Golden Gun and then Robert went home to check on his mail. Later that evening they watched television and Robert spent the night at Ricki's house. On Wednesday morning, Robert drove home to change clothes before going to work.

At 8:45 a.m., Robert was sitting in the kitchen watching the today show on a portable black and white television when he got a call from an Officer Mark Jerome from the Roseville Police. Officer Jerome was a club member who had stopped at the club to get a gun from his locker. He found the Club closed, and several other members sitting in their cars in the parking lot at 8:00 in the morning. Worried, Jerome had his dispatcher call Jozef at his home number but he did not answer. Jerome had tried Robert earlier, but there had been no answer. Robert did not bother to explain that he had spent the night with Ricki. Rather he simply said he would be right there and left for the club.

When Robert arrived, Officer Jerome and two other club members were still waiting. At Jerome's insistence, Robert waited while the policeman went in first, looking for any signs of foul play. Finding nothing, Robert turned on the lights and moved behind the counter. Once the members were seen to, Robert called Jozef at home.

When he didn't answer, Robert spoke to Jerome, asking him if he could swing by and check on the older man. While Jerome was writing down Joe's address, Dave Langston arrived to take over the ranges. Dave was seventeen and had been cleaning the club and running errands all summer. Trusting Dave to run the store for the twenty minutes it would take to go to Joe's house, Robert suggested that he and Jerome drive over and check on Jozef together.

The small red brick house was the only house without a plastic Santa or Snowman on the front porch or lawn. The house had a front bay window with a hedge below the window. Joe's window was the only one with the curtains still drawn. Pulling up in the drive, they saw Joe's Chevy Truck in the single car garage.

"Looks like he is home," said Jerome. "If you don't mind, waiting in the car, and I will see what's going on. I am sure it's nothing, but just in case."

"Here is a key to the back door," said Robert handing Mark a ring of keys. Robert wanted to go with Office Jerome, but he was all business. Jumping out of the car, he quick stepped up the porch and knocked loudly on the door. When no one answered, Jerome walked around the back looking in the windows as he went. By this time, Robert was out of the car, standing by the open passenger door. When Robert heard Jerome using the key to enter the back door, he went up to the front to wait for Jerome to let him in.

It took two or three minutes before Jerome came to the front door. Opening the door, the policeman frowned and said, "You better prepare yourself, he is dead." When Robert tried to push his way in, the larger policeman held him, saying. "It looks like he killed himself; there is a note. I will have to call the Grosse Pointe Woods police. This is a crime scene and they will want to investigate. If I let you in, there will be a stink about my violating police procedure.

"Where is he?"

"Sitting is a chair in the living room.

"I have to see him; I want to see the note."

"Why?"

"Joe might be the only gun smith in Detroit who doesn't keep a gun at home. If he was planning to shoot himself, he had to bring a gun from the club. I am not saying he wouldn't bring a gun home; it is just that I would have expected him to talk to me. Maybe even ask me to stand by him, if you know what I mean. Besides, he was planning to get married."

"Robert, I didn't say anything about a gun. How did you know he used a gun?" Jerome watched Robert carefully as he answered.

"I can smell the cordite."

"Robert, my guess is the autopsy will show that Jozef was sick r had something wrong with him. Perhaps he was in pain and this was his way of ending the pain."

"But why wouldn't he tell me. I would have taken care of him."

"Perhaps that is your answer. Look, I am going to call the Grosse Pointe Woods police. You can take my car and go back to the store if you want. I will be here for several hours.

"I really want to see Joe."

"I don't think you should. I know you were in combat and all, but believe me he is a mess. You don't want to remember him that way. Go back to the store." Jerome pushed Robert outside and then went back in to phone the police. Stepping back out on the porch, Robert sat and waited.

"What did he use, a shotgun?" Robert asked Jerome after the Grosse Pointe Police had arrived and taken over. The two men sat in Jerome's truck.

"No, a pistol. I can't be sure, the body is slumped forward and the gun is under the body."

"Joe talked about having a forty-five from war."

"Actually, it looks more like a smaller caliber. I think, the detective mentioned a Walther.

"A Walther. Shit."

"What is it?" asked Jerome sharply.

"There are three Walthers at the shop, one is George Lewis's P38, Neil Asher has a Walther .22 rimfire, and I have a thirty-two that was given to me as a gift.

"Is that the gun that girl killed herself with?"

"What do you mean by that?"

"I am sorry; I was just repeating some club gossip."

"About my Walther?"

"Look, I am sorry. This isn't the time or place."

"No, please, tell me."

"Well, I heard a story, about you owning a gun that a girlfriend of yours had used to end her life."

"Who told you that story?"

"Actually, it was Tom Wilson. He told me you had a Walther your girl friend used to kill herself."

Robert sat down in the truck with his head in his hands. He could feel the tears although he was unsure who or what he was crying about. In that moment, he wished he were a turtle, able to draw back in his shell.

"If it is my Walther, will I get it back?"

"Probably, if you claim it, but I wouldn't wait long. We sell our guns to a dealer in North Carolina."

"Why not sell them to a dealer here?"

"I guess we get a better price down there, besides, if they are sold in North Carolina or Wyoming, there is less chance they will be used in a hold up in Detroit, if you take my meaning.

"So how many guns do you confiscate a year?"

"Twenty, many be more."

"How often do you sell them?"

"I think it is in the spring, but you'd have to ask the property Sergeant, he handles the whole deal.

"Could be a good way for the club to add to its inventory, are they all Saturday night specials, I mean do you ever see any decent guns."

"Sure we do, but if you want to really buy guns from the police, you should talk to someone in the Detroit PD, I mean they must take in five guns a week. Lately, these drug dealers have been packing brand new military issue. I heard of a bust where they took in four M16s."

Maybe when this is all past us, I will look into it. With Jozef gone, I am going to need a new gun repairman. Maybe I should find someone with experience as a dealer. Buying and sell guns, is something Evert never wanted to do, but there is a lot of money to be made, if you ask me."

Robert raced out of the truck when they brought the body out, but the coroner put up his hand and said under no circumstances was the body going to be viewed by friends. Officer Jerome had identified the man, which was all the law required. When Robert asked about the gun, the coroner pointed to one of the detectives saying, "Ask Carl."

Carl Blum stood talking to a uniform officer. Blum had on a camel overcoat, a herringbone tweed jacket, dress shirt with a red tie and blue wool trousers. Robert thought he looked in his later thirties, but still in good shape. He had on a hat, which was unusual until Robert saw he was bald.

"Detective Blum, excuse me. My name is Robert Cederberg; I understand that the gun used may have come from the store I manage. That is, Jozef may have borrowed a gun. In fact, it may be my gun that was used to kill him."

"What do you mean kill him?" asked the bald detective. "Do you know something more about this that I should be aware of? Because as near as we can tell, no one killed your friend, he fucking put a gun against his head and killed himself." At first, the detective sounded angry, as if he was angry with Robert or Jozef, but finally, he sounded as if he was sad and slightly disapproving. Robert stood his ground but had nothing more to say, as they watched the coroner and an officer load the body into the police wagon. After the wagon drove off, the detective handed Robert his notebook and let Robert read the message he had copied from the suicide note. Jozef had written. "Robert, I am sorry"

"Is that it? Nothing more, no reason, no forgive me. Just I am sorry."

"That's it. They usually are short. Little more than sorry. A lot of them are typed. This one is hand-written on a torn piece of notebook paper. Not even the whole page."

"So, what about the gun?"

"In a week or so," said the detective, "if you want the gun back, you can file a claim."

"Thanks," said Robert. "I know it is hard to understand, but I do want the gun."

"Okay, now let's get out of here," said Jerome.

When Robert got back to the Gun Club, he typed up a note announcing Jozef Kaminski passing. Based on what the detective told him, he knew the body would be at the Allen Brothers Funeral Home in Grosse Pointe. Looking up the number, he called Allen's and said he would be in the next morning to make arrangements. Afterwards he added a note to the front door saying enquires about the Joe's funeral should directed to the Allen Brothers Funeral Home in Grosse Pointe.

When he finished, he called Ricki.

"Where are you?" asked Ricki.

"The club. Have you talked to Lucy?"

"What is going on, you sound funny?"

"Joe is dead. It looks like he killed himself."

"Oh Robert, I am so sorry. When did it happen?"

"I guess Tuesday night."

"Was Lucy there?"

"No, I don't think so. He was alone."

"Perhaps he sent her home. Did you tell the police about her?"

"I didn't, not sure why. I forgot until just now. I think you should call Lucy."

"Of course, I'll call after we get off the phone."

"And, about tonight,"

"Don't worry about it. If you need me I be here, if you need time alone, call me or come and get me when you need me."

"Thanks."

"And, Robert, for what is worth, I love you, and he loved you too."

"Look, I got to go. Wait, I mean, I hate saying I love you, after someone says it, but I love you too, and if I don't come over tonight, I will call you tomorrow."

Robert called Evert Yale next. He knew Evert would want to come back for the funeral if he could. It was 6:30 p.m., dinnertime, but Evert was not home. Robert pictured the old man, eating shrimp at some bar on the beach. Leaving a sign on the front door, Robert locked up and went home. After making dinner and drinking a large scotch, Robert called Evert, but again got no answer. Robert expected to call Evert before he went to bed, but he fell asleep watching Johnny Carson.

Robert called the Gross Pointe Woods police station fist thing in the morning, but the desk Sergeant said information about the deceased was restricted to the immediate family. Robert explained Jozef had no family and Robert was arranging the funeral, but the officer was very clear, about following the rules. Frustrated, Robert called the funeral home and learned that the body was due to be picked up from the morgue either that afternoon or the next day. The man at the funeral home, Mister Vernon Allen suggested that to be safe they assume it would be tomorrow, Friday. Asking Robert about friends, and viewings, whether there would be church service, Robert realized that he didn't know if Jozef had a will or even what he would want done with his remains. Robert was not religious and had only been in a catholic church on Christmas to hear the carols. Telling Mister Allen he would stop in later to make the arrangements, he next called Bruce Cabot.

Robert had asked Evert for the name of a local attorney when he was thinking about buying the house he rented. Evert and Jozef both used the same man, Bruce Cabot. Bruce practice alone in small office on Mack in Grosse Pointe.

"Bruce, this is Robert Cederberg."

"Robert, I wondered if I would hear from you or Joe."

"I am calling about Joe, he is dead."

"Dead, I talked to him on Monday. What happened?"

Robert explained about the circumstances of Joe's death, Cabot, said, he would talk to the police and determine when there would be a ruling about the cause of death. Before hanging up, he asked Robert if he knew about Joe's will?

"No Joe and I never talked about it."

"Well," said Cabot, "I can tell you that you are in Joe's will and he had an insurance policy taken out ten years ago."

"Is that important?"

"Yes, of course. Because it was taken out so long ago, the policy should be in force even if Joe's death is judged a suicide." The idea that an insurance company would pay in the case of a suicide surprised Robert as much as the fact Jozef had a will and an insurance policy.

"What should I do?"

"Just hang tight and I will call you back after I talk to the police."

Robert spent the hour on the phone. First, he tried Evert Yale but got no answer, then he called Ricki, but no answer again, and finally he called the operator looking for a number for Lucy Meadows. There were two Meadows in Grosse Pointe, but neither turned out to be the right Lucy. Finally, anxious for news, Robert called Bruce Cabot.

"Robert, I am glad you called. I checked with the police. I think they are going to rule Joe's death a suicide, but I am certain that will not affect his insurance policy. I didn't tell you before, but I saw Jozef only a month ago, and we went over his will, and his last requests. I don't know the amount of the policy or what is in his bank account yet, but I assume the policy will cover the funeral.

"Let's not worry about that, I will take care of the cost. Why didn't you tell me about seeing Joe a month ago?"

"Well, to be honest, I wanted to check with the police to make sure you aren't a suspect."

"Thanks a lot."

"Robert, you and I have met once. I really don't know you, but I knew Joe. A month ago, he came in and made out a new will leaving everything to you. Now, a month later you call and say he is dead, an apparent suicide."

"And, you think I killed Joe for the money?"

"Joe was my client, and I have to consider foul play, especially after what happened to Evert."

"What happened to Evert, I have called several time, but I wasn't able to reach him."

"Reach Evert. What do you mean?"

"I called, but he wasn't home."

"Robert, someone killed Evert in his home on Saturday night or early Sunday morning; a robber shot him."

"That can't be."

"I thought you knew. Jozef called me on Monday night when he got back from Florida. I think he wanted to schedule a meeting, but when I told him about Evert, he just hung up. I assumed he told you."

"This doesn't make sense. Why didn't Jozef call me?"

"Well it was late."

"Then why not call me on Tuesday or come to my house?"

"Perhaps he did but you were out. Most likely, we will never know, but it is odd."

"How did you find out about Evert?"

"From his son. Paul called me on Monday. He and Becky were anxious about the Club."

"What are they going to do with the Club?"

"Nothing, because they don't inherit the Club. Evert left the house in Florida to his kids, but he left the Club to Joe and You."

"Joe and me. Are you sure?"

"Unless he filed a new will in Florida, I know he left the Club to Joe and you because I made out the will. I'm just sorry Joe didn't live with us long enough to be partners with you. I know it was something he wanted. I guess technically, he did for a day."

"What do you know about Lucy? I haven't been able to reach her. Will she own the Club too? "

"I think Lucy stayed in Florida. Joe didn't really say. When I talked to him on Monday, I got the impression something was wrong.

He said she wanted him to sign papers and I told him to sign nothing without me. Two weeks ago, Joe added a provision in his will for Lucy. I think he wanted to change it back, but it doesn't matter now because it doesn't apply."

"Why not?"

"Look Robert, I am sorry, but this is something we should talk about in my office. Let's meet on Monday morning after the holiday. By then, I will have had a chance to go over both Evert's and Joe's wills and look into Joe's bank account. Do you have a key to Joe's house?"

"I do."

"I will need to get the key, so I can go through any papers. By Monday I should know how much you inherit."

"What about a service funeral?"

"Jozef was very clear, no service and cremation. All he wanted was reading his name his church, you know the big Catholic Church, the one over there by the hospital, off Morris and I94. Instead of a service, he asked that you and Evert throw a party in his honor for the members of the gun club. I guess that leaves it all up to you."

"Sure, but just one thing more. You said Evert was killed by a robber. Do you have any more details? Did they catch the man? What about Evert's funeral, all of that."

"Robert, I have the name of the police officer who called me from Naples. Do you have something to write it down?"

"Go ahead."

"Detective Sergeant Hill, Naples Police Department."

CHAPTER 9

COMPLICATIONS

It took several calls before Robert found Detective Hill in his office. At first, Hill was hesitant to talk about the case, but when Robert mentioned Bruce Cabot, the detective agreed to answer a few questions.

"We think Mister Yale heard a burglar and went to investigate. We found a gun, a Colt 45 registered to Mister Yale. Yale was shot with a smaller caliber gun. Very professional too," said Sergeant Hill.

"Why professional?"

"All I can say is he was shot at close range, and it looked professional." Robert wondered what the detective was not telling.

"Do you have many robberies like that, that end in a shooting?"

"Honestly, because of all the snowbirds down here, we have a lot of break-ins, but a shooting like this one is unusual for us. At first, we thought Mister Yale had committed suicide, because his gun had been fired. But, the bullet that killed him was not a .45 cal."

"So you think it was a robbery?"

"We are looking at that possibility. According to Evert's son, a number of guns are missing from a display case. For now, we are calling it a robbery. I understand Mister Yale owns a gun store up there and you work for him.

"That's right, but he lives full time in Florida."

"Is it possible he was involved in gunrunning, or selling guns to the drug dealers down here? It would explain a lot."

"Sergeant Hill, Evert Yale was a straight as they come. Except for bourbon, he hated drugs. "

"Well, guns and drugs go together down here."

"Do you have any suspects, any leads?"

"Mr. Cederberg, I really can't talk more about the investigation, but unless someone turns over on the robber or he is caught in another burglary or found with something of Yale's in his possession, the case is pretty much dead." Before getting off the phone, Robert asked about the funeral arrangement, learning that Evert's children were planning to bury Evert Florida.

Robert considered calling Ricki, but instead, he drove to the Club, thinking he would clean the club and hold a wake for Joe and Evert. Carl Blum walked in the lobby calling for "anyone," while Robert was cleaning the restroom.

"Mister Cederberg, I need to talk to you about Mister Kaminski," said Blum as Robert stepped out of the bathroom. Dressed in a gray suit, Blum was a little taller than Robert and ten years older. Like Robert, he had a military haircut. He had blue penetrating eyes and when he asked a question, his eyes were what Robert remembered.

"I got a call from Detective Hill in Florida. He says you called."

"I wanted to find out about Evert."

"He said you asked allot of questions, but he wondered why you did not mention that Mister Kaminski was in Florida this weekend."

"Joe in Florida."

"Right, you told me Mister Kaminski and a Lucy Meadows had been in Florida over Christmas. You said they were in Miami." Suddenly Robert realized he did not know if Lucy knew Joe was dead. It was hot in the lobby and Robert unbuttoned the collar on his shirt.

"Did Mister Kaminski mention driving to Naples?"

"No, before he left, I asked if he was planning to see Evert."

"Was he?"

"It was like he did not want to say. He never answered."

"Where were you on Saturday and Sunday? Mister Cederberg?"

"I was here. I mean I was in Grosse Pointe. I was at home on Saturday and I worked in the Club on Sunday. I worked in the club on Monday during the day. Tuesday was my day off. Joe was in the club on Tuesday."

"Are you sure? Did you see Mister Kaminski?"

"No I assumed he worked or I would have gotten a call."

"What about Monday and Tuesday nights?"

"I was with my girl, Ricki."

"Will she swear to that?"

"Yes, and I saw several club members during the day on Monday, so that rules Joe and me out."

"Out of what Mister Cederberg?"

"Killing Evert Yale."

"I didn't say anything about Mister Yale."

"No, but you are wondering if Joe and I killed Evert."

"Did you?"

"Of course not, but we have to be ruled out, because we were in Michigan on Monday.

"How does that rule you out?"

"Because you can't be in Florida on Sunday and Detroit on Monday."

"Mister Kaminski was. He flew to Detroit on Monday."

"Look Detective Blum, are you saying Jozef Kaminski flew to Miami, rented a car, drove to Naples, killed Evert Yale on Sunday, and then flew home."

"It is physically possible."

"If you think he killed his oldest friend, and then flew to Detroit, came to work on Tuesday, acted like nothing had happened, and a day later killed himself? You do not know Joe Kaminski." Robert would have laughed but he could see Blum thought that it was possible. Blum opened his coat revealing a revolver in a belt hostler.

"Money and love do funny things Mister Cederberg. I understand Mister Kaminski had a lady friend who was pushing him to buy the Bullseye. Perhaps she pushed too hard."

"Look, Joe loved Evert Yale. They were like brothers. Evert was his oldest friend. Maybe he went down there, if you say you have the proof, but he could never shoot Evert Yale. If he was there it was for some other reason."

"Perhaps it was an accident. Your friend goes to Yale because he wants to buy this gun club. They argue, and a gun goes off, Yale is dead, and three days later, your friend is dead in an apparent suicide and you are the new owner of this club."

'What do you mean apparent? My Lawyer said it was confirmed."

"Yes, except the murder in Florida got me thinking, so I had an expert look at several other notes and letters that we found in the house. Notes like how to turn on the furnace, that sort of thing, and when we compared those notes with the suicide note, my expert says two different people wrote those notes. So now we have to find out where you were on Tuesday between four in the afternoon and nine that evening."

"I was with my girlfriend, Ricki. We had a late dinner and watched television. We watched the end of Police Story and then Marcus Wellby. Look, Jozef could not have killed Evert and I could not have Killed Joe. I loved that old guy. I was closer to him than my own dad. We were planning to be partners. None of this makes any sense." Robert opened the office door and gestured for Blum to sit.

"Mister Cederberg, here is how it is," said Blum taking a chair in the office. "I want to believe you. I really do, but you're the one who gains here, and in my experience the primary motive in murder is money. Besides, you said yourself, the gun that killed Joe Kaminski was yours. So now I have motive, I have the gun in your possession, and I have you watching Marcus Welby with a girl who loves you. Given the circumstances, I suggest you speak to an attorney, because I think you look good for this whole thing. It was a plan to get the club. Jozef kills Evert, and then you kill Joe." Robert looked at Carl Blum. He was smiling.

"So what now?" asked Robert.

"Don't leave town. And if I were you I'd really talk to an attorney."

Robert wandered about the Bullseye going from room to room. Too late, he realized that he had not asked about Lucy Meadows. Where was Lucy? Robert wondered if he should call Ricki. For a long time he sat in Joe's workroom wondering if any of what Blum had supposed was possible. On Joe's worktable was a shotgun; Jozef was replacing the firing mechanism. In the file cabinet behind the workbench, Robert surveyed the ammunition, both commercial loads and the boxes of customer loads. Sorting through the inventory, the more he thought about it, the less believable it became. He also realized the police in Naples and in Grosse Pointe would do everything they could to prove Jozef and Robert were guilty and do nothing to find out who really killed Evert and Joe. In his mind, that task would be left to him.

Filled with a new drive, self-survival, Robert searched Joe's workroom, the office, and the gunroom for any clues. In the gunroom, he opened his own locker to verify his Walther was missing. In the gun case, he found the silver box he stored the gun in empty. Only the silver silk bag Susan had kept the gun in was left. Robert noticed that one of the two clips that had come with the gun was missing. Thinking about the clip, he realized that someone, whoever took the gun, would have had to load the gun, perhaps leaving fingerprints on the clip and the remaining bullets in the clip, since he never loaded the gun, he knew his prints would not be on the ammunition.

When he was satisfied there was nothing more to learn, he called Bruce Cabot. Cabot listened to everything that Robert said and then gave Robert the name of a good criminal attorney if things went bad. Cabot said he had been planning to call Robert with the news, about Joe's insurance company.

"Robert, Joe had a $50,000 dollar life insurance policy along with thirty seven thousand dollars in the bank. In addition, there is the house and his truck. He owned both outright. All that is required is having the deeds transferred to you. My guess is at current prices, the house is worth twenty-five thousand dollars."

Thinking about what he would do with the money, Robert asked Cabot what he should do next.

"Right now. Stay here and stay close to ground," said the lawyer, "If I can keep you out of jail, you will inherit a fair amount of change."

"Isn't there something I can do?"

"First, I think you and I need to talk to this Detective Blum and convince him to check those bullets. Same thing in Naples."

"Then what?"

"We need to find out what evidence they have that Jozef was actually in Naples. If the police believe there is sufficient evidence that Jozef killed Evert then the slayer rule will prevent him from inheriting."

"The Slayer rule?"

"The slayer rule says that a person who kills another, the slayer, cannot benefit from or inherit anything from the victim."

"So what happens to the Club?"

"My guess is it goes to Evert's children, but I will have to check with an attorney down there to be sure. I have to warn you, a person does not have to be convicted to be judged a slayer, but that usually only applies in cases where the person is insane. A person may be innocent by reason of insanity, but if he can be shown to be the slayer, then he still doesn't inherit."

"So if I was convicted of slaying Joe, which I didn't by the way. Who gets Joe's inheritance?"

"Lucy Meadows."

"Does Lucy know any of this?"

"I told you, Joe was in to see me a couple of weeks ago. He changed his will at that time. He left everything to you, but he added a contingency plan that left everything to Lucy Meadows if you were deceased. If neither of you survived him, he wanted his estate to be liquidated and money be given as a gift to the NRA. Lucy was with Joe when he changed his will."

"Is she likely to be a police suspect?"

"Right now, my guess is you are their only subject. Which makes finding Lucy Meadows critical."

"So, what should I do?"

"We have to establish iron clad alibis for you during the times Evert and Joe were murdered. Give me Ricki's phone number and I will talk to her."

"What about the evidence that Joe killed Evert."

"They may have evidence they are holding back, because what they told me is all circumstantial. Anyone could buy an airline ticket or rent a car with cash using someone else's name. That is why we have to clear you first. We have to prove you were in Michigan Saturday and Sunday. Once you are in the clear, we can try to clear Joe of Evert's murder."

"I think the starting place is finding Lucy Meadows."

"Then we have to determine is who saw Joe in Florida and who was the last person to see Joe alive."

"Besides his killer?"

"Right."

"I can call the club members who usually use the club on Tuesday to see if I can find someone who saw Joe. What about Florida?"

"We may need to hire an investigator down there to ask some of the questions the police didn't ask. Do you know anybody in south Florida who might help?"

"Actually I do. Tom Wilson lives in Coral Gables. I think that is close. He was a policeman in Grosse Pointe. He moved down there when he retired. I have known him since I was a kid."

"Would he help you?"

"He has before."

"That sounds good. Get in touch with this Tom. Tell him everything. Get his take on all this. Perhaps he has enough contacts down there to nose around a little. I will make a few calls and see what

I can learn about the hard evidence that Jozef was in Florida. If you are still on the street Monday, we should meet here in my office."

Before calling Tom Wilson, Robert called Ricki. "Ricki, hi. I am sorry I did not call back last night, but a lot has happened. How did it go with Lucy?"

"She wasn't home. I called, but she didn't answer her phone. Should we be worried?"

"I just found out that Evert Yale was murdered on Sunday in Florida. The police there say they have evidence that Joe was in Naples. The police in Naples there think Joe killed Evert over the Club.

"That would explain the suicide."

"It wasn't a suicide. The note is a phony. So, now the police here now believe Joe was killed and I am the primary suspect."

"But that is crazy. You loved that old man, besides you were with me most of the time you weren't in the club."

"I told them that, but there are enough gaps in my story that I think they may arrest me."

"So, what are you going to do?"

"I have spoken to my lawyer. Right now, I am going to call an old friend in Florida and see if he can do a little looking round.

"Who is your friend in Florida?"

"An ex-cop named Tom Wilson."

"What about Lucy?

"I will call the police and let them know."

"How about tonight, I mean it is New Years Eve. You have to eat and we should see the New Year in together.

"How about late, say 9:00 or 10:00."

"I'll be waiting. And, remember, I love you."

"I do too."

The phone call to Tom Wilson was awkward at first. Tom and Robert had been good friends until Susan Kay. Afterwards, Tom and Robert talked only when the circumstances forced them to speak, otherwise they passed each other with only a nod. When Robert was in Vietnam, Tom retired from the Grosse Pointe Woods Police and moved to Coral Gables in Florida. Tom loved the water so he obtained a part time position with the city police, purchased a home on a canal along with a twenty-five foot fishing boat. When Robert called, Tom said he was sitting outside contemplating taking his boat out for some fishing.

Before Robert could say more, Tom said, "Robert it is great to hear from you. I have been thinking about you. I hear you have a girl. The two of you should come down; the weather is warm and the fish are biting. So, what is going on up there, first I talk to Old Joe, and now you call."

"Tom, did you say you talked to Joe. When was this?"

"He called a little over a week ago. I think it was Wednesday two weeks ago now."

"What did he want?"

"Well it was all a bit confusing, you know Joe. He said he might be coming down, something about getting married and visiting Florida. He wanted to know if he would like it better in Naples or here in Coral Gables. Said he might stop in and take me to dinner, asked me if I had a woman. The old guy sounded happy, actually. He said he was going to visit Evert."

"Tom, hold on. Let me put this together. First, you should know that Evert was killed in Naples last Saturday night or Sunday morning. The police said it looked like a robbery. But they are talking about the possibility that Joe killed Evert."

"Well, that is crazy. You know that. What does Joe say?"

"The thing is, Joe is dead too."

"What?"

"The police found Joe dead. It looked like Joe killed himself on Tuesday after getting back from Florida. There was a note saying he was sorry. But, no mention of Evert."

"I there anything to link the two deaths?" asked Wilson.

"Wait, Tom. You see, the police now believe that the note was a phony written by someone else who killed Joe, and they are wondering if the same person who killed Joe killed Evert."

"And, that person is you?"

"Yes. You see, the gun that killed Joe was that Walther Susan Kay left me."

"Robert, I am sorry, but I have to ask, did you kill Joe, because if you did, I will see you get help. Perhaps all you went through in the war, or seeing your childhood friend killed, or what happened in Canada."

"Tom, how can you ask that?"

"I am sorry, but I had to ask."

"And, what are you talking about in Canada."

"Robert I never told you this, but I looked into your background and I know a man was killed on a beach near where you lived in Canada. I'm not saying you were involved or that you were even at the scene, but the circumstances are there, and then Susan. I guess you know I was the officer on the scene when we found Susan. I knew you were away in basic training, but still I wondered if you had gone AWOL and killed her. Even after reading her note, you were my first suspect, until the reality hit me that she had killed herself."

"Tom, maybe I should not have called."

"No, no, I just think you should know that the file on you paints a dark picture of a man whose life has been surrounded by guns and death. If the locals need a suspect, you are a good one."

"Jesus Tom."

"I'm sorry but that is how it must seem to the police. So what can I do?"

"I don't know. I wanted to see if you could find out how the police know Joe was in Naples. Was he seem or is it just like you said circumstantial. You know, did someone identify him on the airplane or at the car rental, or did someone just use his name. At least that is what my lawyer suggested."

"You already have a lawyer."

"Please Tom, my lawyer is Joe's lawyer, he used to be Evert's lawyer. I have been talking to him because of Joe and Evert's wills."

"Jesus, Robby, are you holding out on me. What about the wills?" Robert explained completely about wills and he mentioned the fact that as of an hour ago, no one had seen Lucy Meadows. When he was done, Tom was silent for a while.

"Robert, I think a good prosecutor would tell the police to bring you in right now. A lot depends on the exact time of Joe's death and the strength of your girl's alibi, but if Evert's death can be pinned on Joe, then all I have to prove is you wrote the letters, or even if they don't match your handwriting, I just have to show you had the opportunity. Like you said, Joe goes to Evert, they fight and Joe kills Evert, and then he comes home to you. You know that if he is questioned by the police, the whole deal goes south, so you kill him to keep him from talking. With any luck the two cases aren't connected and a month later you own the Bullseye." Tom was quiet for a while, waiting for Robert to speak. When he did not, Tom said, "Robert, let me say this again, if you did it, I will help you get a plea of insanity. If you are innocent as you say, I will try to help you down here if I can, but, there is one other alternative."

"What is that?"

"Run for it. My advice is, shake any police on your tail and run for it, because if they arrest you, I think you are going down."

"Tom, what kind of advice is that from a policeman? I am innocent. If I run, they close the books and I am a wanted man for the rest of my life. Like the fugitive, that's no good. What about the club? What about my life with Ricki?"

"Maybe God doesn't want you to have any of those things Robert. Maybe this is his way of punishing you for all the violence you had been a part of." Robert moved the phone away and starred at it. Tom sounded a little nuts.

"Look kid I'm sorry. When you get old, you think about stuff like this. Let me make some calls down here. I will find out what they know and I'll call you back. Where will you be tonight at seven?"

"I'll be at the club," said Robert without thinking.

"Ok, I'll call you at the club at seven tonight."

Robert sat very still for a while, going over the call with Tom, before he called Ricki. When he told her what Tom had said, his talk about God and running, Ricki was silent, not asking any questions, only listening.

"Are you going to run?" she finally asked.

"Of course not."

"I know, but he may be right. The other thing is Lucy. I have been thinking about this. What if Joe did shoot Evert and Lucy knew it. What if Lucy found Joe and a different note, one that said he killed Evert. What if she wrote the phony note and now she in lying low. She doesn't want to talk to the police. She is hoping they will accept the suicide and that will be the end of it."

"Ricki that is crazy talk. You sound like Perry Mason. What if someone killed Joe, and they killed Lucy too and removed her body so Joe's death would look like a suicide. She may be in the truck of a car or some field. Finding Lucy should be one of our first priorities."

"Look Robby, if you have to run, I will join you when it is safe."

"Just like John Dillinger, except he died in an alley. Besides, if I were going to run, I'd need a driver license and a social security card, maybe a passport. Where would I get those?"

"How about Guy Jackson. He will know how to get all of that for you."

"Look, I'm not going to run. This makes no sense, I'll see you around nine tonight and we can talk then. I am going to talk to Tom Wilson tonight at seven. He is calling at the Club. I'll see you after that."

"Ok, but remember what I said. I love you, and I will do whatever you need."

Robert hung up the phone and went to the front windows looking out into the parking lot. He wondered if a police car was sitting somewhere near. Turning over the phone, he looked for signs of tampering. Telling himself to 'get a grip,' he went to the refrigerator for an orange soda. Tom would be calling in three hours, until then he had a business to run.

CHAPTER 10

UNWANTED VISITORS

Normally the Club was be closed on New Year's Eve, but Robert forgot to put out the sign and at four fifteen, Neil Hanson showed up, wanting to used the pistol range for half an hour. Hanson owned a roofing company in Roseville and was a very good Club member. He did not have a permit to carry a concealed weapon, but after two stickups on the street, Robert suspected he always carried a friend.

At the club, he kept a Smith and Wesson Model 10 police revolver. On the range from fifty feet, he was only a fair target shot. Up close, he might hit a man in the stomach, but Robert was unsure. When Hanson finished, he asked Robert if he thought Joe should look at the gun because all the shots were to the right. Robert doubted that there was anything wrong with the guns' sights, rather it would prove to be the shooter, but he said he'd take and look and then put the gun back in its locker, at the same time explaining about Joe.

When Hanson left, Robert put the revolver in his work coat pocket and started to close the club. Locking the front door, he left the back door open assuming he would go out through the ranges. Back in the club, he mopped the lobby floor and straightened the magazines in the clubroom. When he finished cleaning and putting supplies away, he still had twenty minutes before Tom was to call, so he loaded two speed loaders and taking three targets, he walked down to the last range, the one nearest Joe's repair room. While he had the time, he would test the Model 10.

He could have done a bench test, but he hadn't fired a gun in several days and he hoped the practice would take his mind off Joe and Evert. Attaching a target to the pulley, he moved it down to the fifty-foot mark. Sometime in the future, he thought they would have to get electric pulleys. It was already getting dark and Robert should have put the lights on the range, but he liked shooting at dusk. It was like being on night patrol. Once he had the target sighted, he envisioned the bullseye, steadied his hand, held his breath and fired. Nearly a center shot. Relaxing, he took a second shot, again a bullseye, and then he fired the remaining four shots. All hits. Ejecting the shells into the collection can, he reloaded, and then pulled the target down the range. All in the circle, no right pattern. Good shooting he thought. Setting the gun down, he attached a new target and started to pull it down the range, when he heard the back door open. There was a little bell above the door, which sounded when the door was opened. Robert heard the sound of the bell muffled as if someone grabbed the bell. *A robber*, Robert thought. *He thinks the club is closed and I am gone.*

Looking at his watch Robert saw that it was 6:55. He hated to miss Tom's call, but the situation would have to play itself out. Robert picked up the model 10 and the second speed loader. He hoped he could either scare the robber away or call the police and wait. The last thing he wanted was to be involved in a shooting. Given all that was going on, he doubted shooting a robber, even if justified would help his cause, so Robert crouched down and frog walked to Joes' workroom.

In the dark, he picked up the phone and dialed zero. When an operator came on, he explained he needed the Roseville Police. When a Sergeant Vernon answered, he whispered his address, that it was a gun shop, and that he had intruders, hanging up he heard "get out."

Robert heard one of the men whisper "Where is he? He said he'd be here." Then a figure appeared in the doorway to the ranges.

"Keep your voice down," said a second voice.

Robert could have shot the man standing in the doorway, but he was unsure about the other man. The man at the door peeked inside and then silently stepped into the dark gunroom. Behind him, the second man became visible as he too stepped into room. He was much smaller and slight in build. In his hand, he carried what looked like a target pistol, a .22 cal.

Robert thought he saw one man go into the lobby, but he was not sure if both men were in the lobby. If both men went into the lobby, Robert planned will go out the back gate and wait for the police. Robert's army training told him to stay where he was, stay under cover and let them come to him. Robert looked at his watch, 7:07. *The police could be here already* he thought. Knowing they would arrive with their sirens and lights off.

Robert shifted his position to look at the door behind him leading to the hallway and the bathroom. The door might or might not be locked. If it is open, the shooters could come at him from two directions. The alternative was Robert could use the door to come in behind the shooters; he could bring the battle to them. Deciding that he would wait, he moved back in the far corner of the repair room, opened one of the supply cabinet doors and crawled behind it. From the crack between the cabinet doors, he could see both entries, and he had some protection from the steel in the door.

When the hallway door opened, the light from the lobby showed a figure with a gun in his hand in the doorframe. Sighting on the figure Robert calmed his breathing. He could take a shot through the crack in the door, but he wanted to know about the other man before he did.

"We got trouble," he heard the bigger man call out. "I think there are cops outside." From behind his door, Robert expected the other smaller man to answer but he did not, rather he crouched and moved to the workbench where he could see out the shop door.

"Freeze, police," screamed a man. "Put you gun down now." The policeman stood in the lobby door to gunroom pointing his gun at the smaller man in the doorway to the ranges. Robert doubted the policeman saw the second shooter, the big man, come through the hallway door, but Robert did, shouting "get down," to the policeman, as all four seemed to fire simultaneously.

Crawling out from behind the cabinet door with his revolver leading the way, Robert saw the police officer was on the ground in the lobby doorway. The smaller man, the one in the range was invisible from Robert's view, but the other bigger man, Robert heard running down the hall. Robert crawled to the policeman.

"Officer, are you alright, I'm Robert Cederberg." He touched the man; he was breathing, but did not seem conscious; there was blood on his back, which decided Robert's actions. Crouching, Robert ran to the hallway door. Peeking around the corner, he saw a black man wearing a stocking mask standing at the end of the hall. He had an automatic in his hand. Standing where he was, in the doorway, half way out into the hall, Robert was a potential target for both gunmen. Committing himself, he ran to the bathroom, if he had to, he could use the door as cover. The man at end of the hall was less than ten feet away watching the lobby and front door intently. When the front door opened, he knelt and pointed his pistol at the door. Knowing this would end with another policeman shot, Robert ran to the man, intent on taking the gun out of his hand. Hearing Robert, the man turned with the gun pointed low. Without thinking, Robert shot the man in the chest, at the same moment a policeman burst through the front door. Seeing Robert with a gun in his hand, standing over another man, the policeman screamed "freeze, drop the weapon," and dove into the lobby, as a second policeman wearing a helmet came in and pointed a Winchester pump at Robert.

Dropping the gun, Robert put his hands up, and speaking in a quiet voice, he said, "I'm Robert Cederberg, the manager, I called. There is a policeman shot in the room at the end of the hall. He was alive when I left him. I think there is a second gunman still in the building."

"On the ground, Robert. Face down and don't move!" growled the office in the helmet. Turning to the second officer he shouted, "Call for an ambulance and backup."

"Robert," said the helmeted cop, "were do these doors go?"

"One goes to a club room and one goes to the gun room. Both go out to the ranges in the back."

"What about down there, as the officer pointing to the hallway.

"Bathroom and then a second door to the gun shop. It also leads to the ranges. That is where the policeman is, but the room is visible from the range. I wouldn't go in until you know the location of the other gunman." The second policeman, the one without a helmet knelt beside Robert. The man in the helmet said, "Jensen, stay with our manager here." I'm going to check on Anderson. What about him, said the officer pointing to the fallen black man.

"He is as dead as a man can be."

"Robert, why did you kill him?" asked Jensen.

"Because he was going to shoot you."

Well, I owe you my thanks, but you were told to leave the building, not to kill the suspects."

"I didn't think I had a choice.

"We always have a choice. Let's just hope we catch the other man." They searched the entire building twice but found no one. Once Anderson was on his way to St. John's hospital, a detective, the coroner, and a lieutenant arrived on the scene. Ten minutes later, Detective Blum from the Grosse Pointe Woods police arrived. Robert sat in the members room with Officer Jensen while the others walked through the building together and then talked in the lobby until the body of the black man was removed. When the group finally came in to interview Robert, it was 8:16 p.m.

"Robert, I am Lieutenant Cooper with the Roseville Police. I would like you to come down to police headquarters to make a statement.

"Can I come in tomorrow?"

"Normally, I'd say sure, but I understand from Detective Blum that you are somehow involved in a questionable death in Grosse Pointe, and now you have killed this man whom you claim was robbing the Bullseye. Given all that is going on here, I would like to ask you some questions and I think we should do that at headquarters."

"Lieutenant, I am sorry to contradict you, but I never claimed the dead man was a robber or a burglar. When I called the police, I may have said there were men breaking in or something like that, which was true, but I heard them talking. They were here to kill me, plain and simple, no robbery. They were hired killers."

"Why would someone want to kill you Mr. Cederberg?"

"I don't know, but I imagine it has to do with the Club."

"This club, you mean the Bullseye? Excuse me Mr. Cederberg, but why would anyone murder another person over a cinder box gun club on Eleven Mile Road?"

"I understand what you are saying Lieutenant, but, the Club owner, Evert Yale was murdered in Naples on Saturday and Joe Kaminski is found dead in Grosse Pointe on Wednesday and now two shooters attack me at the Club. I think whatever is going on has something to do with the Club."

"Or, something to do with you three," offered Detective Blum. "Maybe the three of you are involved in illegal gun sales or drugs and this black man was here collect, but instead, you placed a phony call and then kill him and then shot Officer Anderson."

"Are you nuts?" shouted Robert.

"Robert, calm down," said Lieutenant Cooper. If I thought there was a chance you shot Officer Anderson, you would be in cuffs already. However, here is my problem. You claim that the black man who you shot in the lobby with this gun is a hired killer. I see there is a gun at his feet and single shot to the back of his head. The only problem is the gun at his feet hasn't been fired and your gun has been fired at least twice. See, the problem Robert, none of us saw the gun in that black boys hand. For all we know, you put it there after shooting Anderson."

"Why would I call the police and then shoot a cop?"

"That is a good question, but think of all the possible answers a prosecutor could provide. You called the police to create an alibi. You planned to kill the black man before the police arrived. He is an illegal gun dealer and you are involved in a deal gone bad. Maybe he was robbing you but he gave up and you killed him anyway. Either way, the officer surprised you and you shot him in the back so he could not talk. You see how easy it is Robert. The DA only needs one plausible answer to convict you."

"Lieutenant, I didn't shoot the policeman, I tried to save him, and I killed that black man to save Officer Jensen. I called the police when I heard men breaking in. I hid in the repair room. I heard them talking about killing me. If you don't believe me then take me to the station, otherwise, I have a girl waiting for me, and this has been a terrible experience, and I would like to either go home or be arrested and charged." Robert sat back and closed his eyes. He could still see the black man turning with the gun pointed low. Robert saw the shot in his mind, he could have tried to disarm the man, but he took the killing shot, because that is what he was trained to do, that is what his experience said to do. That was what he wanted to do. The police officers conferred in the corner of the room for several minutes until only Lieutenant Cooper and Detective Blum were left.

"Mr. Cederberg, Detective Blum thinks we should take you in, but Sergeant Sheets and Officer Jensen, who were here on the scene, think you are telling the truth. In addition, I am sure Officer Anderson was shot with a smaller caliber gun. Therefore, I am going to send you home. If Detective Blum chooses to arrest you in this other matter, that is his and the Grosse Pointe DP's call. We are going to see to it you lock up here and then we are going to follow you home. After that you can do anything you like provided you don't leave the Detroit area, do you understand?"

"Of course."

"Okay, Robert, but there are a couple of other rules. First, until we have a final ruling on what happened here, the club is closed. Michigan law looks down on a possible felon running a gun store." Cooper looked at Robert for a long moment. "Do you have carry permit?"

"Of course I do."

"Yes, well tomorrow you might not, but if you take my advice, if someone sent two men to kill you and they failed, the odds are two more are waiting for you at your home. If you ask for it, I can assign a car to watch your house, but I suggest whatever you do, you carry a little extra weight. Tomorrow morning at 10:00 a.m., I expect to see you, unarmed, and in my office to make your statement. In the morning, we are going to go over everything that has happened and sort this out."

* * *

Robert had not thought beyond what had happened at the club. He had yet to consider who would send two men to kill him and why. He needed to talk to Bruce Cabot and Tom Wilson. In addition, he needed to find Lucy Meadows. Most of all, he needed Ricki.

Before locking the back gate, he checked the phone to make sure it was working. He should have heard from Tom. Whatever he was going to do, he needed a safe place with time to think. What he wanted most was the warmth of Ricki's embrace, but he questioned risking her becoming involved.

When he was ready to leave he looked for the 'closed' sign they hung on the door. Not finding it by the door where it was usually kept, he hand wrote a sign saying the Club would be closed until Monday and taped it to the front door.

Two officers in a Roseville police cruiser followed Robert home and before, he could go in his house, one of the officers entered the house, searching it from attic to basement. When the officer offered to stay, Robert told him, that he would be fine. What he did not mention was he planned to pack a bag, climb over the back fence, and leg it on foot to Ricki's house a mile away.

Turning the lights on in his living room and bedroom, he pulled down the shades in all the rooms and then went upstairs to pack a duffle bag. His bedroom, like his house showed little sign of being lived in. The bed had clean sheets and an attractive bedspread. On either side of the queen bed were matching tables that came with the bed as a set. On right hand table was a reading lamp, and a paperback novel by Ed McBain on the left, a large clock radio, with the new digital numbers.

From the bedroom closet, Robert pulled out his army rucksack and a metal case. Placing the case on the bed, he found a small key on his ring of keys, and opened the case. Inside was a Colt .45 with two clips, and a box of bullets. Sitting on the bed, he quickly loaded the clips, cleared the gun and then loaded a clip in the gun and jacked a round in the chamber. Leaving the gun on the bed with safety on, he closed the case and put it back in the closet. From the closet, he pulled out black jeans, a black turtleneck, a brown belt, and a pair of steel-toed work boots. Even though it was still warm out, he grabbed his army fatigue jacket. Undressing, he put his dirty clothes in a white wicker hamper that Ricki had purchased for his bathroom. Looking at the hamper, he wondered if his life with Ricki, his life as a domesticated man and future husband had just ended.

Into the rucksack, he packed two pairs of underwear, a pair of khaki slacks, a blue long-sleeved cotton shirt, a sweater, blue socks and shoes, clothes for his visit to the police station. When he was finished, he pulled the blind back on his bedroom window and looked down the street in either direction. Streetlamps cast pools of light on snow-covered cars parked on both sides of the street. The bungalows on Robert's street all had one-car garages, but the houses had families with four and five kids, practically every family on the block had a second or third car parked on the street. Looking down the street, Robert checked for any signs of the police, perhaps a large Ford sedan or Chrysler with its motor running and two men inside. At the end of the street, he saw three cars that fit the description, but he could not see if any had men sitting in the dark. All he could see were shadows. As for hired killers, Robert had no idea. Leaving the light on in the bedroom, he went down stairs, all the way to the basement.

In the basement, he went to a workbench with a pegboard behind for tools. Next to the workbench was a tall gun cabinet where Robert kept his Winchester pump, and his fishing gear. From the tackle box, he withdrew a boning knife in a sheave. The knife's holder had a place to put the sheave on your belt. Robert debated undoing his belt and putting the knife on, but he opted to put the knife in the rucksack. Robert looked at the Winchester and hoped he would not have to use it. There was no way he could carry a shotgun through backyards in Grosse Pointe, so he left in the case, it would be there if he needed it.

At the backside of the basement, there was a set of steps leading up to a locked double door. In the old days, they delivered coal and then coal oil down these steps. Robert had a Yale lock on the inside of the doors. Switching off the basement lights, he let his eyes adjust and then unlocking the door pushed it open and stepped into the cold night air. Closing the door, he locked it from the outside and hid the key in the Hibachi barbeque sitting by the back door. If he had to get back in the house, he had a way.

Climbing over his back fence, Robert ran and walked through yards and across streets, until he reached Parkcrest the street where Ricki lived. If her house was being watched, the easiest way to find out was to walk down the block. Deciding that he was not ready for a showdown, he walked quietly down her plowed back alley and knocked on her back door. When she finally opened the door, she was in a flannel nightgown. Before she could say anything, he put his hand on her mouth and whispered "inside."

It took him nearly an hour to explain what had happened. When Robert said he needed to call Tom Wilson Ricki agreed even though it was after ten. Sitting in Ricki's kitchen, Robert drank coffee. He wanted a real drink but he had stopped drinking around Ricki. Instead, he considered aloud who would send gunmen to the club.

"The obvious answer is Guy Jackson," said Robert answering his own question.

"Why Jackson?" asked Ricki.

"The man I killed was black, and Guy was furious over the deal with the club.

"So mad that he'd send men to kill you. That doesn't make sense.

"Maybe not, but with us gone, he could buy the clubs assets from Evert's kids for nothing."

"Sure, but what does he really have except a location. I mean, he has plenty of money, he could build a club next door if he wanted."

"Then why was he so mad?"

"Perhaps it is about race. I'm sorry to say this, but Joe hated Black people," said Ricki.

"I know Joe disliked Negroes, but so do a lot of Detroiters. Guy Jackson has to be use to racism growing up in Detroit. He isn't going to hire men to kill Evert in Florida and then Joe, and me over a racist remark. If Guy is behind this, there is another reason and it involves money. If the man I shot has any ties to Guy, I expect the police will find them."

"If they look."

"You think they are going to arrest me?"

"I'm afraid so."

"Then I need to call Bruce."

"I think you should call Tom Wilson before he goes to bed. Your lawyer gets paid for late calls."

When Tom Wilson came on the phone, the first thing he said was, "Jesus kid, you ask me to do you a favor and then you never call."

"Tom, what are you talking about, you said you would call me at the club."

"Well, maybe that's right, sorry. I have been waiting all night. Now it's almost midnight, let me tell you what I found so I can go back to celebrating the New Year."

"Wait, Tom, let me tell you what's happened here first." Robert then explained about the men at the club and the officer, answering a series of questions, including where are you now, to which Robert answered home.

"Well, that puts an interesting spin on what I found out. First, the evidence that Joe was here is circumstantial, but I'm pretty sure he was in Naples."

"What else did you learn Tom?" asked Robert.

"I learned that Joe or someone using his name stayed in the Naples Beach and Golf Club with a lady. That is a pretty fancy place for old Joe, Robert. Very expensive."

"So what does your cop mind tell you? What's going on?"

"I am not really sure kid. What do you think?"

"I think Guy Jackson is involved. I think Joe went to Florida to convince Evert to sell the club. It is possible, Guy paid for the trip including the hotel for Joe and his Lucy. Joe meets with Evert, but it is no deal. Joe tells Guy it is no deal and flies back to Michigan, his part of the bargain finished. Guy stages a break-in and has Evert killed. Joe flies home and they are waiting for him."

"Why come after you?" asked Wilson

"I am not sure, except it has to do with the club."

"What about Lucy?" asked Ricki from behind Robert.

"What about Lucy?" asked Robert covering the phone. "Did you find anything?"

"Only a lot of maybes. Maybe she stayed in Naples. Maybe she went back to Detroit. Maybe she has nothing to do with any of this.

"Maybe she is dead," added Robert.

"Kid, I don't really see how she fits in. I would forget about her for the time being, and focus on you and Joe."

"How do I prove Joe didn't kill Evert?"

"I don't think you can. Only this Lucy can clear Joe. But,"

"But, what?"

"From what you tell me, the gun that killed Joe was your gun."

"And?"

"And, now you are the man in the crosshairs. The man with the Bullseye on his chest."

"So what now?"

"Tomorrow, I am going to talk to the Detective investigating the case down here. I am going to suggest he look for Lucy Meadows."

"What should I do?"

"You should go to the police headquarters tomorrow and tell them everything, and hope they believe you, because I am not sure I do."

"Tom, how can you say that?"

"Robert, there is something about you. You always have a secret, and a cop can smell a secret a mile away. Take my advice, if you go tomorrow, remember it is in the first few minutes of questioning that most criminal are caught in a lie. So, don't say anything and don't lie."

"What is the second thing?"

"I hate to say this, but either take a toothbrush or run now while you have the chance."

"Thanks, I talk with you tomorrow."

"Okay, good night kid and give Ricki a hug for me."

"Thanks Tom."

Robert hung up and went to the refrigerator for a Vernors. He had too much coffee. Sitting at the kitchen table, Robert pushed his hands through his crew cut.

"Well?" asked Ricki sitting down beside him.

"Tom said to pack a toothbrush." Robert thought about everything Tom had said, including his last comment about Ricki. Robert was seldom afraid, but looking at Ricki in her nightgown, he worried what he might be bringing to her door.

"What is worrying you?"

"I really did not want anyone to know, I was here, but now Tom may know."

"Robert, if you aren't home where would you be?"

"Here I guess, and that is what has me worried. Maybe we should go to a motel; there is that one on Harper at the end of your street?"

"Don't be silly. I have to get to bed."

"You know, this may be crazy, but let's get some blankets and sleep in the basement. Just to be safe."

At Robert's insistence, they carried blankets downstairs and pulled out the sofa bed. Robert placed a loaded .38 special on the floor by Ricki. He would leave the Colt 1911 on the floor by his side. Turning out the basement lights, he said, "Ricki, I am sorry about all of this, and for what it is worth, I love you." Then he went up stairs and proceeded to turn out the ground floor lights and then, leaving the time it would take to get ready for bed, he turned out the bedroom lights out before feeling his way downstairs to the basement.

Kissing Ricki good night turned into passion and they quickly made love with Ricki falling asleep almost at once afterwards. Lying besides Ricki, Robert could still feel the effects of the coffee and needed to use the bathroom, so he picked up the Colt and walked softly up stairs feeling his way in the dark unfamiliar house. The bathroom was in the hallway between the front of the house and kitchen and backdoor. Robert was deciding whether to flush or to wait until morning when he heard glass breaking.

Picking up the Colt, he opened the door slightly and listened. Fortunately, the door opened towards the kitchen, so Robert had a view of the back hall and the archway into the kitchen. From the bathroom, he saw the back door and the stairs leading to the basement. If this was an intruder, Robert assumed it would be two or more men. If they came in the backdoor, they had three options. They could go down into the basement, they could go through the kitchen to the front dining room, and then go up stairs or they could come through the archway to the hall and then go into the front living room and on up stairs. For Robert, his only real worry was one or more would go down into the basement. If their objective was going upstairs undetected, they would come through the archway where Robert was waiting with the Colt. Whatever happened, Robert was determined no one would reach the basement alive.

Three men entered the kitchen. One man was over six-foot tall dressed all in black. In his right hand, he had a semi-automatic. The second man also was small, five foot five. He had on black tennis shoes, blue jeans, and a Detroit Tigers Jacket. He was carrying a shotgun. Both men were black. The third man was a white man, five foot ten, rail thin and wearing black pants and a dark blue jacket.

"You stay here," said the tall black man to the white man. Using hand signals, the big man pointed to the archway for the little man in the Tigers jacket as he pushed into the kitchen and moved to the dining room door. The door into the dining was a swinging door and Robert heard it creek open at the same time the smaller man came through the archway leading with a sawed off shotgun. Giving the man no warning, Robert shot the man in the chest, and ran into the kitchen stepping over the small man now on the hall floor. Robert saw the white man, bolt out the back door, but he did not think the big man had gone out too, so he stood in the archway waiting.

Back in the hall, the small man started moaning and calling out "Sugar, sugar I'm shot." Robert was surprised the man was alive, but he had no time to worry about him, and he wasn't going to shoot him in the back, so he waited. From the alley, he heard a car engine revving, and then the car peel away. Then the swinging door started to swing into the kitchen. Robert adopted a two handed stance and waited. Then the door stopped moving and Robert heard someone unlock the front door and the screen slam. Most people would have followed the man out or found a phone and called the police, but Robert held his breath and waited until he heard the floorboards creak in the dining room. The man was hiding, waiting for Robert. In a test of wills, Robert was convinced he would win, but at that moment, Ricki called up from the basement, "Robert, are you alright."

"Ricki, stay where you are," Robert shouted, placing three shots into the kitchen wall as he moved into the hallway. He knew he had to answer Ricki or she would come up, and he knew the man in the dining room would kill Ricki. The three shots were probably a waste, but the wall was thin and they might have hit the man, however Robert intended them as a distractions, as if he was coming through the kitchen door, and rather than rounding low into the living room.

Letting the Colt lead his way, Robert saw the big man step into front entryway. Robert fired a pattern of three bullets into the man's center not registering the man was already holding his stomach when the man dropped to the living room floor. Using caution, Robert stepped over the small man in the hall and stepped up to the larger black man.

In the darkness, the man appeared dead, but Robert wasn't certain. He considered putting another round in the man's head, but he knew how that would look. "Ricki," he yelled. "Call the police." With the gun on the man's temple, Robert felt for a pulse, nothing. Walking back to the small man, he felt the man's neck. He was still breathing. Picking up the gun, he yelled. "Ricki, tell them to send an ambulance."

Going to the front window, Robert checked for any sign of other shooters. Satisfied that the front was quiet, he checked the back. Stepping outside to listen for the sound of a car or running feet in the alley. Hearing nothing, he assumed the third man had fled. Back inside, he went down stairs to get Ricki.

* * *

Robert came back upstairs, leaving Ricki in the basement, when the police arrived. Before going to the front door, Robert placed his Colt 1911 on the kitchen table along with the shotgun from the hallway. The revolver was still down stairs. Before going up down stairs, Robert suggested Ricki not mention the gun and instead hide the gun in the basement, less the police take it and leave them unarmed.

When Robert went to answer the hard knock at the front door, he heard the officers enter the back without knocking. When Robert answered the door, he did so with his hands raised. Seeing Robert, two uniformed officers barged through the front door, followed by Detective Blum. On the porch steps a pair of fireman waited.

"Stay where you are with your hands up," shouted one of the officers. The man who shouted knelt to examine the large man in the living room. Around the man, a circle of blood was soaking into the oak floor. Seeing the man in the hall, the second uniform ran to the man, checked him, and then, asked Robert. "Are there any others, anyone else hurt?" "No, Miss Williams is in the Kitchen. She is okay.

"Detective Blum, this man is still alive. That one needs the coroner."

After calling in the paramedics, Detective Blum asked Robert to join Miss Williams in the kitchen, saying, "We can talk there while these men do their work." Blum pointed to the kitchen, as the fireman raced in and moved the man in the hall to a stretcher. The man groaned and called out "Sugar, sugar where are you."

"Sugar," said Blum to no one in particular. Blum was wearing a hat like one Frank Sinatra wore on one of his album covers.

"He called out to Sugar. I think that might be the big fellow's name. By the way, there was a driver, but he left from the alley." Robert then explained what happened without being asked.

"Two attempts on your life in one night," said Blum fanning himself with the hat. "They must really need you dead. Did you recognize either man?"

"I am not sure, did you?"

"Well, that large man might be Sugar Ray Jackson, a one-time heavy weight fighter who was promoted and some say used by his brother Guy Jackson. The small fellow may have been one of his corner men."

"Are you saying that was Guy Jackson's brother, I killed?"

"He was and you did."

"Can there be any doubt that Guy ordered the hit?"

"Seems likely, but I still don't see the big picture," said Blum. "I don't see why he wants to kill you. If the small man makes it through the night, we may have the answer in the morning. The problem is it seems to me there has to be something more you aren't telling me." Blum waited for Robert to answer, but he had nothing more to say. Rather he sat at the kitchen table reliving the gunfight.

"So what now?" asked Ricki.

"Miss Williams, I'd like to put you in a motel, with a patrol car outside. I have to take Robert to headquarters for more questioning."

"Can we go check on my house first? My guess is these two went to my house. I would like to be sure it is OK."

"Actually, I would like to check that out too. Suppose I drive you over. In the mean time, I'll have a car take Miss William to a motel."

Leaving Ricki with an officer while she packed a bag to stay at a motel. Blum drove Robert to his house on Oxford. Calling for a car to meet him at the address, Blum was quiet on the short drive over. Parking in front, Blum made Robert wait in the car. Blum had insisted that Robert's Colt be taken in evidence by the crime scene team and he was very complete in searching Robert. Robert, for his part only felt exhaustion, so he dozed as Blum and one of the two uniform officers in the patrol car walked up to the front door.

Peering in, they tried the door and when it did not open, they walked around to the back door. The uniform had his gun drawn. The second officer waited on the street in front. Finding the back door open, Blum drew his pistol. He was a foot behind the uniformed officer when someone shot the officer in the chest. Blum stepped into the house and shot as he entered the kitchen.

Hearing shots, the second police officer, drew his gun and raced back to his car, "calling in 'shots fired," before he ran around to the back.

Robert heard two more shots from the house. One sounded like a shotgun. Odds were the policemen were dead and another hired killer was in the house waiting for Robert. Seeing that the patrolman had taken the keys to the car, Robert knew he had two options, run or bring the battle to the enemy.

Jumping out the rear door, Robert used the car as a shield. It was two in the morning, the street was once again quiet, only a few upstairs curtains pulled back suggesting anyone was aware of the sound of gunfire in the Cederberg house. Running around to the left side of the house, Robert reached the back of the house. Finding the key, Robert quietly unlocked the door to the basement steps. Slipping off his shoes, Robert walked down into the dark basement. Feeling for the workbench, he moved to the gun cabinet; opening it, he debated taking the Winchester, but instead he pulled his army issue Colt 1911 and chambering a bullet, he started up the stairs.

Like Ricki's house, the top of his stairs entered the back of the kitchen by the rear door. At the top of the steps, Robert saw a pair of legs on the floor. Edging around the corner, he saw a shotgun barrel as it rose to fire; ducking back the single blast missed his head and hand by inches. Instantly he pushed back around and fired four shots in the direction of gun, ducking back just as a second blast dug into the stair wall. Again, Robert rounded the corner and fired three times, leaving two rounds in the Colt.

When a third shot didn't follow, Robert chanced a look around the door. On the floor of the small kitchen were three tangled bodies, Blum and the two patrolmen. Beyond them, Guy Jackson was sitting in the archway between the kitchen and the dining room. Jackson's feet were splayed out with the right foot twisted downward. In his right hand, Jackson had the stock of a shotgun that he would never fire again. Knowing Jackson was dead, Robert felt for signs of life from the other three men. Turning Blum over, Robert saw he was breathing, but the wound seemed potentially fatal. Checking, the two other policemen were dead.

"Detective, it is Robert Cederberg. You have been shot but you are going to make it. The shooter was Guy Jackson. He is dead and so are the patrolmen. The police should be on their way, is there anything I can do for you?" Blum squeezed Robert's hand.

"Robert," Blum struggled to talk. "I don't know what is going on here, maybe you don't either, but Jackson wouldn't have come here on his own, I mean all alone, gunning for you unless someone else made him, forced him." Blum struggled for breath. "If I don't make it, you have to get Cooper to understand that someone else had to be pushing Jackson. Don't think it has ended here. Someone else wants you dead, and until you find out who and why, you and that girl will never be safe." Squeezing his hand again, Blum fainted.

The patrol cars pulled up with lights and sirens off. Putting the Colt on the floor, Robert left Blum, stepped over Jackson and turned on the front porch lights. Robert waited at the front door again with his hands in the air. "Call for an EMS, he shouted. There is a policeman shot inside." Running up, one officer, forced Robert to the ground at gunpoint, and handcuffed him, while a second taller man drew his gun and entered the house.

Coming back out minutes later he said, "Its Tyler and Henderson, they are dead man, so is a black man with a shotgun. Looks like the nigger shot them. Detective Blum is in there too, he is unconscious but breathing."

What should we do?"

"Someone needs to put pressure on Blum's wound, with a towel, something to stop the bleeding," said Robert wishing he had thought of that rather than going to the door, "Were either of you in Nam?"

"I was, but I never saw action," said the taller police officer. "I think he is right, Bill. Go find several towels, while I take his cuffs off. Go on, move!" Once he was released, Robert ran back to Blum. Before turning him over, he checked his back for exit wounds. Finding none, he and the tall officer turned Blum over as the second cop entered the kitchen with two bathroom towels. Opening Blum's coat, Robert saw a large hole on his right side below the top of his ribs. When Robert touched the wound, blood came out in a spurt. Placing one towel over the hole, he had the cop use the second towel to apply pressure to the wound. "Stay like that until you can't hold it and one of us will take over. What we are doing is trying to stop the bleeding and help keep his blood pressure from falling." Minutes later another car arrived, this time an emergency medical services truck. Giving the medics room, Robert and the patrolmen moved to the dining room.

"Thanks," said the officer. "I'm Bill Reed."

"I'm Robert Cederberg."

"Robert can you tell us what is going on?"

"I am happy to, but perhaps we should wait for a detective or a sergeant or something, because I don't want to tell this story a dozen times. Also,"

"Also what."

"Well, I just realized no one has searched the upstairs. This might sound silly, but this is the third time tonight someone has shot at me. I wouldn't like there to be a fourth."

"Are you saying there could be another nigger upstairs?"

"Well a person with a gun."

"How about the basement?"

"No, I came in that way."

"Ok, you wait here with the medics. We will check out the house. The two patrol officers spoke to the two medics and another police officer, and then Bill Reed called for anyone upstairs to surrender before he crept upstairs while the others waited with guns drawn. Five minutes later the Reed reported the house was secure.

Robert sat in the living room and waited while police officers came and went. Eventually, Blum was on his way to the hospital and the Sergeant on the scene, Sergeant Barbelli announced that he was taking Robert to the station house to meet with a Lieutenant Cooper from the Roseville PD.

At the station, Robert was taken in through a back entrance into an interview room, where they offered him food and drinks. Robert asked for a hot chocolate and a Clark bar.

Lieutenant Cooper entered the interview wearing a rumpled blue suit with what looked like his pajamas shirt. Behind him, Sergeant Barbelli took a chair.

"Robert, Sergeant Barbelli called me because Detective Blum told him about the shooting at the Bullseye and gave him my number. It appears we are investigating what may turn out to be the same case, and he thought it wise to talk with you together."

"Do I need my lawyer?"

"No, this is an interview," said Barbelli. "You are not being charged, but if you want a lawyer, you have the right to call one, and we will wait until he arrives."

"I am happy to talk. But I think I should have my lawyer here, because he may have information to add that is critical."

"Okay, make the call, and we will wait," said Barbelli, clearly angry over having to wait for a lawyer.

When Bruce Cabot arrived, it was 6:17 a.m., but he was dressed in a pinstriped gray suit, carrying a leather briefcase. Greeting Robert, Cabot introduced himself to other people in the room and then Detective Barbelli explained Robert his rights before laying out the case.

"Ok," said Barbelli. "Let me see if I can put the case in perspective. Mister Cederberg, you are the manager of the Bullseye Gun Club located at Eleven Mile and Bellear in Roseville."

"Yes."

"And, earlier this evening, you claim that two armed men entered you business, that you called the police, and waited in the club. When the police arrived, you claim one or both of men shot at Patrolman Anderson," said Sergeant Barbelli

"I shot at the man in the door to the range. I thought I heard at least four shots.

"Officer Anderson was shot in the chest," said Barbelli. "And, I know you will be happy to learn that he is still with us."

"That is good news."

"According to the ME, he was shot with a .22 caliber. Unusual weapon for a robber," said Barbelli.

"Not for a hit man," offered Lieutenant Cooper.

"Yes, let's move on. After Officer Anderson is shot, your story is you followed one of the break-in men, one…Clive Johnson, who you shot in the back of the head," said Barbelli.

"He was going to shoot another officer. I shot him to save the officer," said Robert.

"Yes, again, let's move on. The Roseville Police escorted you home. However, the next thing we know, you are involved in another shooting at Miss William's house. Imagine, two shooting in one night." Robert looked at Cabot. He sat very still, and Robert took his cue from him, saying nothing unless asked.

"Robert, I don't really have to ask why you might want to see Miss Williams, but tell me about your house and how you left. Did you drive to Miss Williams?"

"No I left my house looking like I was there and walked to Ricki's house."

"And, were you armed?"

"I have a carry permit, and I was armed."

"So you went to Miss Williams' house armed, and then as I understand it, the two of you went to sleep in the basement."

"I thought it might be safer."

"And so it proved, because according to the police report, sometime after one in the morning you heard men breaking into the back door."

"Yes, I was in the main floor bathroom."

"You were waiting in the bathroom with a loaded automatic when three men entered Miss Williams' house," said Barbelli, waiting for Robert to continue. When he said nothing, Lieutenant Cooper took up the story.

"You then shot two of the men, and you say the other fled the scene. These men were Raymond Jackson and Ike Castor. Mr. Jackson was dead at the scene, and Mister Castor is in critical condition at St. Johns."

"When you heard the break in, did you call the police?" asked Cooper.

"No, I was in the bathroom. When the first man came around the corner I shot him."

"No warning, no freeze, or put your gun down?" asked Barbelli.

"Wait," said Cabot. "The law doesn't require a homeowner protecting his property to give any warning, in these circumstances."

"No, that's right counselor, but your client keeps shooting black people in the back. Moreover, he doesn't seem very worked up about it. He is quite a mechanic."

"Detective, one more comment like that, and we are out of here," said Cabot standing up to leave.

"Okay, let's bring it down a notch," said Cooper using his command voice. "Robert, you shot the first man, this Ike as he entered the hallway. Did you shoot him in the back?"

"No in the chest, but the detective is right, I gave no warning. To me, I was in combat. In combat there is no warning and no quarter, front or back, you shoot to kill."

"Did you shoot to kill?"

"Don't answer that Robert," shouted Bruce Cabot.

"Okay, how about the other man, Raymond Jackson?"

"I was concerned when Miss Williams called from the basement, that if I didn't take out the man in the front of the house, she would be killed. Rather than try to talk to man, I shot through the wall and shot the man again as he came into the living room."

"Right, and after this, Detective Blum drives you home where a patrol car meets you."

"Yes."

"So what happened at your house?"

"Detective Blum told me to stay in the car. He and another officer checked the front and then entered by the back door. When I heard shots, the third officer called in and then raced to the back to help. I heard another shot, and then nothing, I decided to take a look."

"So, you entered the house, found the officers down, and shot one Guy Jackson four times in the chest."

"Yes, and he probably saved Detective Blum," added Cooper.

"I appreciate that. The thing is, how many more people are you going to shoot Robert, because I haven't even mentioned Jozef Kaminski, Evert Yale, or Hiram Greenberg."

"Who is Hiram Greenstein," asked Cabot.

"Do you want to tell us, Mister Cederberg?" asked Barbelli.

"I have no idea."

"You see, Mr. Cabot, I had an interesting call this afternoon from one of our past police officers. A man who knew Robert as a boy, and he mentioned how Robert always seems to be close to murder and suicide, beginning when he was only a boy. It seems Hiram Greenstein committed suicide in 1963 on a beach in Canada where Robert's family had a cottage. Funny thing about this case of suicide, the Greenstein family never believed their boy could have killed himself. He was on a driving trip across Canada and the US. He was loaded with cash, and according to the investigators, people in the bar where he had been drinking described him as full of life. According to the police report at the time, the death was judged an apparent suicide, but foul play could not be ruled out." Barbelli ran his fingers through is greased back hair.

"Same with your friend Jozef Kaminski, at first an apparent suicide, but then other evidence comes to light and we have to wonder, if somehow you are involved Robert. Did you kill Joe Kaminski, Robert?" Barbelli almost shouted the question.

"Robert, don't answer that, I think we are done here Detective, unless you change the nature of your questions. If you are going to charge my client, please do so."

"No, Counselor, we aren't going to charge Mister Cederberg, but he is a suspect in the murder of Jozef Kaminski."

"Are there any other suspects?"

"Yes, we are looking for a Lucy Meadows."

"I think she is still in Florida," said Robert

"How do you know that?"

"Your confidential source, Tom Wilson told me Lucy and Joe checked into an expensive hotel in Florida." This information seemed to be news to Barbelli and Cooper.

"Wait," said Barbelli. "Someone connect the dots for me."

"I am not sure they are connected," said Cabot.

"I also talked to Tom Wilson, today," explained Robert, "He told me Joe and Lucy Meadows stayed in a hotel in Naples. Tom suggested that Guy Jackson paid for Joe's vacation in Florida as an excuse for Joe to talk to Evert Yale about selling the Bullseye Club. Tom thinks the meeting went bad and Guy killed Evert."

"Do you believe that?"

"Not with Joe there. Guy would have had to kill Joe right then. What makes more sense is Joe met with Evert and he says 'no'. Joe leaves, he goes back to Lucy. Guy sends someone to Evert's house, fakes a break in, and kills him. Just like tonight. Then Joe flies home and for some reason Lucy Meadows stays in Florida. When they get home, Guy kills Joe or has one of his stooges kill Joe and makes it look like a suicide. Then for some reason he comes after me."

"His whole organization and family came at you," said Barbelli.

"Does Guy have more family or anyone else in his organization who might seek revenge?" asked Cabot.

"We are looking into that question. For now no," said Cooper.

"Robert, why did Jackson want the Bullseye?" asked Barbelli.

"I don't really know. He could have started a club next door if he wanted to and I would have helped him.

"Not really," said Bruce Cabot, "Evert Yale actually owned all the land on the north side of Eleven Mile between Bellear and Chippendale. He owns everything up to the new freeway."

"Is that it?" asked Cooper. "Is this all about land for the new freeway?"

"What do you mean?" asked Robert.

"In the plans for the new freeway," explained Cooper, "they are going to create a new Eleven Mile road on both sides of the freeway. That club must be right at the beginning of the new road. Maybe the club is worth a lot more as land. This end of I696 is supposed to open in the next three years. You probably know, there are property battles going on everywhere. I hear the Zoo is fighting it and,"

"And, I think we may have the answer," interrupted Cabot. "Jackson has apartments in that area. Suppose he got wind of the freeway deal. Somehow, he learned they needed that land. My guess is Evert did not know when he moved to Florida."

"So where does that leave me and Miss Williams. I don't care about land and freeways. All I care about is Miss Williams' safety."

Miss Williams will spend the night at the motel. After that, she is free to go, and in my opinion, she will be safe provided you are not with her. You, I am going to hold for 24 hours or until I speak to the district attorney and a judge. That should be later this morning. I will let Mister Cabot know what the DA decides. Normally, if a store manager shoots someone during a break-in and that person was armed, then the manager is not charged. At the gun club, you should be in the clear because of the officer on the scene reports and the fact the bullet in Anderson did not come from your gun. The shooting at Miss Williams' house is different because Robert is not the homeowner and the Police asked him to stay at his house. The shooting of Guy Jackson is even less clear. Detective Blum told you to stay in the car. The police officer who called it in, told you to sit tight, yet you entered your house when you knew an armed intruder was present, you obtained a gun and killed him, rather than wait for the police."

"Yes and probably saved Detective Blum," said Cabot.

"I was going to add that, and that is what I will tell the DA, however, he may see it differently."

"On what charge?" asked Cabot.

"Look counselor, I can't let your client go until I talked to the DA. Right now, this is the safest place he could be. I will talk to the DA first thing and call you." Shaking hands Cabot left as they took Robert to the cells.

CHAPTER 11

CHANGE OF STORY

They placed Robert in an unlocked cell, but in a locked part of the jail. Lying down on the cot in the cell, Robert immediately fell asleep. When he opened his eyes, a policeman was shaking him, saying his name. According to the officer, his lawyer was here and he was wanted in the Chief of Detectives Office. Before leaving the cell, Robert urinated, washed his face, and hand combed his short-cropped hair. Inside he felt exhausted and confused. Robert just could not understand so many people dying over a block of rundown buildings.

The office of the Chief of Detectives was wood paneled with awards and pictures of policemen on the walls. Behind the desk, the chief was a small blond man with a large broken nose and tobacco stained front teeth. On the desk, Robert saw pictures of children. Sitting down in a chair on the left of the desk, Robert smiled at Bruce Cabot sitting in a chair to the right. Cabot was dressed in his usual gray suit.

"Mister Cederberg. Did you get any sleep?"

"Yes thanks, I did." Robert rubbed his face.

"Robert, I am Chief of Detectives McKenna. I am the second in command. Detective Barbelli and Mister Cabot have filled me in on what has happened, and first off, I want to say thank you for not waiting at your house. The doctors tell me, your actions probably saved Detective Blum. Jack Blum is a good man, a husband, and father, and we would regret losing him." McKenna pushed his chair back and picked up a coffee cup.

"Normally, we would keep you in jail until one of our District Attorneys presented facts before a judge. In a case like yours two shooting at Miss Williams and the one at your house, we would ask the Judge to decide if a grand jury should hear the evidence, but all of us appreciate what you did last night, and there will be no charges brought in either case of home invasion. The deaths will be ruled justifiable."

"How about with the Roseville police and the club shooting? I was supposed to see Lieutenant Cooper this morning."

"I spoke to Cooper and a Chief Granger this morning, and the changes will be dropped in that case also."

"What about the Officer Anderson? Did he make it?" asked Robert.

"He is still in critical condition, as is the man you shot at Miss Williams' house.

"Can he talk," asked Cabot.

"Detective Barbelli spoke with him this morning.

When I told him that Sugar Ray Jackson was dead he broke down in tears." Barbelli was sitting in the back of the chief's office. "I think they may have been what the sex squad call very close friends."

"Apparently," said McKenna taking back the conversation, "when he learned that Guy Jackson had been killed at your house, and that he was facing a felony murder charge, he opened up, especially when we said we might get his charge reduced if he cooperated."

"His name is Ike Castro, aka, "Little Ike," said Barbelli unable to remain quiet. "He was Sugar Ray's ring man, his cut man. Late yesterday evening, Guy Jackson handed Ray and Ike shotguns and a pair of .38's and told them he was going to visit your house, and they were going to be his back up. When they got to your house and found you were gone, Guy told then to go to Miss Williams' house, while he waited at your house. Jackson told them to leave Miss Williams alive, but that you had to be killed. Ike told me he had never carried a gun before and never shot a man, and I believed him. He said Jackson had already hired a professional, but he said the man hired to hit you at the gun club refused to complete the contract. That left the contract up to Jackson and his brother. Work they had done before according to Ike."

"What about the third man?"

"What third man?" asked Barbelli.

"There was a third man in the house who drove away. Did this Ike say who he was?"

"No, but I will follow up on a wheels man."

"Did this Ike, tell you who hired Jackson?"

"No he didn't have a clue. That is where it gets really interesting. You see, I called the police in Naples early this morning and asked the detective in charge of the Yale case if he had checked on this Lucy Meadows yet."

"And," said Cabot.

"And, he didn't know what I was talking about. However he did say that their ballistics people determined that the gun that killed Evert Yale was very likely the same gun used to kill Jozef Kaminski."

"So Joe killed Evert?" asked Cabot.

"Well, that is one possibility, but there is another wrinkle."

"What is that," asked Cabot, before Robert could speak.

"According to the Michigan Crime Lab, the .32 used to kill Kaminski has been involved in at least one other death.

"Susan Kay," said Robert.

"Right, as I understand it, a Susan Kay owned two similar guns. Both guns were actually purchased for her by the same man. According to him, he purchased a new Walther PPK for her in 1964 for her protection. As I understand it, she had been robbed. The crime lab said she used that gun in 1965 to kill one, Edward Krug. Mister Krug was a well-known second story man working businesses in Grosse Pointe. He was accused of rape on several occasions but never convicted. We are not sure what happened to that gun. Do you know where it is Mister Cederberg?"

"No."

"What about the second gun?" asked Cabot.

"Our records show Miss Susan Kay used it to take her life in 1973. According to the police report, the gun was purchased as a gift. Miss Kay wanted to give it to a young soldier overseas, but she used it to kill herself instead. As I understand it Mister Cederberg, you were the soldier in question and you are the current owner of that gun."

"I was. Joe Kaminski gave it to me after Susan Kay died. She left it to me in her will." Robert looked directly at Chief McKenna. Robert knew not to lie, but it was difficult meeting McKenna glare. Robert did not want to talk about the Walther, and talking about Susan Kay made him want to pull back into his shell.

"And how did she come by it? Did she say?"

"All I know is she had it in 1966."

"Yes well, that is where the story gets really interesting. The gun was discovered with her body by the very same officer who had purchased it."

"Tom Wilson," said Cabot before Robert could speak.

"Yes, in filling out his FOID card, Officer Wilson claimed he purchased the gun in a police auction in Winsor. Seems the gun was used in a suicide in Canada in the early 1960's and Wilson purchased it 1966 and gave it to Miss Kay sometime after that."

Robert sat very still in his chair less any sign of emotion take him over the edge. Susan Kay shoots herself with the gun she purchased for Robert. Now, McKenna was claiming Susan's gun could be the same gun from that day on the beach.

"Robert, are you OK?" asked his lawyer.

"Sure, I just wasn't really ever sure that Susan…"

"Right, well, I think there may be more to the story."

"Like what?"

"Like why did Tom Wilson tell you he talked to the Naples police when he didn't? Like, what happened to Lucy Meadows, and where is Tom Wilson. Because he isn't at work and he isn't answering his phone."

"Chief," interrupted Cabot, "is there any way to determine if Miss Kay actually had cancer. I mean what I was told was she left a note, but so did Joe Kaminski, and now we find out it was a phony note and someone killed Joe and left the Walther to implicate Robert. It sounds to me like the same thing might have happened to Susan Kay."

"You mean Wilson."

"They had an affair," added Robert. "I know Tom was very bitter about it being over. You see, the thing is she had the other gun. I guess it doesn't matter, she is dead, Joe is dead, and nothing is going to change any of it. Nevertheless, the silver Walther was for me. I cannot believe Susan would use it on herself when she had the other gun. She never fired that gun, it was for me. She always carried the other gun, a black metal Walther with brown handles. If Susan were going to kill herself, she would have used her own gun. Besides, I never really believed Susan would take her own life. She was a fighter." Robert's thoughts were racing. What did Tom Wilson have to do with Guy Jackson?

"Robert, do you know why Tom left the Grosse Pointe police force?"

"No we didn't talk much that last year."

"A number of women, victims of crimes, complained that Officer Wilson pestered them afterwards, usually starting with an offer to help. Miss Kay never complained, but I knew about her. Stories about married cops who hit on pretty female rape victims, usually reach my desk."

"So what now?" asked Robert.

"When we are done here, I am going to let you go. However, the problem is we still don't know who Guy Jackson hired to hit you at the Club, and who was pushing Jackson so hard he took the job in house, a thing he didn't do anymore. For now, I am going to send you home with a minder. I cannot guaranty your safety, but I am reasonable sure you can."

"What about Naples," asked Cabot.

"Right now, the Naples police believe Joe Kaminski shot Evert Yale and then returned to Michigan where he took his own life. They aren't really interested in Lucy Meadows or Tom Wilson, but I will work on them."

"Can I do something?" asked Robert.

"Ask your lawyer."

"Robert," said Cabot, taking up the thread. "Evert left the club to you and Joe. Until Joe is cleared of Evert's murder his estate cannot inherit the club. What we need is to find Lucy Meadows. Likewise, until Joe's case here is closed and you are clear of all charges, we might have a hard time having a probate judge name you as sole inheritor of the club. As things stand, Lucy Meadows could show up in three months and claim she is the rightful owner."

"Bruce, are you saying I should go to Florida and find Lucy."

"I think someone needs to find Lucy Meadows and Tom Wilson," said Cabot looking at McKenna.

"Robert, I don't think you should go to Florida." Advised McKenna. "In fact, we would still prefer it if you remained in Michigan. I am suggesting you talk to the Naples police about hiring an experienced investigator down there to do the looking for you. Did I make myself clear about staying in Michigan?"

"Understood."

"Good, now is there anything else?"

"About the Walther," said Robert. "I know what everyone must think, but I would like it back." Robert looked directly at McKenna, showing no fear, only determination.

"I wondered if you would ask." The chief took a cardboard box from his desk drawer and handed it to Robert. "I know we should melt this down, but I am hoping that one day when you see Tom Wilson, you will show him this gun, and ask him again about Susan Kay?" Robert took the box without opening it or answering. He needed air.

* * *

When he was back in the club, Robert called Ricki at the motel. When Robert asked her to meet him, she said, "Robert, right now I don't really want to go back to my house or to your house."

"How about meeting at the club or a restaurant?"

"Robert. I need time to think. I was on my way out the door. I am going to stay to with my mother in Ohio."

"I'll come with you."

"What and have my mother murdered?" she screamed.

"Please, I know you are right, but just meet me for ten minutes. You name the place."

"Alright, I'll meet you at the Grosse Pointe Diner in half an hour."

The Grosse Pointe Diner was on Mack between Oxford and Renaud. Inside the white tiled Diner, there were ten stools and four booths. When Robert arrived, he waved at the short order cook, Fred Dillon. Robert had been eating in the diner since he was fifteen.

"Long time," said Dillon.

"How about two chocolate shakes," said Robert seeing Ricki sitting in the last booth.

Walking up to the booth, Robert wanted to hug Ricki, but she remained in the booth, so Robert took a seat opposite her.

"Bruce wants to hire a private investigator in Florida to find Lucy. But, I was thinking you and I could go there and find Tom." he said without any preamble.

"What good will that do?"

"What do you suggest I do?"

"Drop it. Let Bruce handle it. Please, don't go to Florida, don't go looking for trouble."

"What if I have to?"

"Then we are finished. These last few days have been too much. I want a family with a husband and kids. I don't want killers at my door steps or a police guard."

"Why hire an investigator, when you and I can go to Florida. We can visit my folks; swim in the ocean. I know they want to meet you. While we are there, I will take one day and look for Tom and Lucy."

"Robert, if you go to Florida, you go alone. I love you, but I see this ending badly if you go down there. I don't want you to end up dead."

"I don't intend to."

"Neither did Guy Jackson."

"So, what now?"

"Now I am going to my mom's house."

"Can I go with you?"

"No, you can call. Give me a day or two, and then if you decide to be sensible, you can call me." Standing she left the diner without touching or embracing Robert.

Surprising everyone, including himself, Robert did what Ricki suggested. After their meeting in the diner, he visited Bruce Cabot and he and Cabot spoke to the police in Naples and on their advice, contacted a private investigator to find Lucy Meadows. Cabot was convinced Lucy was the key to understanding what happened in Florida. Afterwards, Robert did what he did best, stayed in his shell and waited.

On Monday, Bruce Cabot called to say that he had filed Joe Kaminski's will with the probate court, and he and Robert needed to meet. In Cabot's office, the lawyer explained the process of probating a will. In the will, Robert had been named executor, and beneficiary. Cabot reviewed an inventory of Joe's assets, and gave Robert a copy of the notice filed with the court regarding Joe's death. Once Joe's debts and bills were cleared, Robert would have to wait until the probate cleared, as long as a year, before he could sell the truck or house. Until then, Robert had access to either, and he could spend Joe's money provided the expenses were related to settling the estate.

"I haven't gone to his bank to open his safe deposit. I thought we could do that together. I have his account book and the court notice. Once the probate is finished, the money and the property will be yours."

That afternoon, they discovered that Joe had a safe deposit with a woman's locket and some letters in Polish. The box also contained a hand written note. The note said, "Robert if you are reading this note, I am past caring. You are the son I never had. I left everything to you in my will. Most are just things to be sold. However, there is a key taped to the back of this note. You will know where it goes. What you find, you must keep forever." After reading the note, Cabot, asked, do you know where the key goes?

"There is a locked box in Joe's gun case. I think it is to it."

"Do you know what is in the box?"

"I haven't a clue."

"Well, find out, but only tell me if it helps our case. I don't want to know any dark secrets, okay?"

"Sure, of course."

"Good, let's go check his bank account. As executor, I want you to move it to a new account that you and I have to co-sign. Agreed?"

"Whatever you say."

They waited at the desk of one of the bankers, a woman in her forties named Helen Hammer. When Helen returned, she had a man with her who she introduced as the Manager, Mister Younger.

"Mister Cederberg, it appears that the bank statement you have for Mister Kaminski is from a month ago. Unfortunately, at that time his account showed a balance of thirty-seven thousand, four hundred dollars, and twenty-five cents. As of yesterday, the current balance is nine thousand, eleven dollars and nineteen cents. Unfortunately, when Mister Cabot informed us on Friday that Mister Kaminski had passed away, we didn't check the account, other than to freeze it. In reviewing the account, I see that most of the money is already gone. We are actually holding a check that was cashed on Friday."

"Where did the money go?"

"It appears that Mister Kaminski wrote several checks, for cash two weeks ago in the amount of one thousand dollars, which were cleared. Since then there have been three checks to the same individual each for nine thousand dollars. Technically, the last check cleared on Friday, last week."

"Does that mean there could be one more check, in process or not yet cashed?"

"Yes, but with the account frozen you are safe."

"Can you tell us who the checks are made out to? And where they are being cashed?"

"All three were made out to Lucy Weise and cashed in Naples into her bank account at a Key Bank."

"And, you put a hold on the account."

"I have already done that, but we might be able to do more."

"What more can you do?"

"I will call her bank and inform them we believe she is cashing forged checks, and we want her held for the police if she tries to cash another check."

"Good because I think if you check, she will have already withdrawn most of the deposited money. My guess is she is waiting for the last check to clear and then she will leave town or change identities.

"Lucy Weise," laughed Cabot.

"What is so funny," asked Robert.

"Some crooks are just too clever for words, or with words," Cabot laughed again. "Robert, I guess you do not know it but 'Weise' is 'Meadow' in German. I assumed Lucy Weise is an alias for Lucy Meadows. My guess is Weise is her real name, and Meadows is her alias." Turning to the banker, Cabot asked, "Can I use you phone?"

"Of course, who do you want to call?"

"The chief of detectives here has been in contact with the Naples police. Perhaps he can put a fire under them, and have Mrs. Weise arrested and returned to Michigan."

* * *

Sitting at Joe's workbench, Robert used the small silver key to open the locked gunmetal box in the bottom drawer. Robert found a sealed note with his name and last Monday's date on top of a pile of post cards and letters, keepsakes from the war. Under the pile of letters, Robert found Joe's service pistol, his Colt 1911. Next to the gun were two boxes, inside one was a Purple Heart metal, the second contained a Silver Star. Setting the pile of post cards and old letters aside, Robert opened the envelope with his name. On a torn scrap of lined paper, Joe had written, "Evert is dead and I don't trust Lucy. Don't trust Ricki."

CHAPTER 12

A ROSE BY ANY OTHER NAME

Louise Weise knew she was taking a risk. She should have cashed the final check a day ago, but moving out of her apartment took its toll, so she deposited the check in the drop off box at the main Key Bank branch on Monday and waited two days for the check to clear. Eventually she knew the lawyer in Detroit would put a hold on the account. Normally when she skinned a man, she had all his money cleared out two days before the body was found. In her best jobs, she had the account cleared while he was still alive, and so a suicide wasn't required. In this case, she understood the risk of waiting so long, it was just that she was low on cash and the extra nine thousand would mean two or three weeks of good living in Miami.

The morning was cool for Naples, low fifties. The Key Bank branch on Airport Road was new and shared its parking lot with four other businesses, a Chinese takeout, a used bookstore, and a convenience store. The entire lot was empty, but Louise parked her 1970 Eldorado convertible in an empty space by the takeout, half way down the lot and out of eyesight of the bank. The Eldorado was loaded and ready to go, and she did not want anyone in the bank seeing the car when she withdrew the nine thousand dollars. Louise was dressed in white pants and a pullover blouse with tropical flowers. She carried a large white purse in which a .25 automatic was loaded, should she need. It was 9:17 in the morning and the bank was empty except for a man with Latin features having trouble speaking English. When he finally received his money, Louise and the teller exchanged a knowing look that said, 'Speak English'.

For Louise a woman who grew up in Detroit, South Florida seemed overrun with Mexicans and Cubans. When Louise handed the teller a check made out to cash, the teller started counting out ten-dollar bills, after counting out a thousand, she stopped saying, "I am sorry Mam. I will be just a minute. I have to go to a different drawer for the rest. Do you want any hundreds?" The teller smiled, closed, and locked her drawer, with the check in the drawer.

"Sure give me, ten hundreds, and the rest in fifties and twenties, if you can, that would be great."

"I hope you aren't closing your account because of something we did."

"No I am thinking about buying a used car."

"Well, I will be right back." The teller left the counter and went behind a wall. Louise wondered if she should leave, but her read on the teller said she was just following procedures. Four days ago, in the main bank they had to go in the vault for the hundreds.

Seeing that there was a man in his forties dressed in a suit but wearing a floppy hat behind her, Louise stepped out of way saying, "I am waiting for a teller, she just stepped away. Please go ahead and use the other the teller when she is free." Louise pointed to the teller at the drive in window.

"No that is alright, you finish your business, I can wait," said the man tipping his hat. *Fucking crackers*, Louise thought, *always trying to be the southern gentleman.*

When the teller returned, she opened her drawer and counted out the cash only to discover she was a thousand dollars short. "I am very sorry," she said blushing bright red. "I must have missed counted."

"Well, can't you take it out of your drawer?"

"No, I don't have enough. I'll have to get it from the vault. I am very sorry." Again, she placed the money in her drawer and walked behind the counter.

"Idiot," Louise said to the man behind her.

"Just one of those days," said the man.

"Look you don't have to wait, I am sure if you go to the other window, the other teller will wait on you."

"Thanks, but I'll wait."

"Suit yourself," said Louise thinking, *Another idiot.* This time when the teller returned, she had a man with her.

"Mrs. Weise, I am so sorry. I am Mister Jessup, the Assistant Manager. I understand that Connie, Miss Blake made a mistake in your transaction, and I just want to be sure it is handled correctly, if you can just slide down to this other window, I will take care of you while Miss Blake takes care of this gentleman. Frowning at the delay, Louise pushed her purse in between the two windows and moved to the empty window. The Assistant Manager had Connie count out the money and hand it to him, and then he moved to the second window. As Louise moved, the man in the suit behind Louise stepped up, put his checkbook on the counter, and then put his hand by Louise's purse.

"Alright, now let's count this out together, shall we." The man counted even slower than the teller and Louise found herself counting along under her breath. "Nine thousand," said Jessup, setting the stack of bills on the counter beside him, "Now there is just one more formality before I can release the money."

"What formality?"

"I don't see any record of an IRS form being filed when you deposited the money three days ago. "You see the IRS requires that you fill out a 1099 for any deposit over eight thousand."

"No you have that wrong. It is for deposits over ten thousand."

"Are you sure, I think it is eight."

"No, look I am very sure. Now give me my money."

"Not without a 1099."

"Okay, get your form, and let's get on with this, I'll show you on the form that you are wrong." Louise turned to give the man in the suit another 'can you believe this look' when she saw he had her purse in his hand, and behind him stood two policemen.

"What are you doing?" she demanded using her outraged voice.

"Louise Weise," said one of the uniforms, I am arresting you on suspicion of cashing forged checks." Louise was cuffed and read her rights. As one of the two uniforms took her out to the car, the man in the suit opened her purse, and showed the pistol to the second officer and to the Assistant Manager.

"Sergeant Hill, what are you doing here?" asked the officer.

"I heard the call when I was pulling into lot. I was making a deposit. The dispatcher said the bank manager was delaying the suspect and that she could be armed. At first, when I saw her I thought this must be a mistake, but when she told you, that you were wrong about that tax form, I knew."

"She was right about the 1099."

"That is why I knew she was a crook." Sergeant Hill handed the purse to the arresting officer. "Make sure the detectives know she was carrying. Oh, and there is a car halfway down the lot, loaded with stuff. Check her purse for keys and see if they open the car. If they do, call in a detective and the impound guys, and let's see what in her car."

Using her one call, Louise called a lawyer in Naples. She was prepared to do the time on the check kiting but she was worried after searching her car, the police might expand the case.

* * *

When he got back to the office, Sergeant Hill made some enquiries and learning about Louise's possible connections to the cases in Michigan, he had finger printing send copies of her fingerprints to the Grosse Pointe Woods and Roseville police departments. He also had a copy of her prints forwarded to the Detroit Police Department.

Later that morning he got a call from the DPD informing him that Lucy Weise, aka Lucy Meadows, aka Lucy Fields, was born Louise Weise in Detroit Michigan in 1925. After checking with the FBI, Hill learned that Louise had a long record of arrests for confidence games and Bunco crimes in Florida and Michigan. Louise Weise started her career of crime in Detroit when she was arrested on charges of prostitution and illegal gambling in her twenties. Acquitted, she was arrested again when she was thirty. In that case, she was suspected in a sweetheart swindle of a man twenty-five years older in Florida.

In that case, the man gave all his savings, fifteen thousand dollars to a young German woman named Lucy Weise so she could pay off a personal loan. The man, William Hutchison met Miss Weise at a German deli in Miami. After several encounters they dated and that developed into an intimate relationship, at which time, Miss Weise admitted she owed money back in Germany and unless she could pay it back, she would have to return home. Naturally, Hutchison gave her the money she needed, and she left for parts unknown. Unfortunately, Hutchison died before a positive identification could be made and the money was never recovered.

Five years later a Lucy Fields was investigated by the FBI in a case in which a seventy five year old man in Florida signed a power of attorney to his future wife, so she could help him with his bills. Later, his children discovered that Mrs. Lucy Fields had emptied his bank account of sixty six thousand dollars and sold a boat worth twenty-two hundred dollars before leaving the city of Coral Gables. In examining the checks written on Joe Kaminski's bank account, the DA told Hill he was confident that they could prosecute Louise Weise for forgery.

The difficulty was connecting her to the murder of Jozef Kaminski and Evert Yale.

Interviewing Louise for a second time, Detective Hill took his time, starring at her for several seconds before beginning. He knew she was a hard case, a pro.

"Louise, tell me again how you came to have the checks."

"Joe wrote them before going back to Michigan."

"Why so much?"

"The the money was for a down payment on a home. We are looking for a home in Naples. We planned to pay cash."

"Why four checks each for nine thousand?"

"I knew about the IRS, and I was told this way was easier."

"When did you talk with Mister Kaminski last?"

"We talked about a week ago, but nothing from him since.

"Louise I have very sad news, apparently Mister Kaminski took his own life last Tuesday in Michigan." To Sergeant Hill, the crying and weeping that followed were acting, after which Louise declared she was worried about Joe's recent mental health.

When Sergeant Hill asked about Evert Yale and Guy Jackson, Louise explained, "Mister Jackson paid for Joe and me to come to Naples for the Holidays. He wanted to help Joe buy Mister Yale's Gun Club.

"Did you spend any time with Evert Yale?

"Joe had dinner with him at a restaurant in the Tin City. I didn't go."

"Have you been in Mister Yale's house?"

"No."

"Do you know if Joe Kaminski visited Yale at his house?"

"I believe so."

"Did Guy Jackson visit Yale at his house?

"I have no way of knowing."

"Do you know if Mister Kaminski had a weapon in his possession?"

"I don't think so."

"And, what about you, do you own a gun?"

"Joe gave me a .25 caliber semi automatic. It was in my purse."

"Do you have permit?"

"No, Joe gave it to me because I was carrying so much cash."

"Louise, we obtained a search warrant for your car. In your car, we found drivers licenses, social security identifications, and credit cards in four different names. We also found a suitcase filled with expenses clothes purchased from Jami' on Fifth Avenue three days ago. Can you explain about the false IDs and the new clothes, because it seems to us like you were getting ready to leave?" Louise talked to her lawyer who informed Detective Hill she had nothing more to say.

Based on Louise's criminal record and attempting to cash forged checks in Florida, Hill assumed that Miss Fields was involved in a criminal conspiracy to swindle Jozef Kaminski and was involved with Guy Jackson in the murder of Jozef Kaminski and Evert Yale. The problem was the DA. He only saw the evidence for the check fraud.

Convinced he could break her story, Detective Hill asked for another interview. When they brought Louise into the interview room, her lawyer, Dennis Nunes was talking with Sergeant Hill about baseball. Sitting across from Louise, Hill looked through her file several times before speaking. All the time Louise kept her head down as if in prayer.

"Louise, according to you, Joe Kaminski and you stayed at the Naples Beach Hotel over the holiday."

"Yes."

"Nice hotel. How long did you stay?"

"Five days. We arrived on Wednesday."

"And, did Mister Jackson stay there too?"

"I would not know."

"Did you like the hotel?"

"It was very nice."

"At night did you two go out?

"For dinner, yes."

"Where did you eat?"

"Eat? We ate at St. Georges one night and some fish house another night."

"Did you use the pool and golf course?"

"I went swimming in the pool and ocean."

"How about Mister Kaminski, did he use the pool or play golf?"

"No"

"So, what did he do while you were at the beach?"

"He had meetings during the day. He met with Evert Yale."

"How many times?"

"Two or three I think."

"Ok, now according to you Mister Kaminski wrote you four checks for nine thousand dollars each."

"No, that is not correct."

"What isn't correct?"

"Joe signed the checks. I filled then out. No forgery.

"When did he sign them?"

"When?"

"Yes, what day, and what time, and where did he sign them?"

"In the hotel, before he left on Sunday."

"You are saying Joe Kaminski signed over four blank checks?"

"Yes and you will not be able to prove otherwise. He gave them to me to close on a house. I filled in the amount but he signed them."

"Did you talk to Joe on Monday?"

"No"

"And, when did you cash the first check."

"I am not sure."

"I believe it was Monday or Tuesday."

"And, another on Wednesday?"

"Yes."

"Can you tell me why you didn't deposit all the checks on Monday?"

"No reason."

"Was it because you had to wait for the checks to clear, but you didn't want to red flag the bank in Grosse Pointe? The way I see it, Jackson and you were partners in this sweetheart swindle? He tells you Joe is dead and you decide to empty his bank account before it is frozen.

"I have nothing to say. I have committed no crime."

"And you say, you only learned about Mister Kaminski's death from us today."

"Yes."

If that is true, then why did you try to cash all four checks? If you thought he was alive, why the hurry. I mean what was the purpose unless you knew you were robbing a dead man."

"I have nothing to say."

"Fine! Here is what I am going to do. I am going to ask our forensics people to determine whether there is any evidence you were in Evert Yale's house. At the same time, I am going to ask the Grosse Pointe Police to coordinate with the other police departments up there in Detroit to find any additional connections between you and Guy Jackson, because I am pretty sure you ran swindles up there and somehow you two are connected. I am also going to encourage the police to make a deal with Jackson, laying everything on you. Whatever it takes I am going to see if they can push Jackson into rolling over on you for felony murder down here."

"Good luck with that. How is a dead man going to accuse me of anything?"

"What are you talking about?"

"Guy Jackson is dead, and you have nothing to connect me with any crime including this false charge of forging checks. I am not saying anything more."

"Oh, come on Louise. Just one last question."

"What?"

"Who told you about Guy Jackson?"

"I have nothing to say."

When he finished writing his report, Sergeant Hill called Detective Barbelli in Grosse Pointe to bring him up to speed. Somehow, Louise Weise learned about Guy Jackson. While they were talking, Hill mentioned that they still did not know where Louise had stayed for the week after Kaminski left. The airline claimed she did not use her ticket back to Detroit on the Sunday after Christmas.

"Do you think she killed Evert Yale?" asked Barbelli.

"It is possible, but we think she has a partner," said Hill.

"Someone with a connection to Jackson," said Barbelli.

"Look, I'll check into her activities in Florida, if you will see what more you can learn about her in Michigan." When they got off the phone Barbelli called Bruce Cabot, and Cabot called Robert.

* * *

The news from Florida was both encouraging and disturbing. Once Robert adjusted to the fact that Louise was a confidence artist, many of the pieces fell into place. The question was why Lucy, or Louise as they were calling her, targeted Joe. Thinking back, Robert remembered that Joe met Lucy at one of the church coffees where she spoke Polish. What was confusing was Louise was German so why target a Polish gunsmith? Why not a wealthy German, and why of all the men in the world, why Joe Kaminski? Bruce Cabot had speculated that perhaps bringing Louise into the picture was all a part of Jackson's plan, which Robert thought was certainly a possibility, although very complicated if all Jackson wanted was the Club. In fact, as Robert thought about it the whole deal about the club was over before Joe met Lucy. Thinking back, he remembered that Joe started seeing Louise in August, because Robert began seeing Ricki in September.

Thinking about that first date at Joe's house, Robert remembered joking about Lucy and Ricki. He also remembered that Ricki said her mother and Lucy were old friends. Robert had yet to meet Ricki's mother and that started him thinking. Lucy Meadows was actually Louise Weise. He wasn't sure how long Louise was Lucy Meadows so it was possible Ricki's mother was an old friend, or it could be just a casual phase like "good friend." Robert thought of another alternative immediately, but the implications were too great.

Robert knew that many confidence games required two or more con artists. Three-card Monte actually used a shill and rube. *What if Ricki is a part of the game*," he thought, "*What if Ricki and Louise are partners*?" Later, when he voiced this question to Cabot over the phone, the Lawyer admitted that he had considered that possibility several days ago, and had someone looking into the possibility. Looking at the telephone, Robert wasn't sure if he was angry or glad he had such a lawyer.

"What are you looking into?"

"Who owns Ricki's house. I am also trying to find out if Lucy Meadows, Fields, or Weise owns a house in Michigan or Florida. I asked a friend in the Wayne County Court House to search through the public records, and he said he was a close friend with the owner of a local title company and between the two, we might be able to get an answer."

"I think I should call Ricki."

"If she is playing you, we have to get the police to arrest her before she learns that Lucy is in jail."

"They'd have to find her first. Supposedly, she is at her mothers in Ohio

"Have you talked to her?"

"No,"

"I have is a phone number in Toledo, but no address.

"We need to find her right away. If she is a part of this game you have to be ready for her before she tries to put a bullet in your head."

"If she has been playing me, I will welcome that bullet."

"Robert, we have to find Ricki and see what she does when she learns that Lucy is under arrest."

"What should I do?"

"Give me her phone number in Ohio, and I will call a friend at the phone company. If we can get an address, we will go there. In the mean time, I will call Lieutenant Barbelli and ask him to send a car to Ricki's house in Grosse Pointe. Give me an hour and then call me back and we can decide what to do next."

After Robert finished talking with Cabot, he went to the Club to collect the mail. The police still requested that he keep the club closed. Before going home he checked at Joe's house where he also collected mail and then drove home; it was two in the afternoon. Robert thought about going to Cabot's office but he needed a shower and a change of clothes.

At home, finding everything dirty, Robert loaded some laundry and then, dressed in only his underwear, he made himself a peanut butter sandwich. Eating the sandwich, in the living room, he opened mail and sorted his bills. It made no sense for a team of confidence women to go after Robert and Joe, yet parts of Ricki's story about how she knew Lucy did not seem to gel with the facts. It all made sense, if Lucy and Ricki were hired to go after Robert and Joe, which made no sense. When he finished with the mail, Robert took a shower while his clothes were drying. Once he had on clean clothes, he made another peanut butter sandwich and decided to visit Bruce Cabot in his office.

Greeting Robert in the outer office, Bruce's tone of voice told Robert Bruce was excited.

"Ok, here is what I have found so far. First, Ricki's house in Grosse Pointe is owned by a company called Southeast Properties."

"What about Lucy?"

"Maybe but the title record is unclear."

And what about the building where Guy had his office."

"Yes, that was clever of you. This one will get the police interested. Southeast Properties owns that too."

"So we should assume Jackson is connected to Southeast Properties?"

"I believe so."

"What about an address in Toledo?"

"My contact at AT&T says the address for the number in Toledo is an apartment on Erie street. I did a little checking and learned the apartment is in a very dangerous area of Toledo, so I called the number."

"Did you talk to Ricki?"

"No, a man answered. When I asked for Ricki or her mother, he said they were out and he wasn't sure when they would be back."

"Did you believe him?"

"No so I just hung up."

"What should we do now?"

"I think we have to look in Ricki's house in Grosse Pointe. If she has fled, the house will be empty. If it looks like she planned to return, we will drive down to Toledo."

Just to be sure, they called Ricki's number in Grosse Pointe. When no one answered, Bruce called the Grosse Pointe Woods police and asked them to send a squad car. On the drive over, Robert placed the Colt .45 in his coat pocket under the seat of the car. Driving up they saw the cruiser parked in the drive and a uniform at the door. He had a weapon drawn.

"Is she home?"

"Doesn't look like it."

"What are your orders?"

"Check and wait."

"I know where there is a key. Can I go in?"

"That is up to you."

"What about you, would you like to come in and wait?"

"Let's do it."

Robert went to the garage and opened the single door. Ricki's Camaro was gone. Searching he found a paint can out of which he pulled a key. Opening the door, Robert called to Ricki, but the officer went in first with his gun drawn. Down stairs, the house was clean and ordered, as usual. Upstairs they found empty closets and pulled out drawers.

"She had left in a hurry," said Cabot standing behind officer.

"Do you know where she is going?" asked Jerome

"We have an address in Toledo, but my guess is she never went there. I think she is long gone.

"Detective Barbelli said she might be involved in a confidence ring. We don't see many of those."

"Someone must have called her. Is there any way to check on calls to her house?"

"Ma Bell will know."

"Bruce," said Robert looking a Cabot.

"Suppose we let the officer lock up the house, while I make some calls to Toledo."

"And, when nothing turns up?"

"You go on with your life."

"Back in my shell."

"What?"

"Nothing."

CHAPTER 13

FAMILY VISIT

It took a month for the police to close down the cases in Florida, Grosse Pointe, and Roseville. Most of the detectives involved believed Guy Jackson hired someone to kill Evert Yale and Joe Kaminski. They all agreed that the motive was obtaining the Bullseye, although no one could adequately explain why the club was so important. Left unanswered was how Lucy and Ricki fit into the story.

In Florida, the ADA decided to drop all the charges against Louise Weise except forging checks, for which she received a six-month sentence. In Michigan, Chief McKenna counseled Robert that he should be very careful for a while. As McKenna put, "Robert, you killed several bad men and put two in jail. These are men with friends, bad friends, friends who own guns. If I was you, I might sell the Bullseye and take a vacation or at the very least, keep a loaded gun nearby, at least for a while."

As soon as he was allowed, Robert reopened the Bullseye, hiring several out of work Vietnam vets to help with the club members and to watch Robert's back. Robert didn't try to find a gunsmith. He could handle the ammo and if a gun needed repair, he sent it out. With Joe gone, running the club was no longer fun for Robert. The quiet times were lonely. If he was honest with himself, he missed Ricki as much as he missed Joe. She had drawn him out of his shell and he missed how alive and normal he felt with Ricki.

It took five months for the court in Florida to process Evert Yale's estate. By then a judge in Michigan had cleared the estate of Jozef Kaminski. When Bruce Cabot received the final paperwork from the lawyer in Florida, he called Robert informing him that the Bullseye was his. Robert had already sold Joe's house and truck, and deposited what remained of the money recovered from Louise Weise so he was feeling rather secure, when Bruce called him with news.

"Robert, I had just had an interesting phone call."

"From who."

"I think the question is from whom."

"Yeah sorry, I didn't graduate from college, I went to Vietnam."

"Seriously, I have just spoken to a lawyer at the Department of Transportation."

"Caught you speeding."

"No, that's motor vehicles. The DOT are the folks who are building I696."

"Yes."

"Come on Robert, get excited."

"About what?"

"The Bullseye."

"What about it?"

"They need the land. They are going to move eleven mile, and your piece of property is a lynch pin. Without that little strip of land they can't build the exit to I94."

"What does that mean?"

"It means I just earned ten thousand dollars."

"Why?"

"Because that is three percent of three hundred thousand dollars, and that is what they are offering you for the land."

"Can we get more?"

"I can try, but I have to warn you, the state could just claim the land and only pay the tax value. I think the offer is more than fair."

"Is this what it was all about, someone killed Evert and Joe, because Evert owned land needed for a highway?"

"I think so. So what do you want me to do?"

"Call them back and tell them you will accept four hundred thousand. If they accept, I am prepared to sign the papers tomorrow."

In the end, the developer paid Robert three hundred and sixty thousand dollars for the three parcels of land between Bellear and Chippendale on Eleven Mile road. Land on which sat the Bullseye Rifle and Pistol Club.

A week later, Robert called a club meeting where he informed members that he was selling the club. Most of the members encouraged Robert to immediately open a new larger club somewhere on the east side of Detroit, and several of the wealthier members offered to help back the new club, but Robert said he was going to take some time off and get his bearings. He assured everyone the club would stay open for another month giving the members' time to find a new club and move their lockers. Time enough for Robert to pull back into his shell.

Robert sold the club's entire inventory and equipment to a new gun club in Royal Oak, at the same time turning down an offer to work there. A day later, Robert instructed Bruce to put his house on the market and in less than a month, the house was sold. Flush with cash and nowhere to live, and nothing to tie him down, Robert purchased a new Ford 150 truck and told Bruce Cabot he was going to visit his folks in Florida.

Driving to Florida gave Robert a chance to see America and a chance to clear his head. In Florida, he spent two days in Miami before driving to Naples. The neighborhood where his parents live is on the east side past airport road. Nice, but right on the fringe of being poor. His parents' house was already showing signs of disrepair. Once again, Robert's father had invested poorly. Caroline and Eric were happy to see Robert, until they saw the Ford truck packed with boxes.

That night went to dinner at Kelly's Fish House, and over drinks, Eric asked Robert about his plans. When Robert admitted he had no plans, that he was adrift, both his mother and father said he was welcome to stay with them, but everyone at the table knew that was a lie, and no one, including Robert wanted that to happen.

The next day, Robert moved the boxes from his truck to the covered porch but he didn't bother to unpack a single box. He was simply getting the boxes out of the daily shower that Naples received in the July. Sleeping late, Robert ate his usual three spoonfuls of peanut butter for breakfast and then spent the day walking the beach. Naples had one of the most beautiful beaches that Robert had ever seen.

In the center of the old down town, a pier extended out into the gulf. South of the pier Robert walked by huge mansions and cozy bungalows, all packed fifty feet apart along miles of public beach.

Robert had planned to spend a week with his parents, but he liked Naples and he loved the beach, and a week turned into a month, during which Robert found a gun club where he could shoot, a bar where he could drink, and a beach where he could forget. In Florida, he found a reason to come out of his shell.

One afternoon, Robert decided to drive to Sanibel Island. According to Caroline, people came from miles around to collect seashells on Sanibel and the mile long island of Captiva. The two islands also had several bars. On Captiva a new bar, the Mucky Duck had just opened in a converted beach house.

The Mucky Duck sat on the beach at the end of an unpaved road. Sitting on the beach drinking beer and eating shrimp at the Mucky Duck, Robert immediately understood the allure of island life. Digging his toes in the sand, he wondered what a house on Captiva would cost. Next door, they were building five new houses on stilts. Each faced the gulf, and each had an upper observation deck. Inside the restaurant, Robert found a phone book and looked up 'guns and ammo'. There were listings in Ft. Myers but none for Captiva or Sanibel. Thinking about the possibilities, Robert called Bruce Cabot from the restaurant and asked him to look into the process of licensing a gun club in Florida.

Robert walked across the street from the Mucky Duck to the construction site and spent half an hour talking to the builder. Driving around the few adjoining streets that made up the downtown, Robert wrote down the addressed of existing houses for sale and several sites where new houses were under construction. When he ran out of road, he drove back to Sanibel and did the same at the bridge end of the island.

Robert saw a sign for Ft. Myers and Cape Coral driving off the bridge and on an impulse, he decided look up Tom Wilson. Driving north on Highway 41, Robert stopped at a seven eleven to look up Tom's address and get a map. Crossing the bridge from Ft. Myers to Cape Coral, Robert turned off on the Hancock parkway quickly discovering that Cape Coral was a canal system with houses. Looking for 544 South East 4th street on the map, he saw the streets and avenue laid out in a grid. Fourth Street went across most of the city, but the street stopped and started again divided by canals. It took him thirty minutes to drive to Cape Coral and forty minutes to find the house a ranch style stucco home painted a color of pink they called coral. Behind the house, Robert saw a boat hoist and palm topped Tiki hut.

Robert considered putting his forty-five in his belt, except he was wearing shorts and a t-shirt. Leaving the gun under the seat, he stepped out into the three o'clock sun. Walking up to the house, Robert took off his sunglasses and knocked on a red door. Behind the door, a dog barked and then a woman's voice saying, "be quiet, be quiet Liebchen." Before opening the door, the woman looked out through a peephole in the door. Robert thought he heard the woman say, "Gott im Himmel!" and then the dog started barking again until the door opened and Tom Wilson stepped out forcing Robert to step back off the porch.

"Robert, what on earth are you doing here?"

"Hello Tom. I am visiting my folks. I took the risk and just dropped in. I hope that isn't a problem. I had lunch on Sanibel and decided to look you up, but maybe I am interrupting something."

"No, not exactly, I am entertaining a lady friend, so maybe we should get together another day, how long are you going to be in Florida?"

"Gee, I am not sure. I have been thinking of staying, I really like Sanibel and Captiva."

"Great, let's set a day to get together in Naples. I know a great place for lunch. Do you know the Riverwalk in Tin City?"

"I do actually."

"Great, how about a morning of fishing and then lunch at the Riverwalk?"

"That would be great."

"How about tomorrow, say at eight in the morning. Park in Tin City and I'll meet you at the Riverwalk dock. We can go into the bay. I know a great spot to fish for snapper."

"Sorry about not inviting you in kid, but you know how it is?"

"I sure do Tom. No problem, fishing sounds great, just like the old days on Lake St. Clair."

"Sure, sure, see you tomorrow."

* * *

Tom Wilson stepped back inside and closed the peeling red door. Wilson remained at the door watching Robert through the peephole as he walked to his truck and drove away. Behind him, Louise Weise was holding a small dog by the muzzle.

"What will we do?" Behind her standing in the hallway with a .22 Cal pistol in her hand, Fredericka Weise put the gun back on safe.

"You'll have to kill him, before he figures it out," said Ricki.

"He already knows," said Louise.

"No honey, if that boy had figured it out, he would have…"

"What will he do?" asked Ricki her hand shaking. "Because I saw what he did in Detroit."

"Shut up, I don't want to hear about it again."

"Maybe you should, because after he killed Ray, after he shot that beautiful man, while the police were upstairs cleaning up all the blood from my living room floor, do you know what Robert did."

"Honey, you told me. You told us both."

"Perhaps I need to remind you. He fucked me," she shouted. "He walked down stairs and fucked me while the cops were carrying Ike out on a gurney. He fucked me. He had just killed a man and his dick was as hard as a rock because he likes killing. For him death and sex go together."

"Ricki, I can handle this."

"Yea, that is what you told Mom right before they closed the cell door. That is what you told Guy and Ray. You said it would be easy, now they are both dead."

"Honey, you know I am sorry about all of this. Tomorrow, Robert and I will go fishing. Father and son. After that, no more Robert. For now, let's all have a drink and then we will go out for some dinner."

Robert parked the truck three blocks away. Sitting in the truck with the windows down, he thought about the woman behind the door. "Be quiet Liebchen," he remembered her saying. Liebchen was German for dear or sweetheart. Lucy Meadows use to call Joe, her Liebchen. Robert put his hands on either side of his head, trying to remove the pain as he wiped sweat from his crew cut.

"It all made sense," he thought. The pieces locked in place. Tom Wilson and Lucy Meadows were partners with Guy Jackson. Somehow, they learned the Bullseye was sitting on land the new freeway needed. Perhaps Tom tried to buy the club from Evert Yale, but Evert said no. He tells Tom Wilson that one day he plans to sell the club to Joe, and he mentions his will and Tom starts thinking about a sweetheart swindle. All he needs is the right woman.

Robert could not be sure, but he knew Guy owned the house where Ricki lived in Grosse Pointe and he was certain Lucy Meadows was living with Wilson. Thinking about Lucy made Robert think about Ricki. Was she in the house with the red door? For a moment, he pictured her fucking Tom Wilson, but that was more than he could tolerate. Robert realized if she showed up tomorrow saying it was all a big mistake, he would want to believe her. He would crawl out of his shell and embrace her, saying, "Thank God you are back."

Before crossing the bridge out of Coral Gables, he pulled in into the seven eleven where he had purchased the map. At an outside phone booth, he placed a long distance collect call to Bruce Cabot. Bruce answered and immediately started talking about gun clubs in Florida but Robert stopped him, by saying, "Lucy Meadows is living with Tom Wilson."

"Say that again."

"I just left Tom Wilson's house, he said he was entertaining a woman friend. She was Lucy Meadows."

"Are you sure? You saw her? What did you do?"

"I didn't see her, but I heard her, I know it was her. It all makes sense, Tom was the missing piece. My guess is Guy or one of his boys killed Evert, but Tom was involved and Joe had to die, because he knew Tom was involved.

"What about Ricki?"

"I don't want to think about Ricki, but my guess is she is staying there too. It doesn't matter. What is important is making the connection between Joe's murder and Tom Wilson and Guy Jackson."

"No, Robert, that isn't what is important. It doesn't matter. What matters is getting on with your life. Forget about Tom. Go ahead with what you told me the other day. Find a house on Captiva, start a new club. Start a new life. Forget about Tom. Forget about Lucy and Ricki."

"I wish I could. But, now that they know I am here in Naples, I think they will they have to do something."

"Maybe they will run."

"It is possible, but even if they do. I don't want to go to bed every night wondering if this is the night Tom sends a couple of boys who owe him. One way or another, it needs to end."

"What are you going to do?"

"I am going fishing."

"That is crazy."

"It may be, so will you to do me a favor."

"Anything,"

"Tomorrow is Friday. If you don't hear from me by Saturday, I want you to file a missing persons report and give this new information to the Naples Police."

"Why not do that now. Call that Sergeant Hill. Get the police get involved, let them investigate Tom Wilson. You need to move on with your life."

"Bruce, for years I thought my life ended when I was a boy. Then Tom gave me a new life, he made me look out of my shell and then Joe and the club and Ricki drew me further out. Because of them, I nearly left my shell, I nearly became a real person, but I am back inside, going nowhere, with my arms and legs tucked in, and my eyes the only thing visible. I cannot go back to living this way."

"Robert, let's drop the Psychology 101. If you kill Tom, you will be trading your psychic shell for a jail cell. They will lock you away."

"Maybe I need to be."

"Robert, take my advice. Leave Naples. Find another beach. Find a different island and start your life over. Let me call the locals."

"No, I have a date to go fishing. Remember, wait until Saturday. If you don't hear from me, call the cops. Oh, and one other thing."

"What?"

"I left a letter in case of my death. It is in my safe deposit box in Michigan. If you don't hear from me, I want you call the cops, but you have to promise me, you will wait a year, before you open the letter. It has my final instructions."

"Robert, this is crazy. I can be in Ft. Myers tomorrow afternoon. We can do this together, no guns, no violence."

"Bruce, you are a good lawyer and you are a good friend. Remember, wait a year." Robert hung up, and walked back into the Seven Eleven and asked the grizzled old man behind the counter if he knew of a good gun shop. After getting directions, Robert asked how long it took a boat to make it down to Naples. Back at home, he found a box marked G & A that he carried into his room.

* * *

Tin City turned out to be a collection of tourist shops located next to the marina on Naples Bay. They were meeting at the Riverwalk Ale House, located at the southeast corner of Tin City. The Riverwalk opened at 10:00 a.m., but at 7:00 a.m., there was a line of people, mostly in their fifties, waiting to board Captain Marty's sightseeing boat for a morning of shell collecting and sunbathing. By the time Captain Marty's boat returned, the shops would be open so sun burned northerner could buy shells from Indonesia.

Robert sat at one of the boardwalk tables outside of the Ale House drinking black coffee from a paper cup. On the back of Captain Marty's boat, Robert read the name "Marty's Party." The Captain was in his fifties, dressed in blue jeans and a t-shirt that said

Riverwalk Ale House. Captain Marty looked to Robert as if he spent most of his nights at the Ale House. Helping him were two teenage boys, most likely his sons.

"Are you going with us Mister," asked the older of the two boys.

"No, I am going fishing." Robert shaded his eyes to look at the boy. At fourteen, he already was taking on features of his father, leather skin, squinting eyes, sweat stained baseball cap.

"Well, good luck." The boy ran to the end of the dock making ready to cast off the bowline.

Robert was wearing khaki shorts with a swimsuit underneath instead of underwear. For a shirt, he had on a t-shit he had purchased in Ohio at a competition. The front of the shirt had a four-inch bullseye target printed on the front where most shirts had a pocket. For shoes, Robert was wearing a battered pair of tennis shoes he had worn fishing since he was twenty. Under the table, Robert had a rucksack with a thermos of coffee, a bottle of water, and four donuts wrapped in wax paper. Wrapped in aluminum foil, Robert had a Colt .45 with a loaded clip. The package looked like sandwiches.

After Captain Marty left the harbor, Robert walked down the marina dock checking out the cabin cruisers, speed boats, and fishing boats. The Bayside Maria contained a mix of private and commercial boats. Robert thought if he survived, he might buy a boat.

At 7:52 a.m., an open boat with a center counsel motored up to the dock. The 24-foot boat was built to take rough offshore waters. It was large enough in the stern to bring in fish as large as grouper. The boat had built-in bait wells and fish lockers. Above the center counsel, an aluminum and canvas t-top provided shade for the man at the counsel. Putting the boat in reverse, Tom Wilson ran forward and tossed Robert a line.

Tying the boat to the dock, Robert noticed the boat even had gunnels rod holders. "Sweet boat, Tom."

"Thanks kid. I think so too. I named her Liebchen, which means sweetheart in German."

"Yes, I know."

"Ready?"

"Sure, let me get my bag. I brought coffee and donuts."

"Perfect, I brought chips and beer." Wilson moved back to the center counsel. Robert picked up his bag and untied the line on the dock. Stepping on the boat. He hesitated. "Was he really going out alone with the man who sent men to kill him? Was this going to be the end of the story? One or both men dying out in some back water glade?"

"Step in or step out Robert, you know the rule."

"In for a penny," said Robert stepping over the gunnels into the fishing boat. "Where are we headed?"

"The waters between Naples and Marco Island are filled with canals and backwater bays and channels, mangroves and inter-coastal bays and creeks. This time of year, I know a spot where we should find Pompano, Jacks, Snapper, and Black Drum. Great eating fish."

"Want some coffee?"

"No, let me get us out of here. Find a place to stow your gear. I have coffee cups in the cubby up front, you can pour me some coffee while I steer."

They motored south out of Naples Bay into the intercostals. Clear of the no wake zone, Tom follow the coastline pointing out several of the new mansions before they entered Dollar Bay.

"It is all river ways and a series of bays from here to the everglades. All the way to Marco Island and then on to the keys. Nothing but waterways and canals. Ideal for fishing." Tom pointed to a line of Snowy Egrets and Heron. Enjoying the picture, Robert smiled at the natural beauty around them.

"How far will we go?"

"In about five miles, we enter a large bay called Rockery Bay. At the end of the bay is Henderson Creek. There are a bunch of little islands and sandbars coming off the creek. Ideal for Pompano. The nice thing about Henderson Creek is you can drive close to it even if you don't have a boat. In the future, if you ever feel like a little fishing you will know where to come. Today we will go a bit further, a place you can only get to by boat." Wilson drove the boat with still and care. His eyes never leaving the waterway.

Robert handed Tom a coffee cup half filled. While Wilson focused on driving the boat, Robert moved to the bow of the boat where he sat in a padded fishing seat. The day was already warm. All along the mangrove coast, flocks of winter birds were feeding. Once again, Robert thought this was where he belonged. After half an hour, Wilson slowed the boat, pointing out a number of parked trucks.

"We are in Half Bay. That is Shell Island Road. Up there is Henderson Creek. South of here is Marco Island. If you like, we can go out through the sand bar and come back on the ocean side. But now, we should do some fishing."

"This is great. I really love it here. You are a lucky man Tom," said Robert pointing to islands and sandbars. "This boat, your home on the canal. Paradise." Robert truly meant what he said. He loved the area and being on the water fishing with an old friend. For a moment, he was at peace. In his heart, he hoped all they would do is fish.

"All this is nearly perfect."

"It feels that way sometimes," said Tom putting the boat in neutral. "When I moved down here I was running away from Michigan. I landed here almost by accident. I had a friend who grew up in Naples, before it was a resort town. I came here because of her, and stayed. You know how I loved to fish. In Michigan, you have to either rent a slip in a marina or trailer a fucking boat. Here, I live right on a canal with my boat tied up to my own dock. God, it is paradise. If you wanted to, you could work a full job and still fish every day."

For a moment more, Robert shared Tom's love of fishing and being on the water. "So, what are we going to catch today?" asked Robert.

"Snappers. If we are lucky, Lane or Yellow tail. Maybe Mangrove Snapper. Tough fish to catch but one of the best tasting fish. Mangrove snappers like to hide around piers and bridges, but they also like to sit in the flow." Wilson set an anchor and let the boat drift until the anchor took hold. Turning the engine off, he took two rods from built in holders on either side of the center counsel. Taking the rods to the stern, he opened a bait box and took out a sardine. Breaking the fish in half, he baited each hook with half a sardine. "The oil from the sardines will attract the snappers downstream."

Moving to the bow, he cast the bait out in the center of a narrow flow. Taking up is rod, Robert had to cast several times before he dropped the hook in the same area. The two men settled in sitting in the bow waiting for a strike. They had fished together many times before, often with Jozef Kaminski making it a threesome.

After twenty minutes, Tom caught the first snapper, a four-pound yellow tail. Putting his rod in a holder and carried the dying fish to the stern ice locker. Opening the locker Tom appeared to move items around before putting the fish in the ice chest. Watching Tom at the locker, Robert expected he would come back with a gun in his hand, but instead, he had two Miller Lites.

Opening the beers, he handed one to Robert. Sitting back down, he sighed. "How did it come to this Robert?"

"You have to tell me, Tom. Because I don't understand most of what has happened."

"What do you understand?"

"I am assuming that when I visited you yesterday the reason you didn't invited me in was because Lucy Meadows was behind the door."

"Louise, her name is Louise Weise."

"So how do you know Louise?"

"I met Louise when I was working Bunco in Detroit. She was a suspect in a sweetheart swindler. When I picked her up, I was getting ready to leave the Detroit PD for the Grosse Pointe PD. I had some trouble in Detroit. I was broke, my wife had just left, and I was lonely. Louise may not seem that attractive now, to someone your age, but she was really something fifteen years ago, and she made me an offer. I was thirty-five and she was thirty, but she looked like she was twenty-one. For a while it was all hot and heavy, all passion and sex. After a while, we developed what you might call a working relationship. I would identify possible targets and she would work the swindle."

"How did that work?"

"It's an old story. An attractive woman uses sex to swindle money out of a wealthy old man. In Louise' case she would meet a man and pretend to be fresh off the plane from Deutschland. She would accidentally meet a target at some German American festival or some public event and hook the guy. They would have one or two dates ending in sex. Certainly, the best sex the guy ever had, I can attest to that. Then she'd tell the guy she was being deported because she owed money in Germany. She would convince him that if she could pay off her debt, she would be free to stay with the man in the states. At her best, she took one old guy for one hundred and fifteen thousand dollars. With the money we earned, I was able to buy property in Florida and Michigan. That is how I met Guy Jackson."

"So why go after Joe? He wasn't rich."

"Actually, Joe was the perfect type of mark, good sized nest egg, lonely old man, and a foreigner. But not really in Louise's class."

"Come on Tom, why put Lucy on Joe? Why not Evert?"

"Look, I am sorry about Joe. Guy heard about the freeway from a friend in the planning commission in Roseville. He saw on a map the land they would need. When he drove by, he finds the Bullseye."

"So he drops in with some friends."

"Right, he drops in and he likes you right away. However, Evert and Joe were another story. Evert was a cracker from way back, and Joe was just as bad, calling Guy a nigger."

"So you decide to kill Evert and Joe."

"No you have it all wrong. We tried to use honey. Guy tried to use honey on Evert, but he didn't bite. I never suspected, but now I think Evert may have been a homo."

"Come on he has kids."

Listen, I've seen plenty of married men picking up boys on the streets in Detroit. Whatever the reason, Evert wasn't interested, so Guy had a lawyer in Detroit offered him forty thousand in cash, but he wouldn't sell. We went as high as fifty thousand."

"Sure, because you knew that it was worth seven times that."

"Right, but that was all the cash Guy had at the time and time was running out. Unfortunately, Evert told Guy's lawyer he planned to sell the club to Joe, so Guy sent in Louise play Joe."

"Meaning you always planned to kill Evert."

"No, the plan was for Louise to work on Joe, and through Joe get Evert to sell the Club."

"What happened?"

"Evert turned Joe down and Joe went home."

"Who killed Evert?"

"I assume it was someone Guy hired. It might have been Ray."

"But you didn't?"

"Robert, I swear on the blood of Christ, I did not kill Evert Yale. I liked the old guy."

"What about Lucy, could she have killed Evert?"

"No, Louise had nothing to do with Evert or Joe. I promise you that. The plan was to get Joe to come down and visit Evert. Guy put up the money, but Lucy told Joe she wanted to combine her savings with his to buy the Club. She suggested the holiday in Florida and had him primed to get Evert to sell the club. I was convinced that if Joe owned the club she could get him to sell, but Guy was impatient. On Saturday, Joe had dinner with Evert. When he came back, he said the deal was off."

"Why didn't Lucy go with him?"

"Louise should have been at the dinner, but she had met Evert before."

"She was the honey."

"It doesn't matter. According to Joe, he asked Evert if he was ready to sell, but Evert told Joe when he died Joe and you would inherit the club, but not before. He said he needed the income. Evert kept asking 'what's the hurry?' Apparently, Joe told Evert that he had asked Louise to marry him, but said she would only marry Joe if he had an income they could depend on. Joe admitted that he told Evert that it was Lucy who was pushing him to buy the club. From what Joe told Louise, about the dinner, I wonder if Evert got wise. Anyway, he told Joe, Lucy would have to wait!" Wilson let more line out and then slowly reeled it in before finishing his beer.

"I think I have lost the bait," he said reeling in the line. "These snapper are very good at taking bait off a hook. Apparently something like that happened during their dinner. I don't know, but Evert told Joe he thought Louise was playing him. He told Joe flat out she was after his money. When Joe got back to the hotel, he said he was going home alone, and losing her temper, Louise said he could go without her. I guess she thought Joe was off the hook and a few days without her would set him back on."

"Did she kill Evert?"

"No, she was with me."

"Did Guy kill Evert?"

"Guy was in Detroit."

"What about Joe? Who killed Joe?"

"I assume it was Guy or one of his men, because Louise was in Florida with me when Joe died."

"Tom, Joe was shot in the head by someone working for you."

"Working for Guy. I never told anyone to kill Joe."

"No, but you knew about Evert's will and you knew about Joe's will. With Joe and me dead, it would go to Lucy."

"Kid, I think Guy's plan was for Joe to be found dead, an apparent suicide. In the house the police would find evidence that tied Joe to Evert's murder and that would invalidate the club going to Joe or you. All we had to do was wait, but…"

"What evidence?"

"The gun. Evert and Joe were both shot with the same gun."

"How do you know that?"

"Guy planned it. I think Guy expected the police to buy the murder suicide, but fall back was to blame you. Guy always thought he was so smart. I told him we just needed to wait. Let the club go to Joe and you."

"So, the plan was to make the police think Joe killed Evert and then Joe killed himself or I killed Joe."

"Guys plan."

"So what happened?"

"The Note. It was a mistake. Plus, your lawyer started talking to the police."

"How does Bruce fit into this?"

"After Louise learned Evert was dead, she tried to have Joe sign over his power of attorney. With that, she could sell the land before Joe knew what was happening. You should see Louise in a closing. She has sold more property she didn't own than you could believe."

"Sell to you, to Southeastern Properties Inc.?"

"Sure, that was the plan. Louise gave Joe several checks to sign along with blank a power of attorney form. She was sure Joe would sign them, but Joe called someone in Detroit who told him to sign nothing and come home."

"When was that?"

"Monday morning."

"So Joe flew back in Detroit, and a day later he is dead. Killed by Guy Jackson."

"More likely Sugar Ray or one of the other boys."

"Are you saying one of those fight ring boys killed Joe and left a note? That is pretty thin."

"Perhaps, but when I talked with you on Thursday morning, that was the first I had heard about Joe. I called Guy and when I asked him about Joe, he said he did not want to talk over the phone. I told him I was going to call you at the club. My guess is that is when he called his boys and ordered the hit on you. When that failed, he got personally involved."

"Tom I would like to believe you, but, the pieces don't fit. Especially not about Joe."

"I am sorry kid, but it's the truth." Wilson set his rod down and asked Robert if he wanted another beer? Robert said he was going to have coffee instead, so Tom walked back to get a beer while Robert went to retrieve his rucksack in the front cubby. Robert pulled the thermos out of the pack and then turned with the thermos in his left hand and the pack in his right. At the stern of the boat, Tom stood by an open ice locker with a revolver in his hand.

"I'm so sorry kid," he said as he pulled the trigger. At the same time, Robert fired the Colt .45 from inside the rucksack; the bullet hit Tom in the chest. Tom's shot missed Robert's forehead by inches. Tom had gone for a headshot, a kill, but Robert was moving. Robert had simply wanted to stop Tom, he made a sure shot, the chest; Tom lived long enough to make it back to the marina.

Robert radioed ahead on the emergency channel; informing the authorities there had been an accident and a man was shot. Robert used toweling to put a pressure bandage on the chest wound. Fortunately, they had followed a straight path south. Returning was merely a matter of watching for markers. It took an hour with Tom going in and out of consciousness. When he was conscious, he kept saying, "I am so sorry, so sorry."

When they pulled up to the temporary dock outside the Riverwalk, the police were waiting with an ambulance. After removing Tom, two uniformed policemen questioned Robert. Ten minutes later, a detective sergeant arrived.

"Mr. Cederberg, I am Detective Sergeant Hill." Martin Hill was a Hispanic man in his forties, at one time athletic, he had a barrel chest, large hooked nose and a poor comb over.

"I wondered when you would show."

"What do you mean?"

"We talked on the phone. I was one of the detectives on the Yale case. I happened to be there when Louise Weise was arrested. I had a chance to speak with a lieutenant up north in Detroit who had quite a lot to say about you. As I recalled, you shot four men in Michigan. And now you have shot another man, in my jurisdiction."

"It was self defense; he pulled a gun and shot at me."

"And, you just happened to have a gun with you. You were out with Mister Wilson, fishing, and you took a Colt .45, just in case."

"He had a revolver."

"Yes, and lucky for you he didn't throw it over the side."

"Sergeant, I visited Tom Wilson yesterday. I discovered Lucy Meadows, I mean Weise, living at Tom Wilson's house. Tom asked me to go fishing. I was hoping all we would do was fish, but I knew Tom was involved in what happened to Evert Yale. I found out yesterday he was involved with Lucy Meadows. Because of this, I was concerned

Tom might try to kill me and dump my body in some bay. I brought a pistol just in case. If you like, call my Lawyer. You will find I told him all of this yesterday."

"So why not call the police."

"I was hoping it would not come to this."

"Actually, Mister Cederberg, we knew Lucy Weise was staying with Wilson. We questioned Wilson twice. I was present for the second interview. He was a cop, he knew all the tricks. He had an answer and alibi for everything, but I knew he was bad. If you spend enough time in the police, you can smell a bad cop. I talked to a Sergeant at Cape Coral DP. Wilson left the force before he was arrested. Apparently, his name came up in too many break-ins. He was suspected of targeting homes for a group of thieves. We also connected him with a confidence team, but the judge wasn't' convinced and a warrant fell through. My guess is he got wind of what was coming down and left on half a pension. He was a smart guy, a planner. He used others to do his dirty work. So why take you out himself? Why not just shoot you down in the street? According to you, you fished for an hour before he made his move. Why?"

"I think he wanted to explain. For a while, when I was young, Tom was like a father to me. I think he wanted to talk, he wanted me to understand. We were friends, I don't think he could just kill me in cold blood, he wanted me to understand why."

"And, do you?" asked Hill. They were sitting in the bow of the fishing boat. A team was collecting evidence in the stern. Robert had a length of line that he kept looping. Robert wasn't sure if he was under arrest. Everything depended on what this policeman believed.

"He said Guy Jackson hired someone to kill Evert Yale, and I believe that, but he said he didn't order the hit on Evert or Joe Kaminski, or the attacks on me, he said it was all planned by Guy. I think that was a lie. I think he wanted me to trust him, or maybe he just could not admit the truth. I have known for months he had to be involved."

"Why?"

"Because Tom was the only person who knew I was at Ricki William's house, and yet the hit team showed up there."

"Well, seems to me, if a man isn't at home, he will be at his girl friend, if they had been watching you, going to your girl friend's house might make sense."

"Yeah, I thought that too. However, why not wait outside the house, or just wait at my house? I mean if you hit me at Ricki's house doesn't that mean you have to kill Ricki. Then I understood. Ricki was never in danger, because she was a part of the swindle. When I was on the phone with Tom, she all but shouted out her name. And when I went back home, she had plenty of time to call Tom or Guy."

"When I look back at everything that happened, the one person who knew everything before it happened was Ricki Williams."

"And where is she now?"

"My guess is she and Louise are waiting for Tom at his house in Cape Coral. Either that or they are gone already."

"And, do you plan to shoot them too? If I release you, is that where you are headed? Should I call the police up there and send a car to protect them?"

"I have never killed a woman, and I am not anxious to start. If Ricki Williams came up to me, claiming it was all a big mistake, I'd probably take her back."

"Did you love her that much?"

"I did." Robert watched gulls circling above Captain Marty's boat as it eased into the dock. The line of tourists all stopping to look at the boat tied to the Riverwalk's boardwalk. Several sun burned women pointed to the blood at the back of the fishing boat. For reasons, he could not explain, Robert started to cry.

"Robert, you know she is a confidence artist. She is just a younger version of Louise. She sleeps with men and then she robs them. She is a prostitute and a thief, and now we know, Wilson named her as an accessory to felony murder. For all you know, she pulled the trigger on your friend Joe. If we pick her up in Naples, she will be arrested."

"No, actually Tom only mentioned Louise, but I know you are right. I have no doubts that Ricki is what you say, maybe worse."

"Robert, I am going to take you down to the station. You are going to write down what happened this morning. Explain what happened here and in Michigan. I am going to have you tell the whole story to my Lieutenant and to the Captain. My guess is when you are done, telling your story, they will let you go, provided your permit to carry that gun checks out."

"About the gun,"

"What about the gun?"

"I know it sounds strange, but I would like it back. I used to think it was a lucky gun, I used it in competitions."

"Not what I'd call a very lucky gun. Look, Robert, our policy is to keep all weapons involved in murder. If it were me, I'd buy a new target gun and leave this one with the police. Why keep a gun that killed you friends?"

"I can't really explain it, but if it is possible, I want it back."

"Ok, I'll talk to my Lieutenant, and he can decide about the gun." Robert and Sergeant Hill left the boat and drove to the police station in Robert's truck. When they asked his address, he gave his parents, but asked they not be contacted. By six that evening, Robert had talked to five different policemen, including a Lieutenant and Captain along with the district attorney.

While he told and retold his story, Sergeant Hill sent a detective to Cape Coral where he was met by a Sergeant and a uniformed officer waiting at Tom Wilson's home. With weapons drawn, they knocked on the front door, but on entering the house, they found it empty, in fact, it looked like someone had packed clothes out of two bedroom closets and fled in a hurry, leaving a bra, a pair of women's jeans, and a bathroom full of female products, lipstick, hair stray, and perfume. On the kitchen table, they found two coffee mugs with different colors of lipstick on each mug.

The Naples Police let Robert go at seven that night. For six hours, they questioned him repeatedly about Tom Wilson's admissions on the boat. Each time Robert asked about Wilson, he was told that Wilson was alive but his condition was critical. From Robert's perspective, the police seemed very concerned about what Robert would do next. His impression was they thought he was on vendetta, when all Robert wanted was to sit in the sun and chill out.

Robert's parents were sitting in the family room watching television when he got home. The family room had once been the garage, but wanting more space, the previous owner had replaced the garage door with a sliding door making the room a family room and laundry. The family room had all new furniture, green with floral prints; it was the room that looked the most like Florida. According to his father, the shooting had been reported on the news, describing it as an accident, but Eric said he knew better.

"That cop did this to you. I never liked him," Eric said giving Robert an unfamiliar hug. "I knew this fascination you have with guns would end badly. I told your mother, 'Thank god the club is closed,' and then I see that box in your bedroom. So, is it over now? Can we get on with our lives?"

"Dad," Robert began, "I had to shoot one of my oldest friends. I spent the day in the police station. I am tired and hungry; I need an aspirin. Can we talk about this tomorrow?"

"Of course son, tomorrow is soon enough. And…"

"What is it Dad?"

"Well, your mother wanted me to ask when you think you might be leaving."

"Soon, tell her very soon."

CHAPTER 14

LOOSE ENDS

Seeing Captiva convinced Robert he wanted to live in southwest Florida and start a new gun club. Not knowing what else to do, Robert used the Yellow Pages to find a list of Realtors. One was called Island Realtors. Walking in, Robert was under impressed but once he spoke with, Ellen Benzinger, he was sure he had the right person. Ellen was short, with dyed blond hair and looked like she weighed more than two hundred pounds, but when she talked about real estate she became a dynamo. What caught Robert's attention was her knowledge of commercial properties as well as beachfront. What closed the deal was her pulling a .38 automatic out of her purse and pledging to be the club's first member.

Before they set out to find a house, they focused on finding the site for a gun range. Sitting in the Sunshine Café on Ft. Myers Beach Ellen pulled out an area map with red circles indicating the existing gun clubs. Most of the clubs were in Ft. Myers and considerably inland. There was one club in Naples, and while Robert loved the city, he was determined to live far enough away from his parents they would forget about him. Robert had hoped to locate a building on Sanibel, but Ellen doubted the city council would approve and she questioned why anyone would pay the bridge toll just to shoot a gun.

Their search for a commercial space or property began on Estero drive on Ft. Myers beach. The property values were high, but the flow of tourist might be important. While they were looking for a commercial location, Ellen also showed homes on the beach and homes off the beach. According to Ellen, there were great buys on several of the new golf courses and off beaches like Vanderbilt beach or in cities like Bonita Springs. As an experienced Realtor, she understood how buyers wanted something on the beach, but eventually their pocketbook and practicality took over and they purchased a larger home inland. Robert was different. He wanted isolation and a shelter.

On their second day, Ellen showed Robert a large storefront property on Estero drive. The building had a large parking lot and according to Ellen, the adjacent lot was available for a good price. Robert thought the location was ideal, but everything would depend on getting a license to sell guns.

Robert spent a day filling out forms and answering questions at the Ft. Myer police station. Naturally, he was concerned that the shooting in Naples would end any application, but the officer in charge spoke to Detective Hill in Naples, and assured Robert his application would be approved.

Robert spent three days visiting houses and condominiums. Ellen tried to convince him to look at condominiums on the beach, but he said he wanted a house on Captiva even though it would mean a half hour drives and crossing the bridge every day. Finally, Robert took Ellen to Andy Rosse Lane for a beer at the Mucky Duck. The house closest to the restaurant was nearly finished. When Robert saw the white washed house, surrounded by palm trees and Florida scrub, he knew this was a house for him and Ellen agreed.

Robert knew that living on an island was crazy, crossing on the bridge cost three dollars and most of the homes would be damaged or destroyed if a hurricane hit, but he was determined. Once he had decided where to work and where to live, Robert was anxious to get on with his life, but the mortgage company and title company said it would take a month to close on the commercial property and on the house, so Robert moved into the Sunshine motel on Ft. Myers Beach.

The next morning, Robert had coffee and eggs next door to the Sunshine motel at the Sunshine diner. Using the pay phone, he called the Naples hospital to check on Tom Wilson. According to the nurse on duty, Tom had died three days after being admitted. She said she heard that arrangements had been made by the Cape Coral policemen's association, and Mister Wilson was being buried in Cape Coral. She did not know when or where, but she said it would have to be soon. Hanging up the phone, Robert sat on his motel bed and wanted to cry but he could not. Instead, he made calls tracking down the funeral home taking care of Tom's burial.

In October, the weather could be very mild. The day of Tom's burial was cool for Florida and overcast, a gray day for a sad event. Coral Ridge Cemetery was on Pine Island Road, north of the city, a path of green in the middle of the America's largest network of canals. Robert stopped at the funeral home for directions to the gravesite. The woman at the front desk said they were burying Mister Wilson at 2:30 p.m. Checking his watch, Robert saw he was an hour early. Driving his truck through the grounds, Robert found the spot but seeing the casket was not there yet, his rolled down the passenger window and sat back in the truck seat to wait.

Robert awoke to the sound of the hearse. Wiping salt from his eyes, Robert watched two men set the casket on a wheeled cart and push it up a slight rise to the open grave. There was a canopy over the grave and chairs set out for mourners. One of four chairs was already taken by a woman. Greeting the woman, the men from the funeral home rolled the casket in place, setting it on the mechanism used to lower the casket.

A man walked up to the casket and sat down beside the woman. Robert spent a minute watching them. The two talked for several minutes and then the woman got up and walked with the man in the direction of Robert's truck. As they got closer, Robert saw the man was Detective Hill from the Naples Police Department. The woman looked familiar to Robert.

Stepping out of his truck, Robert said, "Good afternoon Detective." Turning to the red headed woman, Robert said "Mam," and tipped his ball cap.

"Robert, don't you recognize Lucy Meadows, I mean Louise Weise, or is it Louise Wilson. I understand you told the funeral director you were Tom's wife."

"Lucy. Is that really you?" asked Robert pretending surprise.

"Murderer," screamed Louise.

"Lucy, I am sorry about Tom. He didn't give me a choice."

"Why did you come here? Why didn't you call first? Tom, he loved you, you verdammt schildkröte. I spent six months in jail because of you, but Tom said we were to leave you alone? He did not want to hurt you. Even though you got the money, he said you had been through enough. Then you show up at the house; you had to surprise him. Did you know all along?"

"I have known for quite a while now. My lawyer found out that Tom and Guy owned Southeast Properties. He found out Southeast owned Ricki's house in Grosse Pointe and a lot of other land. He also learned that a lawyer representing Southeast Properties made inquiries about the Bullseye but Evert turned them down." Louise stood with her legs apart. She had on white pants and a shirt with prints of flowers and birds. On her feet were gold sandals. Close up it was obvious that she was older than fifty and that her hair was dyed.

"Lucy, I never wanted this, I don't even care about what you did to me, but you and Tom set up Joe." Robert looked at the casket sitting alone under the black mesh canopy.

"That is a lie. We had nothing to do with any death. Guy Jackson killed Joe. He broke into Joe's house and killed him."

"That isn't what Tom said. You see, I was there when the police went into Joe's house. It was locked. No break in. Whoever shot Joe used a key or Joe let the killer in. Either way, Joe knew his killer."

"He knew Guy."

"Guy didn't kill Joe and neither did Ray."

"How can you know?"

"Two reasons. First, Joe Kaminski would never have let Guy or Sugar Ray Jackson in his house, even at gunpoint. However, he let the killer in. because he knew her. Where is she Louise? Where is Ricki?"

"You said two reasons," said Louise ignoring the question.

"Right something Tom didn't know. You see, the ammo clip in the gun that killed Joe had a fingerprint, and so did several bullets in the clip. When the police checked, the prints were not Joe's or mine, not Tom's and not any of Guy's boys including Guy. That leaves you and Ricki."

Detective Hill used that moment to take Louise's handbag. Opening it, he found a roll of money and a .25 automatic. The gun alone was enough to send her back in jail for five years.

"Yesterday Detective Hill had a chance to check the prints he had on file for you and Ricki against the print card they sent from Detroit. It was a match."

"It means nothing, Joe gave me the gun to load and I loaded it for him. That does not mean I killed Evert or him. Besides, I was here. I was with Tom."

"Perhaps, but Tom is dead and your prints were on the bullets in the gun that killed Evert Yale and Joe Kaminski."

"Strictly, circumstantial."

"But enough to charge you, said Hill. "Louise Weise, I am arresting you as an accessory in the murder of Evert Yale."

"But, I didn't kill him. Guy Jackson killed him."

"How do you know?" asked Hill.

"He admitted to Tom that he killed Yale and Joe Kaminski."

"Unfortunately, Mister Jackson and Tom Wilson are both dead, and I have you loading the bullets that killed Yale and Joe Kaminski." Hill took off his dark glasses, giving Louise a hard look. "I don't like murderers and I don't like women who prey on wealthy old men. Maybe you didn't shoot Evert Yale, but I am pretty sure you have killed other men, so all I am doing is closing the circle."

"What are you talking about?" demanded Louise.

"When a murder is committed, my job is to close the case, to solve the crime and catch the killer. It is the DA and the court's job to see that justice is done, to insure that the criminal pays for his or her crime. Taken together, I like to say we close the circle."

"Unfortunately, as you know," Hill tipped his hat to Louise, "the DA and courts don't always do their job and circle is left open. But, I have a theory that sooner or later we all have to pay for our crimes and I think the circle is closing in on you Louise, and one day soon it will close in on Ricki Williams." Hill pulled out a pair of handcuffs putting them on Louise, before pointing her to a squad car that was waiting.

In planning for today's arrest, Hill told Robert that he had warrants for both Louise and Ricki if they showed. When Hill told Robert they were keeping the Colt 1911, he mentioned that both the gun clip and bullets had been wiped clean. Like any professional, Robert had checked the clip in the Colt 1911 before taking it to kill Tom Wilson. The gun was one of several guns Robert used in competition. Unlike his Walther or his service pistol, the Colt 1911 had no memories and no history. He assumed if the meeting with Tom went as he expected, he would be arrested by the Naples police and have to turn the gun over to the police. Nonetheless, he had been careful to wipe the bullets and clip just in case he could walk away from Tom.

Joe Kaminski's killer had done the same. She had checked the clip in the Walther before using it, but she had not completely wiped her prints form the clip when she put it back in the gun. According the Sergeant Hill, Ricki William's prints matched the prints on the ammo clip found in gun used to kill Joe Kaminski. Strong circumstantial evidence, but not enough for the DA in Grosse Pointe. In the District Attorneys mind, loading a gun was not evidence of firing a gun.

Ultimately, that is why the Grosse Pointe Woods police returned the Walther to Robert, breaking the chain of evidence forever.

In Naples, Sergeant Hill and the District Attorney had a different reaction. The gun that killed Joe Kaminski and Every Yale might be in Robert Cederberg's possession, but the bullets and ammo clip were still sitting in the evidence room in Grosse Pointe. After talking with the Chief of Detectives in Grosse Pointe Woods, an arrest warrant was issue for Ricki Williams.

Earlier when Hill told Robert about the prints on the ammo clip, Robert's only comment was 'I should have known.' Now, standing by the police car, Robert was quiet. Once Louise was cuffed in the back of the squad car, Hill turned to Robert.

"Will she really do time?" asked Robert.

"For having the gun, sure, but I wouldn't bet on the murder charge. Still the DA said to pick her up for the murder of Evert Yale and I have. I have done my part of the job."

"Now it is up to someone else to close the circle," said Robert.

"Let's hope," said the detective stepping into the front seat of the police car. "Truth is half the crimes I investigate are never solved. I just hate to leave them that way, but all I can do is hope someone else will see that justice is done. When you called me, I felt sure we had lost any chance of arresting Louise. However, you were sure she would show and you were right. Perhaps she really loved Wilson."

"Perhaps, who can say," said Robert looking around.

"Too bad about Ricki Williams," said Hill.

"She'll turn up," said Robert. Earlier Robert had noticed a blue Ford pickup truck parked two lanes over with its engine running. Robert wondered if Sergeant Hill had assigned a minder or if he had a watcher. The person in the truck was wearing a baseball cap and he thought he saw blond hair. Climbing into his truck, Robert watched the squad car drive out of the cemetery. Hill waved to Robert as he passed by. Turning back to look, Robert saw the blue truck was still parked.

* * *

Sitting in Tom Wilson's blue Ford F100, Ricki Williams watched the police car take her mother away followed by Robert Cederberg driving a new pickup. Under the seat of the Ford, Ricki touched the .22 target pistol with its silencer. She loved the balance of the gun when you screwed on the suppressor.

Louise said Robert would show up at Tom's Funeral and Ricki planned to kill Robert when he did. She had not planned on Sergeant Hill being there and arresting Louise. She debated shooting Robert and Hill, but seeing the squad car and a second cop changed her mind. She decided it was time to leave. Robert would have to wait.

Ricki watched Robert as he turned his head to check both ways before driving north out of the cemetery. *He is heading back to his motel*, she thought. Starting the truck, she considered following Robert and taking him in his motel, but she had seen Robert in action. He sensed an attack, and besides being deadly, he was lucky. That was the reason she told herself for not killing him that night in the Bullseye or later at her home. Robert was hard to surprise. He was always watching, ready to jump back in his shell or reach out and bite. The other thing she realized was that night when he came back down stairs after killing Sugar Ray she wanted him to fuck her. If fact, if she was alone with him in his motel room right now, she were unsure whether she would fuck him or shoot him.

Ricki knew she did not love Robert, how could she? He was responsible for her mother going to jail and he had killed Sugar Ray and Guy Jackson and Tom Wilson, men who had been her lovers at one time. The problem was the sex with Robert was great and she understood Robert. Just like her, he was pretending to be normal. The killer in him was hiding behind a façade: the crew cut, khaki pants, short-sleeve shirt, and penny loafer. Mister Grosse Pointe hiding a killer, hiding in his shell but waiting to be released.

Ricki liked the killer inside Robert, she enjoyed the sex they had, she was excited by the danger he represented. When they were together, she felt balanced, almost normal. In her heart, she wished they could be lovers. She wished they could be partners, but she knew he would come at her eventually; it was part of his nature.

Turning the truck south onto the Tamiami Trail, Ricki settled back as she drove though North Naples on her way to Miami. On the FM, radio they were playing Chicago's 'If you leave me now.' Singing along she was sad to be leaving Naples. The city had more retired millionaires than Beverly Hills. It had been a great hunting ground, but now the police would be looking for her, so the faster she was out of southwest Florida the better. Besides, she thought, *Robert is not going anywhere, he is buying a house; he is going to start another fucking gun club.* For a day, Ricki followed Robert and his fat Realtor looking at houses and storefronts. She should have killed him then, but Louise wanted to wait until funeral, and she would have had to kill the Realtor. Now, Ricki needed a safe harbor, a place to plan, Miami or Key West. Once she was safe, she could take her time, give Robert and the Naples police a year or two, and then one night she would stand over him just as she had Joe Kaminski and put a bullet in his head.

* * *

Driving four cars back behind the blue truck, Robert let several cars push ahead of him on the Tamiami Trail. He was in no danger of losing sight of the Ford. Robert had decided he would let Ricki have the first move. If she came at him at the cemetery or motel, he would kill her defending himself and take his chances with the police. However, if she tried to flee, he decided he would track her and end it on his own terms. Turning south, away from Ft. Myers, she made the decision.

An hour later, they were approximately twenty-seven miles east of Naples with only swamp and mangrove trees for miles around. Robert planned to wait until they were well into the everglades before he would make his move. Under the car seat, he had Joe Kaminski's Colt 1911, a weapon that was untraceable. All Robert needed was the right spot to get rid of the body and truck.

Feeling beside him on the passenger seat, he opened a cardboard box. Touching the silver bag inside he thought about Sergeant Hill's idea that eventually a killer had to pay for his crime; had to close the circle. In the bag was Susan Kay's Walther, her gift to Robert for becoming a man. Pulling out the silver gun with the black handgrips, he still admired its beauty, but he wondered if he had a chance to return to that moment in Canada, if he would hand the gun back to the driver and run for help? *To late*, he thought, as half a mile ahead of him the blue truck pulled over to the side of the road, letting the few cars on the two-lane highway pass by. Picking up the Walther, he pushed the safety off and cocked the hammer. Pulling off the road, some twenty feet behind Ricki's truck, Robert Cederberg turned off the engine knowing that a circle was about to close.

About the Author

Roger Lubeck, Ph.D., is President of Corporate Behavior Analysts, Ltd., a Chicago based leadership and management consulting firm. Roger has over 30 years consulting in real estate services, healthcare, higher education, manufacturing, and mental health. Roger has a degree in Experimental Psychology from Utah State University and M.A. and B.S. degrees in Behavioral Psychology from Western Michigan University. In his career, Roger has been a business consultant, workshop leader, retreat facilitator, public speaker, speechwriter, assistant professor, researcher, parent trainer, and dogcatcher. Roger is married to Lynette Chandler, a University Professor and author. Roger is the author of a number of publications on customer service, leadership, management, marketing, and sales. Roger and Chris Hanson are the authors of *Finding the Right Path: A Guide to Leading and Managing A Title Insurance Company*. Bullseye is Roger's second published novel. His first novel, *To the Western Border: A Fantasy Adventure*, (*Book One in The Council of Magic*) was published in July of 2011.